✦ ✦ ✦

# THE RELUCTANT REAPER

✦ ✦ ✦

# BOOKS BY MARYJANICE DAVIDSON

**STANDALONE NOVELS**

*The Reluctant Reaper*

*Road Queens*

*A Contemporary Asshat at the Court of Henry VIII*

*Really Unusual Bad Boys*

*Doing It Right*

*Under Cover*

*Love Lies*

*Thief of Hearts*

*Dying for Ice Cream*

*Adventures of the Teen Furies*

*By Any Other Name*

**THE BEWERE MY HEART SERIES**

*Bears Behaving Badly*

*A Wolf After My Own Heart*

*Mad for a Mate*

**THE UNDEAD / BETSY THE VAMPIRE QUEEN SERIES**

*Undead and Unwed*

*Undead and Unemployed*

*Undead and Unappreciated*

*Undead and Unreturnable*

*Undead and Unpopular*

*Undead and Uneasy*

*Undead and Unworthy*

*Undead and Unwelcome*

*Undead and Unfinished*

*Undead and Undermined*

*Undead and Unstable*

*Undead and Unsure*

*Undead and Unwary*

*Undead and Unforgiven*

*Undead and Done*

*Undead AF*

**THE WYNDHAM WEREWOLVES SERIES**

*Derik's Bane*

*Dead and Loving It*

*Dead Over Heels*

*Wolf at the Door*

*Love's Prisoner*

*Santa Claws*

*Jared's Wolf*

**THE ALASKAN ROYALS SERIES**

*The Royal Treatment*

*The Royal Pain*

*The Royal Mess*

**THE GORGEOUS SERIES**

*Hello, Gorgeous!*

*Drop Dead, Gorgeous!*

**THE JENNIFER SCALES SERIES (WITH ANTHONY ALONGI)**

*Jennifer Scales and the Ancient Furnace*

*Jennifer Scales and the Messenger of Light*

*The Silver Moon Elm*

*Seraph of Sorrow*

*Rise of the Poison Moon*

*Evangelina*

**THE FRED THE MERMAID SERIES**

*Sleeping With the Fishes*

*Swimming Without a Net*

*Fish Out of Water*

**THE FBI CADENCE JONES TRILOLGY**

*Me, Myself, and Why?*

*Yours, Mine, and Ours*

*You and I, Me and You*

**THE MYSTERIA SERIES (WITH P. C. CAST, SUSAN GRANT, AND GENA SHOWALTER)**

*Mysteria*

*Mysteria Lane*

**THE AFTERLIFE SERIES**

*The Fixer-Upper*

*Paradise Bossed*

**THE INSIGHTER/ REINCARNATION SERIES**

*Deja Who*

*Deja New*

**THE DANGER, SWEETHEART SERIES**

*Danger, Sweetheart*

*The Love Scam*

*Truth, Lies, and Second Dates*

**NONFICTION**

*The Official CaFae Latte Cookbook*
(with C. M. Alongi)

*I Have a Tapeworm and Other Ways to Make Friends*

**ANTHOLOGIES**

*Forgotten Wishes*
(with Joanna Wylde and Joey W. Hill)

*How to Be a "Wicked" Woman*
(with Susanna Carr and Jamie Denton)

*Romance at the Edge: In Other Worlds*
(with Angela Knight and Camille Anthony)

*Charming the Snake*
(with Melissa Schroeder and Camille Anthony)

*Valentine's Day Is Killing Me*
(with Leslie Esdaile and Susanna Carr)

*Faeries Gone Wild*
(with Michele Hauf, Lois Greiman, and Leandra Logan)

MARY JANICE

DAVIDSON

*NEW YORK TIMES* BESTSELLING AUTHOR

✦ ✦ ✦

# THE RELUCTANT REAPER

Published in 2025 by Blackstone Publishing
Cover and book design by Alenka Linaschke



Printed in the United States of America
Originally published in hardcover by Blackstone Publishing in 2025

First paperback edition: 2025
ISBN 979-8-228-59213-1
Fiction / Romance / Fantasy

Version 1

Blackstone Publishing
31 Mistletoe Rd.
Ashland, OR 97520

www.BlackstonePublishing.com

*For my daughter, Christina. She knows what she did.*

People don't change. They just become more of what they are.
The Penguin, *Batman: One Bad Day: Penguin*

The past is never dead. It's not even past.
William Faulkner, *Requiem for a Nun*

# PROLOGUE

*"Don't! Please, it can't be. It can't be my time yet! It's a mistake, please. Please, I'll do anything. Take my mother. Take . . . anyone. Just not me."*

# CHAPTER ONE

Amara Morrigan woke with a single goal: to be fired by lunchtime.

Ninety minutes later, she was well on her way. Goal: crushed.

". . . top of everything else, you were late! Again! This office is literally three blocks from your apartment. If you lean way out the south window"—her boss demonstrated—"you can see the corner of your building!"

"Maybe stop leaning and staring at my apartment window?" Amara was rooting through her purse, which was roomy enough to accommodate several bricks. "It's a cliché," she added in a mutter, "but it's no wonder I can never find anything."

"I've literally given you chance after chance—"

"Two, actually." Amara looked up, considering. "So I suppose that's technically correct."

"—but we're gonna have to let you go."

*Barf, the royal we.* Amara checked her watch: 11:37. "Thank you. Also, you use 'literally' too much. But that's okay, I do, too. That's a literal truth."

"So you better pack up your—"

She nudged the box between them, the one he'd ignored

even while she'd been filling it. (Her soon-to-be-former boss had a gift for ignoring impending unpleasantness.) An hour ago it held six reams of twenty-pound Hammermill copy paper. Now it held (some of) her earthly belongings. Including three crochet hooks. And ninety stitch markers because she kept losing them. And Post-it notes she had no immediate use for. And extra-strength Advil. And a lone Little Debbie Swiss Roll. Missing a bite.

"It's been fun, by which I mean it's been a living nightmare. And I once spent two weeks mucking out stalls full of cows with bovine viral diarrhea."

"Uh." Her soon-to-be-former boss blinked down at her box. "That's a thing?"

"Bovine viral diarrhea? Yes. A thing. Literally a thing. Literally a terrible thing."

"Look, Amara, if you want to stay a couple of days while we find your replacement . . ."

"No can do, William." She slung the purse over her shoulder and picked up the box. "There is no replacing me."

Her newly former boss, who would die of lung cancer in eleven years and thirty-three days, gritted his teeth. "Billy."

"You're a grown man, is my point." And graying at the temples, no less. With a man-bun. Not that she gave a shit about man-buns; it was Billy's inability to keep his hands off it that she couldn't abide.

"Why'd you even take the job here?" he whined. "You didn't like it even before I asked you out."

She laughed so hard she spit a little; Billy took half a step back and wiped his cheek with the back of his hand. "Is that how you're spinning it? You think 'accidentally' brushing my boobs two or three or eleven times while asking me to wink-wink 'work late' wink is asking me out?"

Cue the aggrieved eye roll. "Don't even start with that MeToo crap."

"I'm not. I'm just leaving." She took a long look around the small office she'd spent too many hours in. The gunmetal gray carpet, the secondhand furniture, the vending machine that only took Canadian nickels, the computers with outdated software, the fridge that was barely cooler than the office, the fax machine no one ever used. Fax machine! What year did Billy think this was? "And since you fired me, as opposed to me hitting you with something heavy and quitting, I can draw unemployment. Thank you for that."

"I'll contest it!"

"Please do. I also cracked your server and uploaded all your emails. Work-related, private, the secretly private, the super-duper secretly private . . . nobody's that sneaky unless they're hiding embezzlement or a second family. The digging was worth the migraine." Amara took a last glance around purgatory. "Anyway, I uploaded them to the cloud and gave the password to your soon-to-be-ex-wife. I'm betting her lawyer has them now. And possibly the IRS."

"What?"

"I don't know why you're always whining about what a bitch Shelly is. She was super nice when we had lunch."

*"What?"*

"And she loved my bag. No surprise; every time I'm out with this thing, people ask me where I got it." She patted the felted messenger bag, which she'd crocheted in greens and blues for a "just hangin' in the garden with the lily pads" Monet vibe. "They never believe I made it myself."

Billy's rapid blinking was now a full-on tic. "Did someone get you to take the job to sabotage me?"

"Don't be ridiculous. I took the job because I lost a bet.

Sabotaging you was strictly for fun. Say hi to Shelly for me! You'll be seeing her in court soon."

Most people liked to leave 'em laughing. Amara preferred to leave 'em devastated.

# CHAPTER TWO

"You. Are. Shitting me."

Amara snapped her fingers at her best nemesis / worst friend. "Pay up. Fired by noon, twenty-eight days in. Well, twenty-seven and a half."

Gray let out a sigh. "He only held off that long because he thought he could get in your pants. Let's get supper at Houlihan's."

"You expect me to have an appetite after you put that image in my head?"

"I'll pay you in drinks."

"Good call, since that's the only tender I'll accept."

Twenty minutes later, she and Gray were sucking down virgin mules served inexplicably in regular glasses. Were the copper mugs in the dishwasher? Or oxidating in a cupboard? Perhaps she expected too much from a chain.

"Ka-boom!" he chortled. Graham Gray was currently growing out his buzzcut; as usual, he managed to look disheveled and put-together at the same time. He was dressed in dark blue shorts and a long-sleeved polo shirt in a primary color (today's was jack-o'-lantern orange). As it was March, he was wearing socks with his battered loafers. The long-sleeved shirt wasn't just in deference to the weather; it hid some of the scars.

If you judged him simply on appearance—long, strong legs; swimmer's shoulders; pale green eyes; dark hair—you'd think he never felt fragile for so much as a nanosecond. That no one who looked so good could ever feel so bad.

"Another temp job bites the dust," he said with a snicker. "Pun intended."

"And not a minute too soon. Another day and I was going to set his man-bun loose and use the scrunchie to strangle him. It would have been tough, but you'd be surprised how resilient cloth-covered elastic can be."

Gray chuckled. "That's the only thing I like about you, Amara. Ordinary people burn bridges. You're the human embodiment of the Viet Cong."

"It's not the only thing. Plus, the Viet Cong was actually made up of humans, you delightful dope. And they preferred to be called the People's Army of Vietnam."

He ignored facts. "You blow them up and then stomp all over the smoldering remains. And then piss all over ground zero for good measure, ne'er to return."

"Thank you? What can I say, I don't do long engagements. Sometimes not even short ones."

"I still don't get how you do it. Or why, but that's a conversation for another time. You're always so vague when I try to pin you down."

"I just read the paper and . . ."

"Annnnnnnd?"

"And get a feeling."

"From reading the newspaper."

"Yes."

"Specifically, the obituaries."

She shrugged. He was doing that thing where he knew the answers but asked anyway. "It doesn't happen every time. But now and again I get . . ." A need. An urge. A compulsion. "A feeling. Billy's mother died last month and I felt . . . I just had the impression that he was an asshole doing asshole things. So when he advertised for an assistant . . ." She shrugged again. "And it's a little alarming that you've got such an interest in my employment history."

"Aw, c'mon, after the way we met? I made a PowerPoint," he said brightly. "Which I'll be updating tonight. You should come back to my place and see the updates in real time. This has gotta be a new record for you."

She took another sip. Fresh lime juice, excellent. "Your PowerPoint must be missing a slide: my twenty-two-day stint as a hoser of hounds and catcher of cats."

Gray shook his head. "Doesn't count. You did that for fun and you never got paid. And you had to leave when the full-time gal got back from maternity leave."

"Mmmm." She did have to, but not for the reason Gray assumed. The full-time employee brought her baby to the no-kill pet shelter, which is when Amara realized the infant would be dead before the leaves started to turn. She hadn't wanted to be in the room with either of them after that.

Gray must have seen something on her face, because he leaned back to scrutinize her expression and put down his drink. "Listen, Mar, your deal is your deal . . ."

"Don't get philosophical on me, you doof."

"And maybe this is a dumb question . . ."

"I'm confident it will be."

"But have you tried warning them?"

"It's not just a dumb question, it's one you've asked before.

I'll tell you now what I told you then: It. Doesn't. Work." So she had learned, in the most brutal manner after too many attempts to get in fate's face. "When it's your day, it's your day. And no man knoweth the hour. Shouldn't, anyway."

"What?"

"'Take ye heed, watch and pray: for ye know not when the time is.'" Fine advice which few could be bothered to heed. Not that she was a Bible pusher. Or any sort of pusher. But given that every religion featured her father, she'd made a point of reading all sorts of religious texts: the Bible, the Tipitaka, the Quran, the Torah. And once she'd met Persephone, Greek mythology.

Which was . . . stupid, really. Why study for a job you'll never have?

She rejoined the chat. "Are you rethinking our agreement?" Early in their friendship, he'd made her swear never to tell him the time and manner of his inevitable demise.

"Good God, *no*." Gray downed half his virgin mojito in one gulp, then clutched his head and regretted everything as he waited for the brain freeze to pass. "Don't you dare spoil the surprise!"

"Your death will definitely be a surprise," she muttered into her glass.

"It will? Why—wait. What? No! Don't say anything—okay, a good surprise or a bad surprise? Dumb question, obviously a good surprise . . . do I drown in a vat of DQ ice cream? Don't answer that!"

"Calm down." Time for a subject change. "Drink your drink, honey."

"Honey! You only call me that when you're trying to calm me down or asking if I wish to acquire honey. It just . . . it sounds like it's soon. Is it soon? Don't answer that! Is it now? Ten seconds from now? Or ten years? Don't answer! But you can tell me when Elon Musk's gonna bite the big one. Make my decade and tell me it's this week."

She chuckled. "No idea. That's not how it works."

"Okay, how 'bout our waiter?"

"February 2065. Complications from pneumonia."

"Jeez," Gray muttered, then couldn't look at the waiter when he came back with fresh drinks. "Well, he's gonna live to be a geezer, so that's something. But how can you stand it?" he whispered. It was unnecessary; they were surrounded by the noisy lunch rush. But some things, Amara knew, *should* be spoken of in low tones.

"You already asked me that, too." She didn't mind. Friends who knew about her family's, um, long record of service but stuck around anyway were rare. To be honest, she only had one. The trick was finding a chum who didn't give a shit about dying. Who might even be inclined to speed things up if they thought Death was being a slowpoke. And then rescue them, even if they didn't want to be rescued.

*And keep them safe, as best you can.*

"God, that must be . . ." Gray was still staring after the waiter. "How can you even think about it?"

"I don't," she replied. She clinked her glass with his and took a healthy gulp, filtering the ice out with her teeth to avoid Gray's mistake. "At all. When I have a choice."

# CHAPTER THREE

Amara woke up in one of her favorite places: Gray's office.

His home office, to be exact. After dinner they'd come to his quadruplex, an old Victorian the owner had split into four apartments; the top floor was Gray's. Except the apartment directly below was nearly always empty, so most of the time Gray essentially had the run of half a mansion.

It didn't hurt that Amara had figured out where the owner's late wife had spitefully hidden their combined assets before succumbing to renal cancer. "No prenup," the owner said ruefully. "That was my mistake. That and overlooking her documented history of fraud. She was gonna take it all and leave me with my dick in my hand, but she got sick . . . so when d'you want your friend to be able to move in?"

The sofa bed in Gray's office was, shockingly, comfortable, thanks to the two feather mattresses plopped on top and no fewer than three comforters. She sat up and yawned, blinking at Gray's back.

"Morning," he said without turning around, already at his desk though it was only . . . shit! Ten thirty! She heard the click as he stopped the recorder with his foot, typed something, then hit the play button again. "Gotta finish this transcript by noon. Eat something."

She did, first stopping by the bathroom to wash up and brush her teeth; about a third of the items in the medicine cabinet and the cupboard beneath were hers. The owner, Mr. Lowe, had come up not long ago to fix the leaky faucet, and observed that Gray and Amara were practically roommates. "You can have the lower unit if you want. I'll give ya a deal."

"You're wasting your breath, Lowe. Amara's infatuated with her shithole studio."

"Infatuated's a strong word," she'd muttered.

Mr. Lowe was correct; they *were* practically roommates. It was the rare month when one of them didn't crash at the other's apartment for a night or two. And sure, she'd love to share a mansion with Gray. But that was the problem: *love.*

Living with him . . . too much. For so many reasons. She'd keep her shithole, thanks; the gross carpet, cracked sink, lack of counter/closet space, fourth-hand furniture, and view of the 35E overpass suited her well. Just like her used Ford Fusion with stained seats (on rainy days, she could smell the banana from a long-ago spilled smoothie) and a cracked windshield suited her.

The kitchen boasted the usual breakfast suspects: a plethora of Pop-Tarts, half a loaf of artisan bread, not-quite-expired coconut yogurt, two cases of LaCroix in passionfruit (passable) and apricot (vomit-inducing), half a dozen eggs.

She scored a strawberry Pop-Tart, found her purse, grabbed her keys. "Job interview, gotta run!"

He heard her; she'd caught him between stopping and starting the depo recording. "Why don't you take a break from the temp jobs? It's not like your trust fund's gonna run out anytime soon."

"I like to keep busy."

He chuckled, and she heard the click as he rewound some tape. "You wanna grab a movie this weekend?"

"Sounds good." But then, so did everything with him. She would have had the same response to "You want to help me organize my graphic novels by year of publication?"

✦ ✦ ✦

Amara switched her phone back to Bluetooth and was startled to see she had 429 voicemails. As she'd been studiously ignoring calls from Minot, she was more than a little surprised at the total. *So low.* The last two times her folks tried to lure her home for a family reunion and a fictitious garage sale ("If you want your things, best come home"), she had eight hundred voicemails in seven hours. And that was just on day one.

She shook her head and glared at her phone. *C'mon, guys. You gotta want it! Me. Whatever.* Since she abhorred a vacuum as much as nature did, she shut off her phone. It would be fine. It wasn't like she needed directions. How hard would it be to find a fifty-acre park?

Fifty-two minutes later, she was apologizing for being late because she had, in fact, needed directions. Parks are hard to find!

"No biggie," her next boss said. "There's all kindsa stuff going on right now, I didn't even notice you were late. Lots to do, y'know?"

"I gathered from the posting." *Help help HELP WANTED ASAP, must be able to read and write and other stuff as needed!!!* She'd never seen such a shrill demand for help, and she'd been reading online job postings every week for over a decade.

"So watcha see is watcha get," the boss du jour continued with a vague gesture that encompassed the Angry Beaver RV

Park. It likely would have looked a bit depressing even in high summer, which this was not. Frush (parking lot slush hardened overnight in the shape of tire treads, which made for treacherous walking) was everywhere, the tree branches were bowed down with ice that would sullenly drip only to refreeze that night, and overhead the sky was a blinding blue.

There were about a dozen RVs that Amara could see, as well as an empty playground off to the left. The miniature red barn to the right contained the manager's office and a small grocery store. A six-foot-high stack of wood ran the length of the barn, all neatly cut and shielded with a snow-covered tarp. "Off-season right now, o'course. Chance t'get a handle on the job before we get real busy."

"Sounds fine."

Her next boss, a petite woman with short, graying blond hair who would be dead in thirty-four months, was a recent widow who had scammed her stepchildren out of their inheritance. "A lot of the job is basically bein' a landlord . . . if they're here long-term, you'll have to run their card every thirty days, and if it don't go through, you gotta knock on their door. You're also gonna knock on their door if they break any of the rules. And they're gonna, because these people are—"

"Hi, Mrs. Bennett!" A chubby brunette in her thirties popped out of the nearest RV. "Wanna come over for lunch? I made too much hot dish again."

"No thanks, Miz Dooley, already had lunch." To Amara: "Jackasses. What's with the Mrs. Bennett shit? I been divorced for a decade. Dooley knows that."

Amara had been unaware that RV parks were hotbeds of jackassery, but it explained why her new boss was lying about eating lunch at nine forty-five a.m. She'd stolen the Angry Beaver from her husband's children, though perhaps that was a blessing.

"And see? See?" The former Mrs. Bennett pointed to overflowing garbage bins, beside which were a dozen or so pizza boxes, neatly stacked. "Not even in the cans!"

"Maybe because the cans are full?"

"Yeah, that reminds me, you'll also be in charge of accounts payable. First check you cut you gotta send to Tennis Sanitation."

"Can the second check go to the porta-potty people? I can't see them, but I can smell them."

"West side, behind the office," was the absent reply. "That reminds me, keep an eye on the toilet paper situation."

"The jackasses get testy when they can't wipe their bottoms? Or is it a one-ply vs. two-ply situation?"

"Like you never seen and— *Jesus*!" Mrs. Bennett flinched back so hard, Amara had to sidestep. "More of 'em? Shouldn't they be hibernating or whatever?"

Amara felt a chill, mostly because it was thirty-nine degrees outside but also because a dozen white-tailed deer had come out of the tree line beside the park.

"Never seen so many this close to the highway." Her future boss gave the ruminants a long stare, which they all returned, then turned back to Amara. "Anyways. When can you start?"

Amara blinked. "That's the interview? You complained about your tenants and want me to write checks and now I'm hired?"

"Well, *I* don't wanna do any of those things."

Amara smiled. "It's refreshing to hear that."

"I read your résumé, you seem decent in person, let's get on with it. Besides, you can—what the hell is that?"

Amara sighed. Bennett was gaping at a sizable raptor that hailed from Bahrain. "It's a Eurasian eagle-owl." Over two feet tall, with the characteristic black ear tufts, tawny feathers, and orange eyes of the winged predator. "Mostly found in Eurasia."

"But this isn't Eurasia."

"Correct, ma'am. This is not Eurasia."

"Not a ma'am, call me Bette. Welp, if that's not the weirdest thing I seen today—"

"Wait."

"What?"

"Never mind. When should I start?" *Please say immediately.*

"How 'bout right now?"

"Great, fine, that will . . ." Amara trailed off and sighed, then added, "Before you ask, the ones that just landed are vultures."

Bette gaped. "Those things are vultures? I thought they were pretty big . . . well, I dunno what I thought. What the hell, is there a circus in town?"

Amara chuckled, which went a little way toward easing her dread. "You think circuses routinely travel with vultures and white-tailed deer?"

"Huh." Bette put her hands on her hips and squinted up at her. Amara was used to it. She'd been fetching things from high shelves for people since she was thirteen. "Are you gonna have a smart mouth on you the whole time you're here?"

"Guaranteed."

"Oh." The new boss shrugged. "Hokay. Long as you do your job, I s'pose." Before she could elaborate, the calls of a dozen whippoorwills sliced the winter air. "Now what's this shit?"

Her dread, which had started as a small fiery ball in her belly, was growing. And moving up. If more messages to call home showed up, Amara was sure the dread would move to her throat. She had an urge to call Gray, and squashed it. He couldn't help her. *She* couldn't help her. "It's fine. They're psychopomps."

"Psycho-whats?"

"I shut my cell phone off and didn't return any voicemails, so. Here they are." Before she could elaborate or prevaricate, a sports car rumbled into the far parking lot, then screeched to a slippery stop several yards away.

*Ah. There's the dread in my throat. If I tried to talk, I'd probably choke on it.*

"Maybe call the City of Savage about getting a plow down here, too," Bette added. "Now what's this?"

"It's a Porsche 911."

"That thing's a Porsche?"

*That thing* was a rear-engined sports car with a flat six and torsion-bar suspension; fast and dangerous and as famous for winning races as for getting people killed. In other words, the polar opposite of an RV. So what was it doing here?

The driver's side door popped open and there he was, impossibly tall, impossibly immaculate, impossibly asinine and now (impossible!) strolling toward them. She could see his sharp, sharp teeth from where she was standing. He wasn't smiling.

He'd never come to Minnesota before. Never. It was one of many reasons to love the land of 11,842 lakes.

"That thing would be impractical for anyone else, but not this guy," Amara mused aloud. "It's only a two-door, because it's not like he's known for carpooling. And it's in the top ten of deadliest cars to drive, because he's not subtle, either."

"Who's *that* now?" the new boss asked, sounding not a little dazzled, which was annoying. "Ummm. Nice suit, too."

"Oh, sorry, I should have mentioned. That's a death god. He's here to nag me into going to North Dakota." Amara reached out and patted the woman's arm. "Don't worry. I'll get rid of him and I won't be asking for any time off. Now where's that checkbook?"

# CHAPTER FOUR

"Still neck to heels in all black, I see. Subtle."

Baron La Croix let out a snort. "All my purple is, lamentably, getting cleaned." He stomped toward her and Bette, who was doubtless enjoying a most entertaining morning, scattering vultures and rumpling his suit; Amara was petty enough to be glad. And even pettier to wish he'd slipped and gone down on his ass. "Amara Morrigan. Forgive the cliché, but it truly is always a pleasure."

"We both know that's a lie."

"This guy your boyfriend or somethin'?"

In horrified unison: "Great gods, *no*."

La Croix inclined his head: "Dear madam, I'm an old friend—"

Amara: "He's one of my dad's work buddies."

Bette digested that, blinking. "Oh, yeah? Him and your dad work together?"

". . . Yes."

"Waste management," La Croix added, ignoring Amara's snort.

"Oh. Well. Gotta have that, right?" Bette nodded and motioned to the pizza boxes. "It's not pretty, but it's important."

"The lady is wise," La Croix replied, and swept Bette a bow while Amara rolled her eyes so hard she glared at her own frontal lobe. "We must speak."

"We are."

"I bear urgent news."

"Sounds painful."

"Gods help me." La Croix straightened, grinning. He towered over . . . everyone, really; Amara pegged him at about six foot five. Long and lean and too many teeth and a mop of ridiculous blue-black wavy hair. Blue eyes so pale, he looked blind, an especial irony since he could see in the dark like a jaguar. "Still the smart-ass. It seems to be your default."

"Takes one to et cetera." She made a shooing motion and he laughed at her. "Could you scamper off? I'm working."

"Er." La Croix swept the dilapidated park with a long gaze, then shook his head. "Still with this, hrm, whatever this is? Your litany of jobs? Your tiny trips of vengeance?"

Amara shrugged. "A gal's gotta eat."

"Indeed. Allow me to take you out for a meal."

"I just ate," she lied. "And, again: working."

His grin dropped away. She braced herself for Earnest La Croix, which was always worse than Smirking La Croix. And she'd take either over Scolding La Croix. "I bring urgent news from the Midwestern Fiefdom."

"If it's a tornado warning, we've got the Weather Channel for that. And a thousand, thousand apps. Also, it's too early in the season for tornados."

"Amara—"

"And if it's a family issue, it's none of your business."

"Amara, it pains me . . ."

"Does it, though?"

"Your father is dying."

Amara yawned. Bette, who had been watching their exchange like a tennis spectator, let out an odd sound: part gasp, part groan. "Aw, jeez. That's too bad."

Amara sighed. "It's just another lie. My father isn't dying. He doesn't even get sick. He's never caught a cold, never mind been at death's door."

"Oh, now how would that work?" La Croix cried, and she almost giggled at his exasperation. "Amara. I am quite serious, and you know how ill-suited I am to that."

"I do know," she admitted.

"Your family needs you."

She was already shaking her head. "It's just another trick."

"Amara—"

"It's not true. And you either know it's not true, or you're being duped. Whichever it is, it's not a good look for one of the Gede."

"Amara."

"See? This is me being unmoved." She crossed her arms over her chest. "Literally and figuratively."

*"Amara Morrigan."*

"Stop that!" she snapped. "You're not my father, though you're old enough. My family business is exactly that: *my family.* I can't believe you're letting my father turn you into an errand boy. Where's all that vaunted pride?"

"It's not about him," he replied sharply. "I am no one's lackey. It's about you. Turn around."

Amara didn't move. Bette did, and her gasp was telling.

*Don't do it. Don't look. If you see them, it'll be real. If you see them, everything changes.*

She looked. Where there had been a dozen deer and a baker's

dozen of vultures, now there were ravens and crows and sparrows. They weren't flying. They were simply standing. Looking at her. Thousands of them; an inky, rustling lake covering a quarter mile.

Amara let out a slow breath. "Well, shit."

"Indeed."

"Fine. *Fine.*" She rubbed her forehead and prayed this was some sort of fever dream instead of an oncoming migraine. *Best case, I'm trapped in my studio apartment with a raging temp of 106°, too weak to move, too weak to eat, losing brain cells for every degree my temp climbs . . . heaven!* "You can buy me a meal. Later. I want to finish my shift. Actually, I want to start my shift."

"At last!" La Croix threw his arms in the air like an impossibly tall referee proclaiming the play was good. "She sees reason."

Amara turned away from the silent leagues of birds. "Why don't you go buy something purple and get someone to smoke a cigarette? I'll meet you later."

"I do like buying purple things," he admitted. "And watching people smoke."

"So there you go. Okay?" She could hear the hope in her voice, but there was nothing for it. "You're leaving? Now? Right now?"

"Now I've got my way? Yes indeed. But you shouldn't be surprised. It *is* Monday," he added with a sly smile. Then he bowed to Bette again and spun on his heel, which was needlessly dramatic. If La Croix could die, that's what she'd expect to see on his tomb: *Baron La Croix, lwa of the Dead, Needlessly Dramatic.*

She and Bette watched La Croix leave and, with him, the psychopomps. Their numbers blotted out the winter sun as they took wing. In seconds they were gone, a lake-sized spread of bird shit the only indicator they'd lingered for a visit.

"Jeez," Bette breathed. "It's like magic."

"Exactly like magic. Gross, inconvenient magic. Also, I think I might need some time off."

"Yeah, I figured. Bad news about your dad, huh?"

"You have no idea."

✦ ✦ ✦

*"Don't! Please, it can't be. It can't be my time yet! It's a mistake, please. Please, I'll do anything. Take my mother. Take . . . anyone. Just not me. Please."*

# CHAPTER FIVE

"Amara! Over here!"

"Come to us at once!"

*Sure, sure. I'll get right on that, gents.* Amara had barely crossed the Chart House's threshold when they started hailing her. She cursed herself for being late (the garbage collectors weren't the only vendors her new boss hadn't paid), hung up her coat, and trudged to the table in the farthest corner, where her only friend was getting cozy with a death god for no good reason.

"Gray." She stopped short, stared down at him. From this angle she could see the small white scar he got from being shoved off the swing. One of the times he was shoved off the swing. It was something of a miracle he'd lived long enough to meet her. "I canceled." Which had sucked. She loved eating with Gray. She loved doing anything with Gray.

He raised his hands, palms up, in a *what-can-you-do?* gesture. "Well, yeah, once I was already on my way."

"I was delayed," she grumped.

"Cool, cool. Anyway, I was practically in the driveway by

then and remembered I could enjoy chicken parm without you. And then La Choy here—"

"La Croix," she and La Croix corrected.

"Yeah, yeah. The French pronunciation, right? *La Croix*. What'd I say?"

"Not La Croix. Is what you said."

"He spotted me and came to me," La Croix added, looking surprised yet smug. "It was as though he knew me of old. He saw my nature at once."

"Mostly I saw your sport coat. Is it purple? Is it black? Depends on the light. But, yeah, also your nature." To Amara: "It's gonna sound nuts, but he gave off death-god vibes."

"It's entirely sane since he is, in point of fact, a death god." Her inner thoughts were much less calm. *Fuckfuckfuck! I'm wearing off on Gray. I'm shedding paranormal sight like skin flakes!*

Tomorrow's problem. Meanwhile, La Croix was on his feet and pulling out a chair because he was a slick son of a bitch. "Join us, please. Partake in many walleye fingers and calamari. Or perhaps you wish to sample some of your dear friend Gray's cakes of crab."

"That rotten bitch is entitled to zero percent of my cakes of crab," her dear friend snapped. "Any seafood, actually."

"This?" Amara asked. "Again?"

To La Croix: "She lived in Boston for, what? Three months? Four?"

"Eleven," she corrected. It had been fun, until it wasn't.

To Amara: "Comes back with the accent—"

"I did not!"

"—terrible driving skills—"

"That's fair."

"—and seafood snobbery."

"Walleyes aren't seafood." She was pretty sure. She took her seat and decided not to mention how very much cheaper and fresher calamari was in Boston.

She liked the Chart House, and not just the menu. She liked the lake views and the enormous windows and the way it seemed like you were outside by the lake but weren't, which meant you weren't cold in winter and didn't have to deal with mosquitos in summer.

So she had to ask herself why she'd suggested La Croix meet her at a place she liked. La Croix already knew far more about her than he should. *Should've arranged to meet him at a truck stop an hour after the bars close.* All former truck stop waitresses knew three a.m. was the witching hour, if witching meant barfing.

And she had no idea how to feel about sharing a table with the two of them. No, that was a lie. Watching Gray slap La Croix's hand away as he tried to force a finger of walleye on her best friend was . . .

She groped for it, found it: It was the same feeling she got when someone she cared about was enjoying something she adored: Happy (*this will be cool!*), bewildered (*worlds collide!*), a little—a very little—envious (*it's not my secret anymore*).

"How did you and my 'dear friend Gray' come to—"

"Whoa." Gray nearly choked on his drink. "I could actually hear the air quotes."

"Amara, darling, how could I miss the opportunity to spend time with one of your closest friends?"

"Closest and onliest friend," Gray added, then tipped her a wink.

Discounting Gray's utter fascination with her family's, um, history was a mistake. She should have anticipated it; reason #2 it was dumb to meet La Croix here.

"A drink, *mon coeur*?"

"Stop it, La Croix. I'm not and have never been your heart." She perused the menu, unmoved by his baritone. "I believe I'll be drinking syrup with syrup today."

"Don't you kind of do that anyway?" To La Croix: "She eats her own weight in sugar at least twice a week. When she's done fixing an iced tea, it's got more sugar than a Coke."

"It's March," she pointed out, and caught the waiter's eye. "Cherry Coke, please." As the waiter nodded back, she ignored the newsflash about his impending doom in fourteen months and nine days. Car crash. Drunk driver. She wondered if he had a family. She wondered if his family would die with him.

"So!" Gray said brightly, raising his virgin mojito. "What d'you guys want to drink to?"

Amara let out a snort. "Absolutely nothing."

"Don't let her fool you, La Choy. Somewhere under the sickly pale skin and terrible bangs lurks a sentimental romantic."

"You needn't tell me, friend Gray. When she was a child, she wept over even the smallest creature's demise."

"Yeah, well." Amara took a gulp of syrup with syrup. "I outgrew that by the time I was in fifth grade. Besides, La Croix doesn't toast. Nor does he—oh, yum."

A waitress passed their waiter and handed off Gray's entrée. "Sorry," he said as he got ready to dig into his chicken parm. "Didn't think you'd be here or I would've ordered something for you."

"Could you tell our waiter I'd like the ribeye, medium, with mashed?" Except Gray said "the ribeye, medium, with mashed" when she did, earning a giggle from their waitress and an eye roll from Amara. "So I'm predictable. Fine."

"And whatever this guy wants." Gray jerked a thumb in La Croix's direction.

Even as La Croix shook his head, Amara added, "He can't."

"Vegetarian? Pescatarian? Ketogenic? Gluten-free? Vegan? Flexitarian?" Gray paused. "A gluten-free flexitarian pescatarian?"

"Nothing so—what was the word, Amara? Predictable? I can eat. I *do* eat," La Croix admitted. "Alas, I can only gain, ah, satisfaction if someone else eats what I want."

Gray paused. "Okay, I need to digest that. Shit, I hate accidental puns . . . that explains why you seemed weirdly excited when I wolfed down a crab cake. Related: Please tell me 'gain satisfaction' doesn't mean the deli scene from *When Harry Met Sally . . .*"

"I fear I don't know your friends, nor their deli. As for satisfaction—"

"He can eat for nutrition," Amara broke in. "But to taste anything, to get the total experience, someone else has to do the actual eating. And smoking. So he doesn't order meals in restaurants."

"Sure. What would be the point?" Gray's eyebrows were so arched, they looked ready to climb off his forehead. "Ooooookay. Have I mentioned I love being friends with you, Mara? So much cool shit going on right now." To La Croix: "Okay, how d'you feel about Italian? Like my chicken parm? Because I've got a forkful of breaded chicken here with your name on it."

"I feel 'Italian' dishes should originate in Italy."

"So you can't get the full feels unless someone else chows down, *and* you're a picky eater?"

Amara grinned. "Nutshell."

"Well, when Amara's entrée comes—"

La Croix sniffed. In another moment, he would flounce. "Amara knows full well I loathe bloody meat and despise vegetables mashed into mush."

"So you on-purpose ordered food you knew he would . . . heh." To La Croix: "What about . . ." Gray cast about, then pointed to the nearest table, where a young couple was partaking of salmon with baby potatoes and scallop scampi.

La Croix's eyes lit up, then narrowed. "Oh. *Oh.* Too much garlic, but perhaps . . . that . . . can be overlooked." Then, as one of two women at the table on their other side forked down a mouthful of pistachio crème cake, La Croix's eyes rolled back. "Ummm . . . cream cheese and . . . oh, the drizzle of chocolate ganache, unexpected but quite delightful . . ."

"Okay, now I'm getting a little uncomfortable," Gray admitted. "Also, is it a proximity thing? Because you didn't really notice anyone else's meals until I pointed them out."

"It is a proximity thing," La Croix acknowledged. "I have to have my attention on them and the closer the better. But in a pinch, so to speak, a nearby table will—ohgoodGodthat's-realwhippedcream—suffice."

"The thing I like best about this dinner," Amara sighed, "is how it's not even a little bit weird. Can we just get to it, please? Why have you come? How is my father?"

La Croix's blissful expression dropped away. "Quite ill. I confess I was startled to see his deterioration. And even more startled that he thought to summon me to his bedside. And your poor mother is beside herself."

Amara said nothing.

"He speaks only of you." La Croix leaned in, which was alarming. The eyes, the deep voice, the intensity . . . could be a lot. Was almost always a lot. Even Gray looked a bit dazzled. "He wishes to see you at once, Amara. As does your dear mother."

"Oh?"

"But more: He has called the Gede."

"Oh."

"My strong suggestion is that you do not delay."

He was a manipulative bastard, but knowing that didn't

help. She could *feel* the force of his will pressing against her own, and fought it off while keeping her expression as close to bland/bored as she could. "Just stop, La Croix. Death deteriorates? No bullshit, please. I know that's an impossible request, but . . ."

Even as La Croix dipped into his pocket and placed the thing in front of her, her heart dropped. More than dropped; it felt like her heart was beating around her ankles, which was weird and dumb and . . . She should have run when she spotted the vultures.

*Run where?*

Anywhere. Seattle. Mexico City. Mars. Arrakis.

"What the hell is that?" Gray asked, sounding not a little tense.

"My father's crown," she breathed, staring at the seven-inch ring of owl feathers before her. The crown was woven from feathers from all parts of the owl. Not just the tail feathers, or even the greater wing coverts. Her father had plucked from every part of his sigil creature: tail feathers, secondary wing, breast, nape . . . crown.

Death kept it close to hand at all times. Not necessarily on his person, but never far away. If La Croix had handed over her father's kidneys, she couldn't have been more shocked.

"Shit." She stood, and La Croix leaped up as well. Gray looked at both of them, shrugged, and stood. "I have to pack. Right now."

"Oh, God, packing." To La Croix: "She is the worst packer. She brings full-sized shampoos and conditioner when she flies! Who does that when everything comes in travel size? Lotion, cotton swabs, deodorant, gasoline, probably . . ."

"I'm a great packer," she replied without much heat. "I just . . . know what I need. And what I don't."

# CHAPTER SIX

*Look ye upon the daughter of Death's packing list and despair.*

7 boxes L'Oreal Paris Excellence permanent hair color in dark neutral brown
2 boxes Little Debbie Swiss Rolls
7 pairs leggings
2 pairs jeans
17 black T-shirts
1 white T-shirt
28 pairs heavy socks, various colors
1 pair black boots
2 pairs flats, the navy and the red
32 pairs panties, various colors
1 white bra
1 black bra
Double Stuf Oreos (indeterminate amount, whatever fits)
1 bottle Milk Shake Color Care shampoo
1 bottle Milk Shake Color Care conditioner
1 bottle Milk Shake leave-in conditioner spray

2 disposable razors
3 boxes chocolate fudge Pop-Tarts
1 case beef jerky
4 spare contact lens cases
2 gallons contact solution

# CHAPTER SEVEN

Well before 9/11 made flying even more of an ordeal, Amara loved trains. The speed and comfort. The leg room. The dining car. The lack of shoe removal, full body scanners, and cavity searches. The way farmland slid by at all hours. The way you could lie in your sleeper bunk in the dark and listen to the great and terrible machine as it took you away, away, away.

"Oh. My. God." Gray couldn't contain his pleased amazement, doing a Julie Andrews–style twirl on the platform. *The hills are aliiiiiiiiive* . . . "Your dad has his own train?"

"Not his own train." She poked him in the back so he'd board the damned train already. "His own railcar."

"It's cute how you're trying to downplay all the awesome. And those are real? I've only seen them in movies. Well, one movie." Gray had been unbearably cute since he wore Amara down and invited himself along. "How have we been friends so long and I'm only now seeing your private car?"

"Yes, they're real. Amtrak will let just about anyone latch a private car."

"That's so cool! You guys are like a royal family!"

She sighed as she followed him into the car. "Are you seriously taking pictures right now?"

"I hate when you ask questions when you already know the answer. You know, that thing you say I do all the time? Smile!" Click.

"Never." She took the three lush, carpeted steps downstairs, stowed her carry-on in the first bedroom, and came back up. "I still can't believe I'm letting you come along."

"I still can't believe your posh railcar has stairs and you packed six suitcases."

"Four, you doof. We'll probably just be there over the weekend, anyway."

Amara doubted it would matter to Gray if they were stuck in Minot for a month. He employed multiple side hustles: legal transcriptionist, medical transcriptionist, paid surveys with Prolific, and the occasional book review for *Kirkus*. Well before the pandemic, Gray had a viable work-from-home setup, one he could take on the road whenever he liked.

"And what d'you mean, 'letting' me come? Like you could've stopped me."

"I could have. You wouldn't have liked it."

Gray waved away her casual threat, walked past the kitchen to the lounge at the other end, ignored the plush couch, and flopped onto the nearest La-Z-Boy hard enough to make it rock so violently it almost pitched him to the floor.

"Tell me you have a private chef and a bartender," he gasped, holding on as he stared up at the dome. Her second favorite spot in the railcar. At night, the stars streamed by, maddeningly close.

"There is no bartender. And we don't need the chef for this trip."

"Ah-ha! So the private chef exists, elsewhere for now."

Amara shrugged.

"Cooooooool. So if you have a private train—"

"It's just the one railcar."

"—I'll bet you have a private plane, too."

She shook her head. "It's unnecessary. My father is old-fashioned and never leaves the Midwest."

"Because he's Death for Minnesota and Iowa and Wisconsin."

"And Michigan and the Dakotas and Illinois and Nebraska and Ohio. And parts of Kentucky. We don't follow strict geo-political boundaries. At least, not Midwestern ones."

Gray started to reach for his phone. "And Missouri? I think Civics covered that. I might've missed that day . . . actually, I missed a crap ton of days."

"The US Census Bureau decided Missouri counted as the Midwest. Not my father."

"Ma'am?" She turned to see the friendly porter and had to resist the urge to turn her back. "Your other guest is ready to board. Can I get you any—"

"No. We're fine."

"Oh." She was earnest and redheaded and sweet and Amara couldn't stand the sight of her. "Okay. Well, if you n—"

"We're fine. Thank you."

Gray sat up and waited until the porter was out of earshot. "I know that look," he stage-whispered, which wasn't whispering. "You gave her the shoulder earlier, too, and you almost never do that. You're pretty polite for a sociopath with great hair."

"Thank you. And yesterday you said I had terrible bangs. Be consistent with your casual criticisms, please."

"So when's that poor girl gonna bite it?"

"Tomorrow."

"Jesus." Gray leaned back in the chair. "Do I even want to . . . ?"

Smoke inhalation. There was small comfort in knowing she'd be spared burning to death. "No. You do not."

"I'm sorry. All this stuff—" He waved vaguely at the plush carpet, the soft chairs, the lamps, the view, the dark wood, the gleaming brass accents, the large windows so clean it was like there *were* no windows, the four bedrooms, the double beds . . . "It comes at a cost, right? Some days maybe it's not the best trade-off."

"Most days." She smiled, because she adored the idiot. "But I like that you like it."

"Yeah, well, I—oh, look, here comes the Marlboro Man. I don't know what's worse, that he's gorgeous or that he knows he's gorgeous."

"I heard that!" La Croix bounded up the steps, beaming and immaculate and hilariously puffy. The moment he felt the warmth of the car, he shrugged out of the pile of Gore-Tex he called a winter jacket.

"You know that's a woman's coat, right?" Amara teased.

"It was the only one that covered my knees." He flung the green jacket toward an empty chair and sighed. "Thank the gods both ill and blessed, they allowed cigarette smoking in the lounge! Well. Not really. But I was persuasive."

"A death god smokes," Gray observed.

"He doesn't smoke," Amara pointed out. "But he likes it when other people do."

"Right, right, the food thing extends to smoking. Got it."

"I also like the scent of rum, friend Gray, if you're feeling generous."

"I'm . . . not. So purple and black, that's kind of your thing, huh?"

"What gave it away?" he asked, shooting his cuffs, which were purple, and adjusting his suit jacket, which was also purple.

"Have a seat," Amara said. "We're pulling out soon."

He crossed his legs and flashed them his lavender socks.

"Hmmm. More terse than usual. It could be the hour, but if I know my Amara—"

"Not *your* anything."

"—you're sad about the girl who will asphyxiate tomorrow before dawn."

"Oh, God." Gray had been spinning his chair; now he planted his feet to bring the La-Z-Boy to a shuddering halt. "She doesn't even get a whole day?"

Amara and La Croix shrugged in unison, looked at each other, and then Amara looked away. "I warned you not to come, Gray."

"Oh, please. I don't have to stow away on your ritzy train—"

"Car. One car."

"—for you to talk about sad deaths. Full disclosure is the only way this friendship works. That's the rule."

"That's the program," Amara corrected. "Your program, not our rule."

"Yeah, well. Program's why I'm still alive."

Not an exaggeration. He had the scars to prove it.

"You have to admit, the young lady's manner of death *is* a bit farcical." La Croix shrugged. "Given the young porter's family history."

Amara stomped the urge to stomp him. "It's good that you're reminding me of alllll the reasons I dislike you."

"You wound me! You've always found me delightful."

"Um. No."

"Your mother would charge you to be kinder to me."

"Leave my mother out of it," she warned. "And my father. And everyone. Leave yourself out of it, while you're at it."

La Croix brushed invisible lint off his black pants. "Surely you have a kind thought to send my way when I'm not around, after all this time?"

"Nope. Not only am I fresh out of kind thoughts, I don't actually think about you when you're not around."

"Ouch." From Gray.

"Okay, not entirely true. I think of you every time I drink fruit-flavored seltzer. So, twice. Once it was blackberry, which was overdressed, and once it was peach/pear, which was disgusting. That's the last time I thought of you, La Croix."

"Ouch!" From Gray. "And am I crazy, or is there some weird vibe I'm picking up here?"

La Croix snickered. "Both of those things can be true."

"All vibes in the death car are weird vibes. Speaking of, La Croix, why are you here? I told you I'd go home, and you know I never lie."

"It's true!" Gray piped up. "It's almost pathological with her."

"I'd think you would have wasted no time getting back to your territory," she went on. "Especially because it's sunny and seventy-five in New Orleans right now. You could have gone back to Minot without me."

La Croix chose the La-Z-Boy opposite Gray and sat with a flounce. How he could make flouncing so masculine was an eternal mystery. "I missed you," he replied simply. "As does your mother. I'm not just here on your father's behalf; I promised your mother I'd see you to the train. It's been too long."

"It hasn't, though."

The train was pulling out. Gray cleared his throat in what he always assumed was a subtle way, but it sounded like a bulldozer in low gear. "I think I'll go downstairs and pick out my room. Which is nothing I thought I'd ever say anywhere, much less on a private train. I know there's no way to stop you from talking behind my back once I'm out of earshot," he added, slipping past them and down the stairs. "All I ask is that you temper the snark with the sweet."

Amara laughed. "We're not going to be talking about you even a little, you vain slug."

"Yes you are!" Gray punctuated that by shutting the first door he saw. Amara waited, heard his muffled curse, and then the door swung open. "Okay, obviously Amara's room. The eighteen suitcases tipped me off. Maybe one of the other nine bedrooms will be unoccupied . . ."

"Four," she protested.

After another door slam, La Croix shifted in his chair and crossed his legs. "I like friend Gray."

"What's not to like? He puts up with my weirdness and I put up with his generous nature and his twelve-stepping all over the place and love-me-love-my-dog loyalty. We both bring something to the table. Him more than me, obviously."

"I would have thought you would share a bed."

"It's not like that," she snapped. "It's never been like that. And even if it was, it would be none of your fucking business."

"Mmmm. Well, as I assured your mother, there's plenty of time for you to take a lover and birth an heir."

"Please please *please* stop discussing my reproductive future with my mother. Or anyone."

"It's a fine thing to have such a good friend, in particular one who knows what you are. What a pity you'll soon bid him adieu."

"Shut up."

La Croix scrutinized her over tented fingers. "You haven't told him."

"Shut. Up."

He sighed and had the gall to look sorrowful. "Must you do this dance every time?"

"Apparently."

"Your window where denial serves your purpose is sliding shut," he warned.

"Your metaphor sucks and also, shut up."

Gray often wondered how she put up with her heritage and the baggage it brought.

She'd never told him: The only way to put up with her heritage was to deny it. Every day.

# CHAPTER EIGHT

*Five years ago . . .*

✦ ✦ ✦

When you feel like barfing into the abyss, the abyss barfs back into you.

Or something.

Graham Gray stared into the abyss, which in this case was the muddy ground thirty-some feet below behind the Rolvaag Memorial Library. He wasn't sure how he'd ended up on the library roof—a walk? A dare? A trance? But he knew why, of all the places to explore the St. Olaf campus, he went for a roof.

*It doesn't matter, none of it matters, and it's not like I'll be missed and I'm so so so tired and maybe this wasn't such a dumb idea after all God knows my folks will be thrilled but even so it's a mess of my own making AGAIN and I can't even blame the booze since I quit last year so what's my excuse now?*

Simple. He didn't have one. And he was tired of blaming everything—the substance abuse, the depression, the inability to connect, the oily T-zone—on his parents. It was past time to hit the Reset button, maybe come back as a muskrat or blue whale or medical transcriptionist or cotton candy vendor.

Or would that be the Delete button? Because he was pretty sure there wasn't a benevolent God looking down on humanity, giving them little jobs to do so they could trundle about the earth like ants, earning their tiny heavenly merit badges.

"I can't believe I'm gonna die like this," he marveled aloud, and the sound of his own voice—small and scared and disbelieving—startled him.

"Not to worry." The voice came from fucking nowhere and he nearly went over, because that was *way* more startling. "You aren't."

"Excuse me," he snapped, turning. "You can't possibly—huh."

A ridiculously pretty woman was standing about eight feet away. She was tall and slender, with shoulder-length brown hair and a pale face, sporting a bright-purple raincoat and black boots with white skulls on the toes. As she stepped closer and he got a better look at her (and at the Jack Skellingtons on her Wellingtons), he was startled all over again. It was probably the light, but it looked like her hair and eyes were . . . deep red?

Then a lightning flash lit up the roof, and her eyes and hair were ordinary brown. Prob'ly why he'd never heard her come up behind him in the first place. Stupid spring rainstorm! Not only was he about to die, but he'd die wet and shivering and goosebumped. And in his rattiest pair of underwear.

*It's possible I didn't think this through.*

"You look cold," she observed. "And I am, too."

"Wow, you suicide hotline people don't just use the phones to do your thing, huh?"

"I'm not with the suicide hotline. Or any hotline. But you're chilled through, so you need to get off this roof. Come have hot chocolate with me."

Annnnnd of *course* a pretty stranger would ask him on a pity date during his last five minutes on Earth. "You can't trick me!"

"Pointing out we're cold isn't a trick." She smiled. Smiled! Like this wasn't a matter of life or death! Like she thought he was doing something . . . cute? "It's an observation."

"And don't try to grab me, either," he warned, though under different circumstances, he would have welcomed all the grabbing.

"There's no need to grab any part of you. I told you. You don't die today."

He liked her voice, a calm, confident contralto. "You can't possibly know that."

"Of course I can."

"I don't recognize you." He pegged her at about ten years older than he was. Maybe more. A line from his mother's least favorite movie came to him. "You don't even go here!"

"Correct. I'm here for the funeral."

"So I *will* die."

"Not tonight." She laughed. "But that's quite the ego on you, assuming I showed up early just to attend a stranger's funeral."

"Fair," he conceded. "Sorry. I'm not usually this self-centered."

"It's fine. And it's Ms. Gardiner's funeral. I worked for her for a couple of weeks."

"Couple of—" He blinked. Then blinked more, because the rain wasn't letting up. "Ms. Gardiner? The bio prof? She's dead?"

The stranger had no reply. Just crooked a finger at him. "Come down. Let's get cocoa with a shot of Frangelico. Two shots."

"I quit drinking."

"Oh. Good for you. Straight cocoa it is, then."

She didn't ask, but he went ahead anyway: "Because I kept doing dumb destructive stuff and couldn't stop."

"It's a good thing you quit, then," she replied, po-faced, and he had to laugh. "My name is Amara."

"Graham Gray. And I'm not coming over to shake your hand. So give it up already."

"As you wish. But—stop me if you've heard this—you aren't dying tonight."

He was surprised to see she was only a couple feet away, though he would have bet money she hadn't moved the entire time they talked. Had she hypnotized him, like a gorgeous spitting cobra? And if she had, what did that make him? Mongoose or mouse?

"I still don't see how you could possibly know that."

"No need to take my word for it. Here, I'll prove it."

She was *right there*, and even as he processed that fact, she slapped her palm against his chest and shoved. The world went upside down and then righted itself with crazy speed, and he had time for one panicked thought—

*Why did I think this was a good idea????*

—before he felt *and* heard the impact:

*Splorch!*

"Mud," he groaned. He wriggled in the mess for a few seconds, amazed he could move, then managed to flop over on his back and gasp at the night sky while wiggling his fingers and toes. The breath had been punched out of his lungs by the impact, and he sucked in air so quickly he was light-headed. Or maybe that was the concussion. "God damn. A four-foot pile of muddy slime because they broke ground on the new annex this weekend. I walked past it to get to the stairs!"

He heard footsteps, but he was in no hurry to try to walk, or even stand. Then she was looming over him, which was startling all over again. He'd thought she was older, but now realized she was closer to his own age. And how'd she get down so fast?

"See?" she said with a smirk. "You're fine."

"I've got mud inside me."

"Mostly fine," she amended. "So . . . hot chocolate?"

They had hot chocolate. Then tea. Then more hot chocolate, this time to go, and they ended up in his dorm room. And he told her everything. And she told him unbelievable things that he believed because, in a crazy-stupid way, they made sense. And then he passed out in his bed because he hadn't slept in three days or eaten in two.

And she was there when he woke up.

# CHAPTER NINE

La Croix disappeared just after the train pulled into the Minot station, off wherever he lurked when he wasn't irritating all living creatures in his immediate orbit. But her old Mustang was easily spotted in long-term parking.

"A convertible," Gray observed. "In March. In North Dakota. Is your dad tricking you into coming home so he can kill you with pneumonia?"

"Oh, please, he could kill me with a thought."

"Uh, what?"

"Don't worry, this car has an incredible heater."

"Sure, sure, could we get back to how your dad can kill you just by thinking about it? I mean, I know he's the Reaper, but how can he think you to death?"

Given Gray's childhood, mentioning a potentially murderous parent was a dumbass move. She cursed her lack of tact even as she ignored the question and talked up the car. "This heater? It could warm up the Arctic. More than climate change already is, I mean. C'mon, let's go. The Mustang won't hurt you. Most likely."

It wasn't just transport; it was an inside joke. Her dad had procured the Mustang her senior year in high school so she could drive it to prom. He'd never gotten around to selling it despite the fact that Amara hadn't lived at home in a decade. But she still had the key. She wasn't sure what that said about him. Or her.

Prom had been a bust, anyway. Her date showed up two hours late and left early with another girl. The knowledge that Amara's replacement would OD before she hit voting age hadn't been especially comforting. Nor had throwing her room-temperature Coke in the guy's face. The worst part? The cheating SOB was going to live well into his eighties.

The drive to her parents' place took half an hour, which was fine because she hadn't been kidding about the heater. It was colder than Minneapolis here—colder than almost anywhere, getting colder by the minute—and crisp. Dusk was quickly shifting into night, and the uncountable stars over their heads were brilliant pricks of fire. It was impossible to take them in and *not* feel insignificant. And Death's daughter liked feeling insignificant.

She understood why so many dismissed the Dakotas with tired scorn ("flyover country"), but it only ever evinced pity in her. *That's fine. You're missing out, but it's fine. Stay in New York. Stay in LA. We'll take all that room and clean air.*

Gray yawned again, apologized again, and kept chattering while she wondered if she was losing her mind. Going home—bad enough. Exposing Gray to the dangerous chaos ever-present in her parents' home—bad and possibly stupid.

She didn't have to bring him. Easy enough to ditch him, in fact. But if she was going home in a long-overdue attempt to stop running from her problems—if that's even what she was doing—abandoning Gray spit in the face of that.

Far more worrisome: Ditching him would put an unwelcome strain on their friendship.

Also, she was lonely. Even with her parents. Even when the house was full of death gods and their accompanying shenanigans. But it was impossible to be in Graham Gray's orbit and feel alone.

"Gah, sorry," Gray said after another yawn. "Long day and I didn't nap on the train. Too busy marveling at the big soft bed to actually sleep in the thing. So what am I in for?"

"Sorry?"

"Besides your folks. Who else is gonna be there? I'd love all the dirt ahead of time."

She snorted. "It's not a class reunion."

Gray shuddered. "Thank God. I'll sit down with death gods before any of the shitheads I went to school with. Also, La Croix said something about calling the guide?"

"Gede. Pack of death gods. The usual gang of suspects."

"Uh-huh. Pretend I've never met a death god."

"Well, La Croix, of course. His territory's south, but he's fond of my mother. And if Death really is sick"—she was still having trouble swallowing that one—"he would hurry to her side. Hades and Persephone, too."

"Wait. Greek mythology Hades and Persephone? Demeter's daughter? The reason we have winter? That Persephone?"

"Yes, but the myths don't get everything right. Sometimes they don't get *anything* right. She adores her husband, and her mom was always overprotective. Demeter made the classic mistake; she made the Lord of the Underworld forbidden fruit."

"'I forbid you to see him again, young lady.' Like that?"

"Exactly like that. Oh! And my favorite. If I had favorites. Which I don't, but I can't wait for you to meet my old teacher, Scáthach. And you'll like Chernobog, but you probably won't meet him right away; he's always late and he comes at night."

"And they're your dad's friends?"

"Colleagues. My father doesn't have friends."

"Oh. Yeah, I guess that would be weird. Is that why you don't want the job?"

*"Don't! Please, it can't be. It can't be my time yet! It's a mistake, please. Please, I'll do anything. Take my mother. Take . . . anyone. Just not me."*

"That's one reason," she replied carefully.

"Because, Amara, we'd still be friends if you—God forbid—had to take over for your dad."

And then they were over the small bridge that marked the start of her family's territory, thank Christ, and it was a relief to climb out of the car and suck in the cold air.

That's how you knew you were back in NoDak; you inhaled and your esophagus hardened instantly.

Amara was seeing the farm with fresh eyes thanks to Graham Gray: Unabashed Tourist, which needed to be a podcast. And she had to admit the three thousand acres were splendid, even this time of year: all fallow fields and leafless trees, the monotony of white and gray broken by acres of evergreens. The grounds were vast, the driveway snaked for three miles, and the two-story, ten-thousand-square-foot house—

"House? That is not a house, Amara. That is a stadium with bedrooms!"

—was on a private lake, and somehow designed so that every window had a water view. Even the basement! (Amara chalked it up to dark magic or genius architecture.)

If you stepped out the back door, you had your choice of four docks and half a dozen canoes and kayaks. The barn and outbuildings were on the other side of the driveway.

"Holy shit, this is a compound!"

"A hub and a homestead," she agreed. "My folks entertain. And they get a lot of pop-ins. Sometimes by the dozen. So."

"Death throws a potluck," Gray mused, and giggled.

"My mother would never allow a potluck. She would take mortal offense, in fact." Amara knew it was a cliché, but it was too quiet. "There should be people out here to greet us. Well, me."

Gray shrugged. "It's late."

"It's only nine p.m."

"Yeah, but they're old, right?"

"You have no idea." Still. Worrisome. "Come on, this way."

She led Gray up the heavily salted front walk and into an entryway that was larger than most living rooms. She relieved Gray of his coat and boots, took off her own, then tossed the bundle in the nearest closet and led him to the parlor, also larger than most living rooms.

"Jeeeeeezus," Gray breathed.

"Yes, it's . . . uh, well, it's our house."

The parlor, like most of the rooms, was all gleaming wood and glossy floors and heavy leather furniture, with loads of floor-to-ceiling bookshelves (complete with sliding ladders child-Amara definitely didn't ride while pretending they were horses), thick throw rugs, a fireplace, a wet bar, and the de rigueur dead animals on the walls: deer heads, a bobcat, a bison, drake and hen mallards . . .

"Holy shit, that's a cougar!" Gray was beneath two of the heads, craning so far back to see, she wondered if he'd tip over. "And . . . a grizzly?"

"Tacky, right? Sorry, my folks are old-fashioned."

"No, I mean—did he shoot them here? On your farm or whatever this place is?"

"Sure. A while ago, but yes."

He spun and stared at her. "North Dakota grizzlies and cougars are a thing?"

"Like I said, he killed them a while ago." She cupped her

elbows and rubbed, trying to chase the chill that had nothing to do with the weather. "Also, this is odd."

"Did you just now notice?"

"No, I mean . . . where is everyone? There's a reason the homestead is so big, and why my folks have a staff to help them with it."

"Because of course you have servants."

"Yes, and where are they? I should have had to introduce you to half a dozen people by now."

"So what kind of benefits package does Death offer? Full dental? Paid leave?"

"You can ask him yourself. My suggestion is that you not lead with that."

"Oh oh oh oh oooooooh!"

At the familiar trilling, Amara turned toward the far doorway and smiled. "Hi, Mom."

"Ohhhhhhh!"

Amara braced herself for the clutch, and her mother did not disappoint, rushing across the room and hugging her hard enough to lift her off her feet. A good trick, since Amara had towered over her since she was twelve. "*Herregud*, my darling!"

"Nnnnnf." Amara gently extricated herself. "Nice to see you, too, Mom. You know you're getting shorter, right? This is my friend, Graham Gray."

"Of course, of course, Amara's told us so much about you, *velkommen*, Graham!"

"Thank you, ma'am. Please call me Gray."

"As you like, dear."

Her mother was . . . changed. Short and stout, with shoulder-length red hair shot with gray, her normally tidy braid was carelessly done up, dozens of straggling hairs sneaking loose. Her eyes were still lovely, a clear green like beach glass, but the shadows beneath them were so dark, she looked like she'd been double-punched. She had always looked extremely well for her great age, but today, some of the years showed. But she was still strong and sweet and smelled like soap and honey and home.

Amara stopped staring long enough to remember her manners. "Gray, this is my mother, Freyja Brunhilde."

"Thanks for having me, Mrs. Morrigan."

"Hilly, please, everyone calls me Hilly. Has Amara given you the tour?"

"She just started. This is all amazing." Then, "Oooof!" as she picked him up in a hug. When she put him down, he was flushed and smiling. "Wow! Great grip."

"We'll get you set up in one of the guest suites, don't fret even a little. Unless you'd prefer the Caretaker House? It's empty right now so you could spread out . . . or maybe Amara's tower? Where's your luggage, dear?"

"The Mustang. Amara said someone would be along to help—"

"Well, you and Amara can bring it in and sort out the sleeping arrangements."

"Mom, where is everybody?"

"Are you hungry?" she asked with a bright, bright smile. "We've got lots of leftovers. Oh, let's see . . . venison stew, some duck, lasagna, lots of sandwich fixings. Or I could make something. Do you like lefse, Gray? They have lefse down in Minnesota, right? It's good with brown sugar and butter and we have so much! Or are you a vegetarian? There's salad and pasta and—"

"Mom?"

"—and you just help yourself and make yourself at home."

The sick feeling that had hit her when she saw the psychopomps at the RV park had never entirely left. The birds of prey, the crown, La Croix's urgency, the quiet house, and her mother's determined cheer were popping too many red flags.

"Mom, what's—"

"Later, dear, your father needs to see you right now."

*Needs. Not wants. And he wasn't here to greet us, either. That's never happened before.*

"Gray, dear, why don't you head over to the kitchen—take the doorway behind me and you can't miss it, but if you find yourself in the wine room you've gone too far—and I'll be in there straightaway to fix you something. And I just brought up a batch of mead from the wine cellar, won't that be a treat?"

"Mom, Gray doesn't drink."

"Oh, how stupid! I forgot!"

"Don't even worry about it, Hilly. I wasn't in the mood for fermented honey anyway, and I'm almost fully self-sufficient. Amara can vouch for that."

"Can I, though?" The sarcasm fell flat, not least because she had trouble keeping her tone light.

"And then you can pick out a room. I'll get Amara settled with her father and be right back, okay?"

"Sure. I'm guessing it'll take you at least an hour, given the size of the place. I'm pretty sure your house exists in two counties at the same time."

"Don't be silly," her mother replied, then seized Amara's hand.

"Ack! Easy."

Her mother hauled her toward the doorway. "Uh, Mom? I know the way."

Her mother clamped down harder. "It'll do him *such* good to see you," she replied, and her tone—hopeful yet uncertain—alarmed Amara all over again.

"Mom."

"I'm just so happy you're home."

"Mom."

"And he will be, too."

"*Mom.*" She'd known her mother was preternaturally strong—as a child she'd assumed every mother could move a loaded china hutch with one hand—but she hadn't manhandled Amara in years. "I wouldn't say you're scaring me, but you're definitely uneasying me." That was a word, right? And if not, she'd make it one. Right now.

"It's just so lovely that you're here."

*Lovely.* Not the adverb she would have chosen.

"It's just such a—a thrill!"

Another descriptor that didn't fit.

As her mother hauled her down the hall and into the next wing, Amara had time to take in the walls and note that they had changed exactly nothing in the decade since she moved to Minnesota. More dead mammals and waterfowl, stuffed and mounted, including the lesser scaup drake, Amara's favorite due to its purple head, and the trumpeter swan, her least fave, because swans were jerks. And hey! Can't forget the hunted-to-extinction birds (*great job, Dad, really*) also adorning their walls: the Labrador duck, the great auk, and the Eskimo curlew, which was just dumb. Who killed curlews?

Now the art: The occasional federal duck stamp painting long before there was a federal duck stamp. Some of John James Audubon's original sketches. Van Gogh's *The Kingfisher* (the one in the museum was a brilliant fake).

And there, just before her father's door, the sketch of her mother, courtesy of Loki and never intended to be seen by Death, never mind mounted in his house. It was part of the reason her folks decided her dad should go be Death in North America. Amara used to worry the trickster god would come for it, but it had been centuries.

She planted her feet. "*Mom.* Stop *dragging* me." Home five minutes and she could already hear the teenager whine creep into her tone.

Her mother released her, then grabbed her again, since Hilly hadn't anticipated immediate obedience. "Sorry. Oh, I'm sorry. It's just . . . I know it will do him good. Seeing you." Her mother yanked the bedroom door open and all but shoved Amara inside. "Look who finally showed up!"

Then her mother shut the door. And Amara trudged toward the bed for a long-overdue face-to-face with Death.

# CHAPTER TEN

Death was lying in the middle of his beautiful bed, and had been tucked in with no small amount of care, which almost distracted from his ghastly visage. His vivid, bloodred hair was fading to a mottled dark pink. His eyes, normally a match for his hair, were a muddied red. His hand, when he lifted it in greeting, was a bundle of sticks and dry skin.

"How're you so pretty when you do that to your hair and eyes?" he croaked. "Enough with the dyeing already."

"You took the words right out of my mouth." Amara swallowed her shock at his appearance. "And a backhanded compliment right out of the gate? Thanks, Dad."

"It's just silly, is all I'm saying. Be *you*. Look like *you*."

"You mean look like you. If you've got a problem, take it up with the good people at L'Oreal and Bausch & Lomb."

Her father let out a wheeze that might have been a chuckle. "Missed you. C'mere."

"If that's my social cue to say I missed you, too, you might have a bit of a wait." She sat on the bed and accepted the (alarmingly) weak semitriangle hug practiced by nonhuggers the world over: elbows out, cheeks not-quite-touching while leaning away from each other. Death smelled like cotton, cough drops, and Vicks. "The kind that taxes even your patience."

"Smart-ass."

She grinned. "I am as you made me, Father."

"Oh, stop it, cripe's sake." She laughed as he scoffed, and then he was seized with a dry coughing fit so sudden and sharp it bent him in half and scared her off the bed. She hurried to the en suite bathroom, got him a glass of water, came right back. He waved her away, but after a few more racking coughs . . .

*If he yarks up a lung I am OUT.*

. . . he accepted the glass and drained it in three monster swallows. He cleared his throat, then chased the last few drops. "Thanks. I've got a little fridge right over there, y'know."

"What idiot put it so far out of your reach?" she snapped, even as she knew she wasn't angry at said idiot. She wasn't sure who she was angry with. Her father, maybe. Her mother, often. Herself, always. She went to the teeny fridge, opened it, beheld bottles of ice-cold water and fresh-squeezed orange juice. "I think this is the fridge you got me when I left for college."

"It is," he croaked. "Had to scrub all the spilled Coke out of it."

"Oh, please, like you were the one doing any of the scrubbing. And it's not my fault the thing was permanently set to Arctic."

Death rolled his eyes. "The 'not my fault' mantra."

"So one or two or ten cans blew up. It was years ago and I regret nothing because it was how I discovered the joy of homemade Coke slushies. Now please hush and drink more. Your voice sounds like a mudslide."

As he guzzled, she went to the corner, grabbed a chair, dragged it over. Death's suite was mostly the same, even if he wasn't. Tall ceiling, big windows. Reclining chairs in gray velvet on either side of a red love seat. Hardwood floors polished until they shone, a four-poster, king-size bed. Marble-topped side tables were cluttered with Kleenex boxes and lamps lent a golden glow throughout the room. The fireplace across from the bed was banked to coals.

He was in his favorite flannels, the green-and-black plaid (Death adored Lands' End), and the covers were pulled to his chin, so he looked like a bundle of homemade quilts topped by a wan moon. His vividly colored eyes, a shade Amara shared and referred to as Satan Red, were washed out, as if he was going blind, and his vibrant hair was being co-opted by silver strands.

"So what's all this?" she asked, indicating Kleenex boxes, the fridge, and Death's disheveled appearance. "You wouldn't believe the huge lie that La Croix La Shitbird told to get me here."

Death closed his eyes. "Your mom hears you talking like that, she'll shit a brick."

"I'll rephrase but the intent behind my words remains the same."

"I'm dying."

"That's it! That's the huge lie La Croix foisted on me. And he co-opted my friend Gray, too. Charismatic SOB," she added in a mutter.

"Your friend? Or the baron?"

"Both."

"Yeah, I wondered if you were gonna bring a guest."

"Couldn't have kept him away if I'd tried. So I didn't."

"Admirable. Or suicidal."

Amara smirked. "Both those things can be true about Graham Gray."

Death laughed. "I'd like to meet him."

"Incredibly, the feeling is mutual."

"Well, good for him. I'm glad you have a . . . friend. You never—"

Death cut himself off, but she knew the rest. "I was never one for cliques, let's leave it at that. Also, you're not dying."

Her father ignored her declaration. "Worse, the fair-weather friends are gonna start deserting."

"I did notice no one's around," she admitted. "There's usually some housekeepers and grounds staff, but I've only seen you and Mom so far. That didn't even happen during the pandemic. Or the one before. Or the one before."

"They're all gonna leave. If they even bother to show up." Death heaved a sigh and managed to look still more pitiful, which was almost as alarming as La Croix whipping out the crown of owl feathers.

"You're not making a lot of sense. And since when have Anus, Scat, and Chernobyl been fair-weather friends?" She deliberately invoked her childish nicknames for the death gods, in hopes of provoking the *real* Death lurking in the sickly body on the bed. "You've known them for a thousand years."

"They can smell blood in the water."

"What, you think they might try a territory grab? Why would they? Literally no one wants your job. Death gods least of all."

Death ignored her logic. "They're getting their ducks in a row. Your mom's fixing them, though. Got a big breakfast planned, and they're too scared of her to blow it off."

She rubbed her temples. *Stay away, migraine.* "Your mixed metaphors just get worse and worse."

"We can't all be English majors who never use their degree."

"First, ow. Second, drink more; I don't know if Death can get dehydrated, but let's not take any chances. Third, why am I here? Do you really think you're going to die? Because that's not how it works. For anyone, and especially you."

"Now you're an authority on 'how it works'? You've spent your life running from it. From me. It breaks your mother's heart."

"Annnnd now you've dragged Mom into it. Well done, Dad; you're checking every box."

"Amara . . ."

"You're the one who butchered her sisters back in the day," she retorted, already heading for the door. "But sure. Moving out when I was eighteen was somehow worse."

"Amara!"

*Go. Put your hand on the knob and go-go-go.*

"I—I'm sorry. I just . . ." Her father gestured helplessly at himself, the Kleenex boxes, the room's general disarray.

*Doesn't matter. Go-go-go!* Her arm was suddenly too slow and too long. The doorknob was about a mile away. *Streeeetch! You're almost there.*

"I don't know what to do," he whined. "Neither does your mother. Please don't go. I—I'm thankful you came home. We both are."

*Dammit! So close to a clean getaway.*

She turned back with a sigh. Smelling victory, Death was heaving himself up to a sitting position. "I am. And I apologize again. Being overwhelmed is no excuse to belittle my last child. Any child," he admitted.

*Argh, don't let him off the hook, don't let him off the hook, don't . . .*

"Okay. That's . . . I understand. You're having a difficult week. I accept your apology."

*Dammit!*

"But Dad, in all seriousness: What do you expect me to do? Fluff your pillows and ply you with orange juice while you don't die? Because, obviously, you're not dying."

Silence.

Her desperation was a palpable weight, pressing the air from her lungs. "Death can't die," she whispered.

"No, but Death's avatar can." He blew his nose and looked even more woebegone than before. "And I am. And so the time has come."

"No."

"At long last."

"Nope."

"The passing of the torch—or scythe, if you prefer."

"You hear the noises coming out of my face-hole, right? The way I keep saying no, no, a zillion times no? And shaking my head like I'm trying to dislodge a tick? Dad? Are you listening?" *Dumb question. He never listens.*

"Don't worry." He coughed again, wiped his mouth with a Kleenex that came away bloody. "You're a natural. I've known that since you were six."

"No. *Nyet. Non. Nie. Não.*"

"If not you, then who?" he asked, and she had no answer.

# CHAPTER ELEVEN

She left the Reaper and bypassed the Valkyrie on her way out.

Well. That had been the plan. But her mother was on her almost before the bedroom door closed.

"He's better, don't you think?"

"What are you basing that on, Mom? Better compared to what?"

"I knew your coming would help."

"He looks ghastly compared to the last time I saw him. I don't know what he looked like last week or last month. My baseline's way out of date."

"And whose fault his that?" she snapped.

Amara blinked and took in her mother's denial / sudden fury / helplessness. "That's fair," she conceded. "What did Paeon say?"

"Paeon?"

"Yes, the god of godly medicine. Why are you saying 'Paeon?' like you have no idea who I'm talking about?"

"It hasn't come to that yet."

"Oh. That's . . . good, I guess." Amara's knees wanted to buckle from relief. If Mom had declined to bring in the big gun, her dad couldn't be in too much trouble. "But maybe you should—"

"I put your friend in your tower."

Amara giggled in spite of herself. "Thanks. That's not a sentence you normally say. Anyone normally says."

Her mother grabbed a piece of her hair and gave it a tender yank. "You must be tired. Go rest. See to your friend. And we'll talk about everything and anything in the morning, when the others get here."

"Okay." Amara tried to do the polite triangle hug but her mother was having none of it, giving her a squeeze that left her breathless. "Good night."

✦ ✦ ✦

It was stupid, given the size of the compound, but everything looked smaller, starting with her mother and ending with the tower, three stories high and artfully covered in vines, an Insta-worthy picture if there ever was one, but she didn't so much as glance up. Instead, she unlatched the unreasonably tall and heavy egress and shoved, and in seconds she was hammering on Gray's door.

She jumped at the scream.

"I'm coming! Don't harvest my soul, I'm coming!"

"Jesus," she said when he swung the door open. "How long have you been greeting people like that?"

"Two seconds. C'mon in." He let her enter, then waved his arms like Vanna pointing to the right letter on *Wheel*. "You believe this place? Of course you do. You were spawned and raised here. But *wow*."

She borrowed a line from Olivia Goldsmith's *Flavor of the Month*. "It's not home, but it's much."

Gray was in his normal sleeping attire: shirtless with shorts. Thank goodness they were just friends, because it had to be said: The man had an outstanding physique. It wasn't fair; Gray counted ignoring the McDonald's drive-thru and going inside as a workout.

He'd been given the smallest of the tower chambers and she was glad. Better the tower than the house; sharing the same space with death gods didn't always work out well. This way Gray had a separate space to retreat to if needed.

The chamber was simply furnished with a double bed, an end table, and two overstuffed, wine-colored chairs. There was a small table between the chairs, and the brass bathtub was directly across from the bed, adjacent to the fireplace. The built-in bookshelves were bare, the carpet a deep brown, the windows shut tight against the March chill.

"This place is like the fanciest of fancy B and Bs. Gotta say, the tub's so cool, I don't mind not having an en suite bathroom."

"There's a bathroom on this level," she replied absently.

"Yeah, I know. Your mom—"

"It's the second door on the left just after the door to your room."

"Um, Amara? Preeeeeetty sure you're not listening."

"But if you don't like that, you're welcome to come up to the top of the tower and use mine."

"Okay, now I'm getting a 'she's not listening' vibe *and* a Rapunzel vibe."

She laughed. "Don't be an idiot; my hair's not nearly long enough."

"Yeah, 'Rapunzel, Rapunzel, let down your bob' won't work. C'mere, have a seat in one of these ludicrously puffy chairs and tell me about this tower. Your family tower!"

"Pass. There's a reason my room's at the top. It was given to me so I could look over the kingdom I'd one day inherit."

"Couldn't give you a ground-floor room and a ladder, huh? So tell me about your dad. Wait—first, check this out, your mom got me settled and left a platter of—well, it sounded like she said *loofah*, but that can't be right."

"Lefse with fresh butter and brown sugar," Amara said, smiling to see the snack setup. "She used to bring it to me when I was studying. Or grounded. Or sulking. So every couple of days, now I think about it. Once it was four times on the same day."

"Do I even want to know what constitutes a grounding offense in *Casa El Death*?"

"Your Spanish sucks, and the usual. Lying about giving my lutefisk to the dog. 'Forgetting' to get their signatures for the in-school-suspension slips."

"Slips, plural, huh?"

"And hiding the crown. I was young and dumb and thought Death couldn't do the job without it."

Gray raised his eyebrows. "So you thought a world without Death was a plan?"

"Young and dumb." She shrugged. "Like I said."

"I know this isn't helpful right now, but everything you say is fascinating and scary and wonderful and terrible."

"Warned you. You know you're ridiculously brave, correct? Because most people would avoid Death's domicile. Most people would have dropped me like a bag of dirt when they found out what I was."

"A cute bundle of nonsense wrapped in a bow of bitchery?"

"Stop it." She plopped down on the chair, then spread butter on a small triangle of lefse, sprinkled it with a staggering amount of brown sugar . . .

"Oh my God."

. . . then rolled it into an eight-inch cigar . . .

"Ohhhhhh my God, Amara! You're gonna unhinge your jaw now. I've never been more terrified."

. . . and gobbled it down in two bites.

"I saw it and don't believe it. Do me, too, please, but instead of half a pound of sugar, maybe half of an eighth of a cup max. And instead of eight inches, maybe three?"

"Boring." But she obliged, and smiled to see Gray's enjoyment.[1]

"Your mom says this is made out of potatoes. Super-thin potatoes."

"Potatoes and butter and cream. Don't tell me you've lived in Minnesota for years and never had lefse."

"I've lived in Minnesota for years and never had lefse. I guess it's more popular up here by the border. Don't worry, I'm rectifying even as we speak. How's your dad?"

"Concerning."

". . . Okay. Is he really dying?"

"He thinks he is. Or he wants me to think he is. Or maybe he is." She fixed herself another brown sugar / butter / potato cigar. "Coughing up blood—nobody does that for fun."

"That is true. Nobody coughs up blood for the hilarity factor."

"I don't know what's going on, but he wants me to take over the family business." She masticated, then added, "Which, to be fair, I already knew."

Gray, who'd just popped the last lefse inch into his mouth, nearly choked. "Yeah. It's one of the reasons you left . . . what? A decade ago?"

"One reason, yes."

1 Lefse is soooo good. Don't take my word for it; try some.

"So you're taking up the scythe? Or the twenty-first-century equivalent?"

"Of course not. I'm going to find out what's making my dad sick and fix that instead. With luck, by the end of the week, we'll be back in Minnesota guzzling virgin margs by the pitcher and wishing we had lefse on the side."

"Sure, sure. End of the week. It's Thursday night, but whatever. Not that this is about me, but visiting your folks is a nice reminder that mine aren't nearly as weird and damaging as I thought."

"They *are*," Amara corrected, ignoring the coil of anger in her belly when she thought of Gloria and Greg Gray. "And they are damaging."

"See?" Gray gave her a friendly whap on the arm. "Bad as you thought it was here, it could've been worse. Death and Hilly never abused you, they just want you to spend the rest of your life murdering everyone in the Midwest."

"I was wrong not to realize Death's tankard was half full, not half empty," she intoned, and got another whack on the arm. "Let's talk about anything and anyone else besides your family. Or mine. Abortion? Who was really behind January sixth and/or on the grassy knoll? Why Harry and Meghan are the worst?"

"Harry and Meghan are *not* the—ugh, point taken. You want a subject change. But hey! At least my family is keeping their word. No contact until they're ready to apologize."

"Since they never will, you'll never have to see them again."

Gray shrugged. "Their choice."

"And their loss." She stood and stretched. "See you in the morning, I'm going up. Also, my mother will make a seven-course breakfast and if you leave so much as a crumb on your plate . . . well. Lie awake in terror and contemplate alllll the wrath."

"Jesus Christ."

"Sweet dreams. Ha! That pillow missed me by a mile."

# CHAPTER TWELVE

*Years earlier . . .*

✦ ✦ ✦

Gloria Gray struggled with three bags of groceries and her keys, then bit back a scream when her apartment door opened from the inside because some bitch was in her goddamned entryway.

"Let me help you with those," the stranger said, then grabbed two grocery bags, took a few steps back, and slung them into the kitchen. Didn't even *try* to dump 'em on the counter.

Gloria was so pissed and bewildered, it took her a few seconds to lodge a protest. "What the fuck are you doing? There's eggs in one of those bags!"

"There still are," the stranger replied, eyeballing Gloria like they were gonna fight or fuck. Then she walked into the living room, dropped her pink-and-green tote bag at her feet, and made herself comfortable on the good chair.

"Bitch, you've got five seconds to get your narrow ass out of my apartment before I call the cops."

"Excellent plan," her uninvited guest replied. She had boring hair, chalky skin, and skinny limbs like those scrawny models strutting down runways. And weird eyes, so bloodshot they kinda looked red. "And while we wait for the sound of sirens, we can discuss how you avoided indictment across several states for multiple counts of felony child abuse."

Gloria stopped. Not just walking or reaching for her phone. Stopped thinking, stopped blinking. Her heart stopped. Her breath stopped. Everything just fuckin' . . . went still.

After a long silence, the stranger said, "The number is nine-one-one. If you were trying to remember."

Gloria realized she was gripping her phone so hard her fingers were going numb. "How—how did you know about that?"

"I worked in Fairview's medical records department for five days."

"You can't do that! You can't use your job to—to spy on innocent people."

"Two counts of felony neglect and child endangerment."

"I forgot my keys! That's all that was."

"You locked your eleven-year-old son outside because he forgot to do the dishes. At night. In Minnesota. In December."

"He was fine! The doctors all said!"

"One count of misdemeanor malicious punishment of a child."

"My husband did that, not me. How was I supposed to know Graham was in the basement for two whole nights?"

"Your testimony suggested otherwise. And he was four years old at the time. And the basement wasn't soundproofed. You knew."

"How the *fuck* did you get my testimony?"

"I worked for the Ramsey County courthouse for nine days. And Itasca. And Dakota. And those are just the ones in

Minnesota. Three counts of felony child abuse. That was back in 2010. You gave him a concussion and broke two of his teeth."

"Oh, for—they were baby teeth! Fuck's sake!"

"Shut your mouth, Gloria. Or I'll help myself to some of *your* teeth."

Gloria shut her mouth. The last bag of groceries had gotten heavier than the world, somehow, so she shuffled into the kitchen to put it on the counter. Took her time, too, put everything away nice and neat, even the booze, and emptied the dishwasher to boot, but the stranger was still sitting there when she returned to the living room.

"I don't understand it," the stranger said, like the conversation hadn't stopped for ten minutes. "I've been over it and over it. He's wonderful in every way a human being can be wonderful. He's thoughtful and clever and fun and hygienic and a good cook and not exactly hard on the eyes and beautiful. He is, somehow, the best. While you . . ."

"I don't—"

"What is wrong with you?"

What to say? *Welp, got knocked up with Ginni in high school, married the twenty-five-year-old fuck-o who did it, tho' I had to show him the DNA test first, got pregnant with Graham three months after Ginni was born, and she was dead before he started walking.*

*Found out I was in an "open marriage," which meant my ex could cheat but not me. Found out you don't get alimony when you're still married. Found out he had no intention of helping. Ever. With anything. Found out my family didn't want to hear about any of it. Found out the social services people did want to hear, but cared more about filling out forms than me or my kids. Kid, now.*

*My future was set a year before I could vote and it's such a fucking cliché I can't stand it. And I took it all out on my boy. And now I don't see him or talk to him and that's prob'ly for the best and I shouldn't care but I do, a little.*

"It just . . . all . . . got away from me."

"A pity he could never get away from you. Whenever Child Protective Services got too snoopy, you bailed. You'd uproot him and lug him around like a plant you don't like but feel compelled to keep because it was a gift. Even so, I think your deeds would have caught up with you. You are not a subtle woman. But your son wouldn't cooperate with any of the investigations."

She'd been scared of the stranger, this judgy bitch lurking in her apartment for fuck knew how long. Some of the fear had gone away when she realized the woman was young, maybe her son's age? But then her anxiety came roaring back, and Gloria couldn't figure out why. What, exactly, was there to be scared of? If the stranger wanted cops, they'd be there. If she wanted to pull a knife or a gun, she could have. If she wanted to beat her up, she would've started already, not talked for-fucking-ever.

But she wasn't doing any of that. She wasn't making moves of any kind, much less grabbing for a weapon. Her voice just got colder and colder, and the tone, the temperature, it *spread*, somehow. How could she make Gloria cold from seven feet away?

"The worst, most dreadful part? Not the bruises or the concussion or the broken bones. Not the terror of being locked outside while two inches of snow fell and the wind chill dropped. None of that."

"I don't—"

"Your son didn't lie to CPS because you threatened him. That's the worst. He didn't throw sand in the gears of every social worker for *fear* of you. Quite the opposite. He loved you. He didn't want you to go to prison."

"I know," she said dully.

"And so here you are."

"Yeah."

"But I won't have it, Gloria. I refuse." The stranger clasped her hands together and hunched forward, like Mr. Burns with tits and hair. "You're too close, for one thing; you only live an hour away. And he's kind. Which is wonderful, when you think about it . . . he's *kind*, Gloria, because you and the abusive shit you married couldn't brutalize his essential goodness away. So if you were to call him for help—the only circumstance you would ever reach out, I imagine—he might feel compelled to act."

"I wouldn't—I—I—"

"Which is entirely unacceptable."

"No, you've got it all—"

"And so you're leaving."

"I can't just—where would I even go?"

The stranger pulled a fat, legal-sized envelope out of her tote and threw it at Gloria. When she didn't move to catch it, the envelope hit her chest and thumped to the carpet.

"Open it."

She did. And stared at the contents.

A trick. Had to be.

"That's twenty thousand dollars. More than enough for your credit card debt with plenty left over to cover your moving expenses."

"I don't get it."

"No, you *are* getting it. That's the *point*. The cash is yours, and every month you don't contact your son, I'll wire another two thousand to your bank account."

"You . . . can do that?"

"Are you asking if I'm rich or if I temped at your bank to get all your account information? The answer is yes. However. The minute—the *second* you break our deal, we're done. And not only does the money spigot close forever, I'll do everything in my power to make sure you stand trial for your monstrous actions."

"But you can't—"

"The statute of limitations for felony child abuse won't kick in until your son is dead. He can sue you and press charges anytime he likes. Sorry to keep cutting you off, but I hate the sound of your voice."

"Did you take another temp job to learn that? About the limitations thing?"

"No, you worthless shitpile, I looked it up."

Gloria let the envelope fall and thumbed one of the packets of cash while the stranger watched. "There's gotta be a catch."

The stranger rubbed her eyes and sighed. "You mean *another* catch, don't you? Because most parents would assume cutting off all contact with their only living child to be a sizable catch. Two."

"What?"

"Two states between you and your son at all times. Minimum. Big ones. Rhode Island and Delaware don't count. Neither do Massachusetts and Vermont. But wherever you go, if you're only one state away, that's a deal-breaker and you'd better get a phenomenal lawyer. If Gray moves out of state, I'll contact you and give you the new boundaries you will abide by."

"What's wrong with your eyes?"

The stranger stopped rubbing and glared red. "Nothing. I left my contacts at home and I'm getting a migraine. I wanted this meeting to be memorable, Gloria. Stamped on your brain for the rest of your life, so there are no misunderstandings, now or ever."

"So you're just gonna give me two grand a month forever? What if I live to be eighty?"

The stranger made a sound that might have been a laugh. "You won't."

"What?"

"Live to eighty. You're waaaaaay off. Your son won't, either. That's the other reason you need to get the hell gone. If there are fewer than ninety miles between us, I might eventually give in to the urge to beat you to death. I want to do that *now,* Gloria. I want to see if you're an ugly crier. I want to hurt you very, very much. And so you're going."

Terror had shrunk the already tiny apartment to a pinhole. There wasn't anything in her world except the stranger's burning gaze.

Gloria bent, picked up the envelope, stuffed the cash back inside. "It wasn't just me, y'know. I'm not making excuses . . ."

"Of course you are, you useless twat."

Gloria felt her face get hotter and hotter, bit her lip, glared at the carpet. "I'm just saying, my ex-husband—"

"Oh. Him." The stranger stood and speared Gloria with one more bloody glare. "He's my next stop. I'm aware there is plenty of blame to go around."

She left, and Gloria listened until she heard the door at the far end of the hall wheeze open and slam shut. Then she stacked the cash on the counter, ran to the bathroom, and threw up.

# CHAPTER THIRTEEN

Amara's tower rooms were unchanged. The setup was beautiful; even at her most angsty, she could never deny the trappings were sweet. The queen-size bed with a semicircle headboard (still sporting the clamp reading lights she would attach, her mother would hide, she would find and reattach) was square in the middle of the room, and the curved wardrobe was opposite the fireplace.

A chandelier with artificial candles hung over the middle of the room, and there were the de rigueur overstuffed chairs (two, upholstered in forest green, with matching, uncomfortable throw pillows) but no end tables. Her mother felt they would look awkward in a round room, comparing them to skin tags.

She went to the wardrobe, opened it, observed the few outfits she'd left behind on her last visit, two—no, three—wait, five?—years ago, and wondered what the hell she was thinking when she'd paired cream-colored clogs with baby blue bike shorts.

There'd be time enough to burn her old clothes later; what she needed was the bathroom mirror. That room, too, was unchanged; the marble sink still sported a faint mint-colored smear from her green-hair phase, and the drawer of her vanity was stuffed with eyeshadow palettes in various shades of violet. *Why did I keep buying the same basic colors over and over? A fortune! A fortune on mauve!* She rummaged, then scowled down at the tube of Milani's Pink Frost lipstick. *Why? It made me look like I just guzzled a Pepto-Bismol smoothie.*

She made a mental note to have a long soak in the whirlpool tub, then opened the cupboard beneath the sink and pulled out two towels. Then she opened the medicine cabinet: Tums, Visine, ibuprofen, a box of Band-Aids, a nail clipper, deodorant, Jo Malone's Sweet Milk perfume. And a box of L'Oreal Paris Excellence permanent hair color in Dark Neutral Brown. Not that she needed it, given the stash she'd lugged from Minnesota. But still: good to know.

She checked the expiration date, replaced it with a newer box, and got to work.

# CHAPTER FOURTEEN

All the bad news hit at once: Breakfast was savory oatmeal, death gods were in attendance, La Croix was en route, and Penny had just stabbed her husband in the throat.

"Don't make that face," her mother coaxed. "Try it."

"I'm making that face *because* I've tried it. Brown sugar and cream, Mom. That's what belongs in oatmeal."

The kitchen could have been out of a high-end restaurant, huge and all shining chrome and gleaming counters, a spotless floor and meticulously organized pantry. Brass pans and hand-woven baskets hanging overhead. An industrial-sized fridge and freezer. Three stoves with six burners each. Sinks deep enough to bathe a calf.

"Maaaaaybe blueberries," Amara allowed. "Or strawberries in season. That's what belongs in oatmeal. Kale and a fried egg and mushrooms, not so much."

"Amara doesn't speak for me," Gray said, on her heels as always. He was the one person she didn't mind almost tripping over. "Bring on the weeds and fungus." He was barefoot, his hair still damp from the shower, sporting one of several pairs of knee-length cargo shorts and a long-sleeved polo shirt (sunshine yellow this time).

*How does he never get sick?* she marveled. *Not even a head cold?* She'd asked him, once. He'd just laughed at her and pointed out that she never got sick, either. Except for the migraines.

"Everything smells so good, Hilly. I can't wait to—Jesus Christ!"

"He'll walk it off," Penny snapped. She'd been straddling her husband's corpse and now yanked the knife out of his larynx and stood, her insteps pressed against each side of his ribcage. She showed her teeth in a grin and extended a hand. "Lovely to see you after all this time, Amara, but who is your friend? I confess I'm surprised to see you— Child, what are you doing?"

"Calling nine-one-one!" Gray screamed. "What the hell else would I be doing?"

"This is my friend, Gray. He's, um."

"gak."

*"Why am I the only one freaking out right now?"*

"agh ack."

Gray saw their bemused expressions, cleared his throat, and continued in a calmer tone, "And FYI, just to throw that out there, it wouldn't have worked anyway. I can't get a signal."

"And won't. Or at least not consistently, and not for very long," Amara said. "I warned you last night, there's a reason the homestead is so isolated."

"Yeah, but I prayed you were exaggerating or that your folks took a few hours sometime in the last decade and upgraded."

"Ahem."

"So if we can't call anyone, should we, um, put him somewhere? I mean, it's still a crime scene, even though I'm guessing it's a crime scene the cops will never hear about. Not sure how I feel about that . . ."

"Where do you suggest we put him?" Penny asked, seeming honestly interested in the reply. Like most of her ilk, she hadn't aged in any noticeable way. She could still pull off cropped sweaters and leggings and an eyebrow piercing. And she'd always been petite—not much taller than five feet—and slender and fine-boned. The kind of woman who looked like she could break if you glared at her too hard.

Her concessions to the modern world were chopping her titian hair (it really was the best word to describe her riotous red waves) severely short on the sides and disdaining a bra. She looked like some people's idea of a forest fairy, if forest fairies could rock a buzzcut and routinely stabbed their spouses. "I should like to hear your suggestions."

*"Ahem."*

Gray blinked. "Oh. I dunno, drag him out of the kitchen? And into . . . a ditch? No, that's cold. Literally and figuratively."

"Also unnecessary," Amara replied, "as you'll see in a minute. Do you want a gloppy pile of oatmeal loaded with mushrooms and kale?"

"I know you're trying to calm me down while also making it sound gross but it sounds pretty great."

"You're a good boy," Amara's mother said with an approving nod. "And you're handling this quite well, considering."

"Sorry, I'm new to all this stuff," Gray said as the corpse began to stir. "Amara told me some of it but it's still oh *fuck*!"

The corpse was sitting up. "Dak! Ack! Da—darling, I swear." Hank coughed up a little blood and took Hilly's proffered napkin with a nod of thanks. "She—ack!—was nothing."

"Don't you 'nothing' me," Penny snapped while her husband blotted his blood. "You went to such lengths to gain my hand, you wooed me like you were getting paid and broke my dear mother's heart to have me—"

"With all respect and reverence, love, your mother overreacted. Punishing the entire planet for the actions of one—"

"Scoundrel! One ass, one kidnapping wretch! One faithless dog! And now you're tired of me—"

"Never!"

"—you'll abandon me for an ordinary skink?"

The corpse seized her ankles and pulled; Penny landed on top of him and they groaned in unison. "Aggh, my ribs . . . it's 'skank,' dear one, and of course not."

"And this is Penny's husband, Hank," Amara finished.

"There's—there's no way those are their real names," Gray managed.

"They are now. But they used to go by Persephone and—"

"Hades." Gray nodded, trying (and failing) not to stare. "Sure. Of course. Makes perfect sense. Yep."

"Well, it does, kind of," Amara replied, then shoved a heaping bowl of savory oatmeal at him. Gray instinctively grabbed it, dropping his phone as he did so. Amara moved quickly; it slapped into her palm and she tucked it into his shirt pocket. "Penny, Hank, this is my friend Gray."

Hank blinked up at them with eyes that were unrelieved black. Looking into Hank's eyes was like staring into a couple of miniature tar pits. "Friend? Huh."

"I have friends," Amara mumbled, resisting the urge to scuff the tile with her toe.

Gray was still goggling down at the couple. "I'm sorry for your loss?"

"No more so than I," Penny huffed. She was wriggling and trying to get back to her feet, but Hank wouldn't let go. "Unhand me, you rutting cretin!"

"She was nothing," Hank soothed. "All of them, nothing."

Gray nudged Amara and mouthed, *All of them?*

Amara shrugged.

"So you keep saying. And yet inevitably I'll catch you following the wrong pair of panties down the lane."

"Dalliances!" Hank protested. "Fripperies! Ouch!"

Penny had somehow gotten the leverage to jam a bony elbow into his side. "I've had enough. You may return to your solo rule of Hades, that cold and dreadful place; *I* shall return to sunlight." She looked up and glared out the kitchen windows. "Somewhere warm. Somewhere the sun is up more than six hours a day."

"Now, Penny, that's an exaggeration," Hilly soothed. "Next month the sun will be up for a good seven hours. On your feet, both of you. There's quite a bit of food, and our other guests have arrived."

Then: the cacophony. Shrill yapping and the brittle sound of claws on ceramic tile.

"Swell," Amara said dourly even as Gray squeaked in alarm as the claws skittered closer. "Must Arawn always be preceded by his trio of hellhounds?"

"Hellhounds? Oh shit, oh shit, what do we d—awww!"

Amara groaned. *He got rid of those magnificent blue Labs for . . . for . . .*

"Wieners!" Gray said, delighted. The hellhoundlets had bowled him over, and all three were frisking about on his chest and legs. "Oh my God, the cutest hellhounds ever!"

"Still hellhounds, Gray," Amara pointed out. "However, in this house at this time, if you're not a badger, you should be fine."

There was a low chuckle from the hall, and then a familiar and uncomfortably deep voice: "I find the smaller breeds to be much more vicious."

"And lame, Arawn," she pointed out as the Celtic god of death swept in. "Deeply lame." She gestured at the tiny horde.

"First, who replaces awesome blue Labrador retrievers with long-haired wieners?"

"But they're so silky and shaggy and cute," Gray protested from the floor. Then: "Gargh!" as a hellhoundlet jumped on his balls.

"All the annoyances of a small, yappy dog," Amara continued, "without the convenience of the short coat. Be ashamed, Arawn."

"I decline." He dropped a casual bow. "Always a pleasure, Amara Morrigan."

"I, um, like your dogs, Mister . . . um . . ."

"My thanks, you poor child," Arawn rumbled.

"Poor child?" Gray asked. "Aw, c'mon. I'm old enough to vote. And rent a car, even, mister . . . um . . . death god."

"Arawn." He was as tall as Hades, but not nearly as gaunt, and sported his usual black long coat with the bristly black fur ruff that looked like glossy raven feathers. His leather gloves were bright red, and when he stripped them off, his hands were, too, with unnaturally long fingers and the nails filed to points. "A-R-A-W-N. But when Amara was wee, she pronounced it Arwen. And so."

"There are worse nicknames," Amara said. "Also, I might have been obsessed with *Lord of the Rings* when I was a kid. Thank God Tolkien eventually had a daughter, or it would have been more of a sausage-fest than it already was."

"Ah, I hear the dulcet tones of Amara on another feminist rant."

Amara ignored the annoyed shiver that La Croix's familiar voice brought on. "Swell. The gang's almost here."

"Hi, La Choy!" Gray called, still on the floor being harassed by hellhoundlets. "Have you seen these awesome dogs?"

"I could hardly miss them. You got rid of the Labradors?"

"They died, La Croix." Arawn spread his red, red hands. "Even our abilities have limits."

"And replaced them with—ah—well, friend Gray seems to like them."

"I love them!" Gray cried from the floor. "They must be magical hellhoundlets because I never cared about dachshunds until this minute." To Arawn: "Sir, if you ever need a dog-sitter, call me."

"That'll add some pizazz to your résumé," Amara observed.

"And my new business cards! Please remind me to get new business cards."

Amara giggled in spite of herself even as Hades said, "Your friend remembers his manners when he's not shrieking profanity in your lady mother's kitchen."

"Sir, when I met you, you had a knife planted in your jugular. I'm just saying."

"That's still no excuse to swear in front of a lady."

"Disagree. I think that's the perfect time to swear in front of a lady."

"All of you, shut the hell up and go sit down and eat all this food I've made," the lady ordered and, to her credit, no one wasted time arguing.

# CHAPTER FIFTEEN

*I'm normally not at a loss for words. Or so freaked out at the breakfast table.*

It was the empty seat at the head of the table. Actually, it was worse, because for a long moment, the others looked at her like they thought she might take her father's spot.

Never. Fucking. Happening. She sat so abruptly, the cutlery rattled.

"I can't remember the last time we all gathered for a meal," Hilly said brightly.

Her mother's happy expression and everything-will-be-fine-now air was so startling, Amara nearly choked on her bacon. How long had her mother been in such a state of extreme denial? "Been a while, Mom."

"But we are always happy to be invited," Penny put in. She and Hank were well into the cooing phase of their I-love-you-I-hate-you-I-love you drama. If the pattern held, they would hold hands all through breakfast, nuzzling and gorging themselves, then disappear for three days, eventually emerging flushed, dehydrated, and more in lust than ever. "You put on such a lovely spread, Freyja."

Like the other rooms, the dining hall hadn't changed. The table alone was ridiculous: a bulky thing that could seat twenty, hacked and planed out of ancient trees, polished and pampered until it gleamed. The chandelier overhead was a dozen lightbulbs tucked into a nest of pronghorn antlers. The fireplace at the end of the hall could have accommodated half a cow. And not a smallish cow, like a mini Hereford. A real monster, like a German Angus.

"It *is* overdue," her mother agreed. "And as I said, it's nice to have all of us together, however belated and brief."

"It's not 'all of us' without me." This from the woman no one noticed until she spoke.

Amara dropped her fork, which only added to Gray's surprised alarm: "Gaaaaah, where did you even come from?"

Amara ignored Gray's yelp, and was out of her seat in a flash and hugging the new arrival, a tall, broad-shouldered woman with a long red braid, wide green eyes, and a gorgeous explosion of freckles from forehead to shoulder blades. She was wearing cargo pants with what appeared to be a hundred pockets, a short-sleeved black Henley, and black knee-high mukluks.

"Gray, Gray! This is my teacher, Scáthach. The only living creature who can pull off mukluks."

"Sorry, I didn't quite—Scat-hock?"

"Call me Skye," the new arrival replied. "It's easier."

"I think I've heard of you."

She laughed at him. "Doubtful. So! This is Amara's dear friend we've heard so much about."

"That's a little terrifying, but it's nice to meet you." Gray stood and looked up at Skye. "Is it a death-god rule that you all have to be lava-hot and larger than life?"

"Oh, yes," she replied with a grin. "Our oldest and most sacred rule."

"Skye was my martial arts teacher. She taught me all sorts of things, actually." Amara gave the latest arrival another quick hug. "It's so good to see you!"

"Whoa." Gray made the time-out motion because he was a referee now, apparently? "I've never seen you come this close to gushing. Not even when you figured out how to make mango sticky rice."

"Mango sticky . . . ? Sounds vile. But I'm sure it's lovely. Perhaps you can show me the recipe, Amara. Skye, come dish up and then take a seat," Hilly coaxed. "We've saved a place for you and there's still lots of bircher muesli."

"Cold oatmeal. That's what my mother means. Cold oatmeal and mushrooms swimming in hot oatmeal. That's what you're looking at, Skye. Be warned by me."

Hilly sighed. "Yes, hon, you've made your feelings clear."

"It's her thing," Gray said.

"Overnight oats are stupid and gross. I regret nothing!"

"See?" Gray grinned. "Also, Skye, I understand how an ordinary mortal wouldn't hear you coming, but how'd you sneak up on the others?"

"That's *my* thing." Skye had been busy filling her plate, and wasted no time sitting and falling to. "Sorry to keep you all waiting."

"No worries," Hank said. "We waited for you as one pig does another."

"Speak for yourself," La Croix said coolly, gesturing at his empty plate. For one of the Gede, he sure bitched a lot.

"At least I got here before Chernobog," Skye chortled through a mouthful of ham.

"That's a low bar," Penny giggled. "He only comes at night."

"We didn't know, actually," Gray said. "I mean, not all of us knew. Okay, just me. I'm the only one who didn't know."

"Liar; I went over this with you already." Amara plopped another piece of gravlax on a cracker-thin slice of rye bread, took a bite, chewed, swallowed. "Pay attention."

"Sure, sure. I'll just jot all your notes in my death-god-shenanigans notebook."

"I've said it before, dear, but it bears repeating," Hilly said, refilling Gray's grape juice. "You're handling this so well."

"Hanging out with Amara is good practice when it comes to shenanigans."

"Arawn, what happened to your glorious blue Labs?" Skye speared another chunk of ham and popped it in her mouth. "I liked them very much. The older they got, the more they resembled furry barrels on legs."

"I'm afraid as they got older and more incontinent, I had to put—"

"Shhhh! Not in front of the houndlets," Gray begged, jerking his head toward the attentive trio.

"I'll say this, it's nice that the new bunch doesn't produce puddles of drool," Penny said. Her husband reached for a berry from her plate and she playfully slapped his hand away. "That was their only bad quality. That and the flatulence."

"That's endemic in all Labradors, Persephone," Arawn chuckled. "Especially as they get older." He tented his fingers and gave Gray a long look. "And congratulations, youngster. I cannot recall the last time I was hushed."

"I'm sorry. I was just looking out for your houndlets."

"Understood." Arawn settled back in his chair. "And so I let the impertinence pass."

Hilly cleared her throat. "As I was saying before Skye joined us, it's a delight to see you all, even under these, er, circumstances. Especially Amara and her . . . her friend."

"Why do people keep doing that?" Gray whispered to Amara, who shook her head.

"Did I not guarantee her presence?" La Croix asked, all expansive mood and relaxed air. His default arrogance never failed to make her want to bite something. "You wished for it, Hilly, and I made it so. And to Amara's credit, she did not hesitate."

Amara raised her eyebrows.

"Once she understood the severity," La Croix remedied. "Your idea to bring the crown was well done."

*Oh, for the love of. . .* Of course it had been her mother's ~~plot~~ idea. She served Death in all things. So did every living thing, to be fair, but her mother tended to go overboard.

"Amara's too jaded for one so young," Hilly said. "But the immoderate always made an impression on her."

Amara dropped her fork and it hit her plate with a clatter. "Gosh, this is all so swell. Truly. I love being discussed like I'm not even in the fucking room. Yes, I'm aware I used profanity, Mother," she snapped. "Did you ever consider it's on purpose as opposed to a slip of the tongue? I'm pushing thirty, for God's sake. I'm allowed the occasional F-bomb."

"And the occasional S-bomb, C-bomb, and X-bomb."

She snorted (which was Gray's intention) and got up for more food. Her mother had laid out a traditional breakfast on the sideboard, a ridiculously long and ungainly piece of furniture someone chopped out of mahogany a couple of centuries ago. The wood was so dark it was nearly black, with dragonvine carvings and the marks of hard service. Sooo many water rings.

Gray in particular seemed pleased to see the vast buffet: scrambled eggs and salmon, more of the dreaded savory oatmeal, several loaves of various breads, cold cuts (Amara had been eight before she realized most Americans don't normally have roast beef sandwiches for breakfast), gravlax, miniature loaves of dense rye bread, bowls of yogurt, platters of berries, a ham shank brushed with brown sugar and butter, nine pounds of bacon, and brown cheese.

"Everything's so good, Hilly," Gray groaned. "And there was a ton of good food last night, too. That you just had lying around! How are you guys not really, really fat?"

"Hard work and exercise," her mother replied, then laughed. "Just teasing. Metabolism."

"Well, it's working for you. Hey, Amara, after seeing where you grew up," Gray continued, waving his fork at the dining hall, "I get now why your apartment is a tiny minimalist modern craphole."

"Is it?" Hilly asked. "Her father and I have never seen it."

"Whose fault is that, Mom? And I think 'craphole' is unnecessary and unkind," Amara sniffed. "I like small and I like cluttered. So it's perfect."

"But why move a state away? We understood your need for your own residence—"

"Did you, Mom? Because you went from your dad's house to here. You've never had your own place."

"By choice," Hilly pointed out sharply. "My point stands; there was no need to move so far."

"I could have picked San Diego. Or Paris. Or Moscow." She could hear the petulance in her tone and was getting as irritated with herself as with her parents. *Home barely twelve hours and we're singing the same old battle songs.* "Count your blessings, Mother."

"Yes, Hilly," Penny giggled. "Count all those blessings."

"Wait, Amara. You could have gone to Paris but you picked Minneapolis?" Gray asked.

"You're missing the point."

"Am I, though? Look, all I'm saying is, I get why you wanted a small place after growing up here."

"And all *I* am saying . . ." Hilly continued.

"I feel like I shouldn't have brought up your living arrangements," Gray confessed.

"Agreed." It wasn't the conversation, however annoying. It was how the others were 100 percent focused on the conversation. Most of them were even leaning forward, so as not to miss a word. Ridiculous. You'd think death gods had higher priorities than her living arrangements and her parents' notes on the same. "Besides, my mother has a rule, no psychoanalysis during meals."

"Among other things," Hilly replied. "Such as the rule about feeding animals while at the table. I see you, young man. You never mind those hounds."

"What? Hounds?" Gray's exaggerated innocence reminded Amara why he was a terrible poker player. "Ohhhh, *hounds*. That's what you were talking about. Y'know, I forgot they were even there."

Even Arawn snickered at the bold lie. The hellhoundlets had followed them into the dining hall, then taken their spots beneath the bank of windows, where they remained bright-eyed and attentive, their silky ears cocked, unwavering gazes following the food. Gray kept sending them longing looks and was discreetly (ahem) pushing a small pile of dachshund-sized bits to the edge of his plate.

"Oh, Hilly, what a pity your husband can't join us for breakfast," Penny said.

"Agreed. But. He's indisposed."

"Indisposed," La Croix repeated, as if he was tasting the word.

"So it's true?" Hank asked. He'd torn up his rye bread and was feeding Penny tiny pieces, but now his gaze went to Hilly. "I mean, I got the impression from you that it was bad, but . . . that bad? Death is dying?"

"No," Amara replied even as her mother said, "Yes."

"This is not encouraging," Arawn observed.

"Failing," Amara clarified. "Not dying."

"Yes. Failing. Would anyone like some venison? I could get a roast started."

"Please don't cook more food, Mom." To Hank: "He'll be fine. We're just working out some family issues while he recovers. I'm not even going to be here that long."

No one agreed. And no one demurred. La Croix just sat there with his habitual smirk. Penny and Hank, after looking at her, her mother, and then back at Amara again, resumed being lost in each other's eyes. Arawn simply sat and looked at her over steepled fingers. And Skye, shoveling bacon in like she was getting paid, kept her head down and ate.

"Of course, we all wish for Death's swift and thorough recovery," Arawn finally said smoothly. "And it is a relief to finally discuss the pachyderm in the dining hall. But with the utmost respect, we all know you would downplay his condition regardless of the severity."

"Truth," Skye announced, coming up for air and ham. "He could be hemorrhaging out his ass and you'd dismiss it as indigestion. You know it's true, Amara."

"And so," Arawn continued with a pained sigh, "Skye's revolting example aside, I have to give more weight to your dear mother's diagnosis."

"You wait," Amara replied. And she didn't sound nervous. Because she *wasn't* nervous. Because there wasn't anything to be nervous about. Death would be fine and this—all of this—was unnecessary. "He'll get better. You won't have to pretend to care much longer."

"How dare you," Penny huffed. "Your father's recovery is our top priority. Your insinuation otherwise is *nnpphh* not *now*,

Hank." Penny chewed and swallowed the brown cheese Hank had stuffed in her mouth.

"My father's your top priority—I believe that. But to what end? You can't want his job. And you're not pals. So why are you circling like vultures?"

"Your mother invited us. Hardly 'circling.'"

"Yes. Great. Here you all are."

"Except the guy who comes at night," Gray put in, and if she hadn't been proud of him before, she would have now. He was stressed and surrounded by death gods, and he was paying attention to all of it.

"We were invited," Hank pointed out. "It would have been rude to ignore your mother's kind invitation."

"See? We *are* concerned."

"So are vultures, Penny. Now throw down your napkin and storm off while your husband keeps trying to feed you salmon and get to second base while the rest of us try and look *anywhere* else."

Penny, who was already on her feet, sat so quickly it looked like she'd been hit over the head. "I'll do no such thing, Amara."

"More juice?" Hilly asked with forced cheer. "Or a smoked turkey? I could bring one in from the larder."

"Aw, man," Gray said, polishing off the last of the bacon. "Next time, lead with 'smoked turkey.' I've never been so full in my life."

# CHAPTER SIXTEEN

After breakfast, Hilly had declined all offers of help with cleanup, so Amara had taken Gray up the stairs and across the bridge.

"A little bridge. In your house." He bounced a bit, testing the weight. "Sturdy, too."

"Stop making the bridge bounce, you twit. Come on."

"What's next? A secret tunnel? A mysterious elevator that only works during a full moon? An enchanted pantry?"

"Nothing like that. Well, maybe the tunnel." She took his hand and led him across to the other tower, which held the library. His ecstasy was on full display and she loved to see his joy.

"Oh my God. Stand back, I'm gonna do a Belle-type whirl. 'Ohhhhhhh, isn't this amaaaaaaaazing?'"

And he did.

"I wanted to show you last night, but . . ."

"Yeah, I get it. Yesterday was a lot. Speaking of 'a lot,' you have so many books they have their own sections! And you've got two stories to hold them! Watch out; I feel another twirl coming."

*I'd like a lover who looks at me the way Graham Gray looks at a great big stack of books. Just for a little while.*

Nope. Such things were not for her. The thought of falling in love with someone and knowing exactly when and how they would die? Knowing the date she would be alone again? If it was a bad marriage, she'd be counting the days. A good one, and . . . she'd be counting the days.

Unsupportable. Especially when it came to Graham Gray.

The library was one of the few rooms with wall-to-wall carpeting. The bridge was a nod to the fact that the place was two stories high, with rows of built-in bookshelves ringing the room. A spiral staircase led to the lower level, where there were comfortable couches, chairs, plush footstools, and two antique desks, each long and wide enough for a grown man to stretch out on. A chandelier hung overhead, and there were three-way lamps scattered around the room, with switches set to bright, brighter, and operating room. A wooden cabinet across from the desks held a printer and (quaint!) a fax machine. The two-story windows offered a view of the lake, and in winter, it was the coziest place imaginable. Summer, too.

Her family's collection boasted everything from a book of twelfth-century Norwegian literature to Joe Hill's *Locke & Key* graphic novels, and Gray wasted no time plucking books from shelves and sinking into a couch.

*I should go see Dad again. I should. Maybe bring him some fruit. I know Mom fed him, but it was probably savory oatmeal, poor bastard. I should . . . but it's nice in here. With Gray. Maybe we could stay a bit longer. Until Tuesday. Maybe Wednesday.*

She was startled by the difference her best friend's presence made. The place didn't seem like a luxurious tomb with him there. She wondered what that meant.

After half an hour or so, Gray came up for air. "So I knew about your dad, but I didn't know your mom was famous."

She had sunk into the chair across from him and let out

a sigh. "Yes, Gray, that's usually how it works when the myths are written by men."

"Could you not right now? I get it; we're all terrible."

"Finally! A bald admission of guilt. I'll make sure to tell all the other feminists during the next blood moon."

"Ho-ho-ho." In deference to his status as guest, Gray was as dressed up as he ever got: knee-length cargo shorts and a sunny-yellow long-sleeved polo. No socks, natch.

"Your folks are in a lot of these," he continued, brandishing *D'Aulaires' Book of Norse Myths* in her direction. "Listen, and I don't mean this in a nasty way, but isn't your mom—who I think is awesome—but isn't she a little—um—I mean, I didn't expect—but she's kind of—"

"Cough it up already."

"A cliché?" he whispered. "She fusses and feeds and that's it? Maybe that's not fair; we've only just met. It's just, she's so different from you. From what I expected."

"She's not a cliché, she's the archetype. She's where the myth of the perfect homemaker comes from."

"Oh. Wow." Gray shook off the concept like a dog shaking off water, and tapped the book again. "Skye's probably in here, too; I haven't finished reading it."

*I am, too,* she thought but didn't say.

"And Arwen's hellhoundlets are here!" he exclaimed, and tapped one of Sapkowski's tomes, *Baptism of Fire.* "Listen: 'At that moment sounded the howl of the fell beann'shie, the harbinger of imminent and violent death, and across the black sky galloped the Wild Hunt—a procession of fiery-eyed phantoms on skeleton horses, their tattered cloaks and standards fluttering behind them.' Doesn't that sound adorable?"

"Not even a little. Don't discount them because they're small. Those adorable teeth are basically weaponized sewing needles."

"I can't help it! I want one so bad. Say, since it's just the two of us in here . . . I didn't want to put you on the spot in front of everybody, but when d'you think I could meet your dad?"

"Now," she replied, almost before he'd finished the sentence. "I'd love for you to meet him. He'll like you, I think. But be warned: He's blunt."

Gray just looked at her.

"Like me," she admitted. "But that's the only thing we have in common. Well, maybe not the only thing. Look, we don't have more than a dozen or more things in common, all right?"

"Okay. Maybe we could bring him his lunch? I don't want to meet him by myse— I mean, that's an intimidating thought. Just me and Death, chilling in his bedroom. He can reminisce about the plague and I can be terrified."

"You've already talked to him on the phone."

"Oh, yeah!" Gray snapped his fingers. "That time you forgot your phone at my house. One of the times you did that. He kept yelling into it like he didn't know how phones work. It was a real 'Sir, this is an Arby's' moment. What a geezer. An adorable geezer," Gray elaborated, likely hedging his bets.

"Nothing to be worried about." *Provided Death keeps his mouth shut. But he's like me: He only tells people their fate if they ask. And Gray won't.*

"I'm not worried. Well, not too worried. You'll protect me. You always have."

"What?" She was flattered and appalled at the same time. "No. No, I haven't."

He laughed at her.

"Okay, I protected you once," Amara admitted. "But 'all the time' is a gross exaggeration."

"My ass. You've gone to bat for me how many times over the years? And I've borrowed how many hundreds of dollars?"

"One."

"What?"

"That's how many hundreds of dollars. And you paid me back four days later."

"Shut up, my point is I love you and you're a great friend and I trust you completely, which is why I'm not entirely terrified to meet Death."

"That's good to—"

"It's all those other death gods I don't trust. Hank and Penny knife each other for fun, Arawn runs around with hellhoundlets and wears red gloves to hide his bloody hands, Skye could fuck me up like a chainsaw through paper towels, and Chernobog only comes at night."

"Accurate," she said, then stood and extended a hand to pull him to his feet. "So then, no time like the present. Let's swing by the kitchen, I'll bring him some raspberries and condensed milk."

"Oh, yuck."

"Tried it?"

". . . No."

"Well, then."

"D'you know, Arawn's dogs like blueberries? Not that I, um, fed them any. They just look like the kind of hellhoundlets who would appreciate a handful of tiny berries. God knows what he feeds them. Dead doves? The blood of innocents? I should rescue those poor little—ow."

Halfway to the stairs, Amara stopped and stuck a finger in his face. "Get that idea out of your head right now, Gray. No one here should be rescued. Ever. For any reason. We've shat our bed and now we all have to lie in it."

"Okay, super gross. Here's what I don't get. Behold!"

"Oh my God." Amara was equal parts amused and horrified.

"Who gave you my junior high school yearbooks? Have you been carrying that around the whole time?"

"I swore I'd protect my sources unto death. But look." He began flipping through the pages documenting her period of public-school imprisonment. "Look at all the activities! And lots of friends—so many people signed this thing, there's not room for even one more person to wish you a great summer. 'Raider Princess,' whatever the hell that is. But then . . ." He held up her senior high school yearbook. "A year later, no activities, and maybe five people signed, and it looks like three of them were teachers."

"Your point? Other than I need to set those things on fire?"

"No one in this house can hide their amazement that you brought a friend. But it wasn't always like that. These books prove it. What happened to *this* gal?" He jabbed a picture of fourteen-year-old Amara emoting like crazy on the set of *Into the Woods*. "Where'd she go?"

"She found out when all her friends were going to die and under what circumstances and realized there was no point."

"Utter bullshit, Amara."

"It's *not* utter—"

"Ah! I knew I'd find you here."

They both turned as Skye came down the spiral staircase. "You, Amara, I mean." To Gray: "I had no idea where you'd be. I'm indifferent to your location."

"You're just in time!" Gray cried, and Amara prayed that meant he was going to quit with the yearbooks. "I told you earlier I recognized you."

She grinned. "I assumed it was a craven lie."

"Not this time. Check it."

Skye peered over Amara's shoulder. "A comic book."

"A graphic novel," Gray corrected. "See? *Red Sonja*."

Flip-flip-flip. "Here she is invoking Scáthach. And here she is praying to Scáthach. That's the goddess who gave her such prowess in battle. Here she is asking Scáthach to do her a solid, and here she is yelling at Scáthach."

"I know all these things," Skye said, handing back the graphic novel. "I'm just surprised you do."

"Are you kidding? My dad has a Red Sonja tattoo between his nipples."

"Good God."

"Don't judge, Amara. Dad could have used that two hundred bucks either for groceries or for Red Sonja. He made the right choice."

"Good *God*."

Gray ignored her revulsion. "Anyway, Skye, I've been hearing about the She-Devil with a Sword since—wait. You know? What does that mean? Are you implying that Red Sonja was real? Oh my God! Please *please* tell me she was real."

"Many myths are based in reality," Skye replied. "But I'd worry your brain would implode if we take this any further."

"I wouldn't mind! And that's as good as a yes." To Amara: "I fucking love visiting your family."

"Wait," Amara advised, as Skye laughed.

# CHAPTER SEVENTEEN

Figuring it was best to postpone visiting her dad and leave Gray to his research (though she prayed he wouldn't unearth more yearbooks or, worse, old book reports), and wanting to work off bacon calories, Amara asked for a sparring session. Her old teacher lit up at the suggestion, so they went to the caretaker's house on the south end of the property, where the upper floor had been converted to a gymnasium when Amara first began learning to fight.

And hadn't that been the source of many a squabble? Death and his Maiden, a.k.a. Hilly, could think of no reason why their daughter needed to learn a proper palm strike or master the spinning back fist. *Because I won't ever be Death*, teenager Amara had wanted to shriek but didn't. *And you know that!*

It had been one of the few arguments she won, and though her parents essentially oozed "It's unnecessary but why not humor the silly darling, let her get whatever this is out of her system," Amara took the training seriously.

A good thing, too, as Skye wasn't just an expert in all sorts of wonderfully dangerous pastimes like underwater fighting and cooking over an open flame, she was mistress of the Gáe Bolg and passive/aggressive shit-talk during fights.

"Your friend seems nice," Skye began pleasantly. "For a doomed mortal."

Amara dodged the blow—barely. "Thanks, I'll tell him."

"And it's nice to see you haven't let your appetite for pastries slow you down *too* much."

"Stop." Amara blocked, then blocked again. "I'm blushing."

"The only reason I came today was to see you."

"Awwww."

"No, that's bad. You made me lose a bet with one of the Gede." Jab. Block. "That purple-wearing shit. I was sure you'd stay in Minnesota." Hammer fist. "Now I have to hand that smirking jackass twenty dollars." Hook punch. Uppercut.

"You could at least pretend to be out of breath, you crone. And would it kill you to sweat just a little?"

"What's that saying your generation loves? Cry more?"

"You leave my generation—ow!—out of it."

"Mmmm." Skye looked down at her onetime pupil, whom she'd just tossed to the floor, gasping like a gaffed lake trout. "And then there's the other reason I came."

"If it isn't for the pleasure of my company, I will cry and cry. That's what those tears will be. They won't be tears of pain at all."

"I won't lie, I've always coveted your family's land."

"I know."

"So I took the chance to see it again."

"I know."

"And that's why—what? You do?"

"Uh, yes." Amara propped herself up on an elbow. *Argh, my bruises are going to have bruises.* "You've told me many times. My parents too. You are not subtle, in case no one has shared that with you. It's how we know the place reminds you of your home on the Isle of Skye."

"Ah."

"What I never got was, why not stay in Skye? It's still yours."

Skye tossed her a towel. "It's a shadow, a scrap of a shadow of what it was," she replied simply. "It's almost worse than having nothing, because I can recall the former glory. I can almost see it at times. Close and far. And how are the migraines?"

Amara blinked at the subject change. "Frequent and nauseating."

"Hmmm."

The migraines: a twisted gift from . . . well, she wasn't sure. First the spots would show up in her left eye, black irregular ones she couldn't see through. A dime-shaped blob crackling around the edges like miniature lightning balls. The blob would grow until she was more than half blind in that eye, and each tiny lightning strike felt like it was hitting the middle of her brain.

Then the aphasia: an utter inability to speak in coherent sentences. Not drunk incoherent: "We shhh, mmm, w'should keep in touch better. Mmm serious, we gotta hang out!"

No, the aphasia rendered her really, *really* incoherent: "Bllp mmttttti jabbey killy berg."

The most maddening thing about it? She knew exactly what she was trying to say. She could see the words in her mind, there was no confusion. But there was a breakdown somewhere between brain and speech.

The only good thing about migraine-induced aphasia was that it was transient. Though when you're trying to ask for help, or just sympathy, and all you can produce is gibberish, "transient" is relative.

Then the headache, which would start at the back of her

neck and gradually swallow most of her skull, the trigeminal nerve throbbing in perfect pace with her heartbeat.

Next came the aural sensitivity. Dropped pens sounded like bowling pins falling over, then blowing up.

Then the photophobia—a night-light might as well be a spotlight. And finally, the nausea and accompanying vomiting.

But they weren't real. Because Death doesn't get sick. Not even a head cold. And neither does his heir.

"Everyone gets headaches," her mother had insisted, bewildered. "Just take some ibuprofen."

"A warehouse, a *stadium* full of Advil wouldn't touch what's in my head, Mother!"

Then, later: "Is this about getting out of your chemistry exam?"

"Mo, tz moot meh brin!" (Fuck aphasia. Seriously.)

Amara shook off the reverie. "I'm dealing."

"Perhaps the headaches will lessen with time," Skye suggested.

"That's what the research says. Thank you, though."

"Pardon?"

"When I was a teenager, you were the only one who believed my migraines were real. You were the only one who supported me when I tried to get Mom and Dad to help."

"Well, as you know, I'll take any excuse to visit. On your feet, Amara. I'll help you hobble back to your tower."

"How are you simultaneously the best and the worst?"

"Yet another superpower," Skye began, but the horrified shrieks cut her off.

# CHAPTER EIGHTEEN

"Mom!"

With Skye on her heels, Amara nearly collided with Gray as he shot out of the library. "There's no way that racket means anything good."

"Keep behind me," she ordered.

"Sure, sure. Except I'm not gonna, so."

The clichés had it right: No matter how fast she tried to move, it was like trying to sprint through molasses. Her urgency was in direct proportion to her difficulty in getting to her mother's side. She had never heard Hilly sound like that. The only time she came close was when Amara accidentally drove the family SUV off the cli—

*Oh, shit.*

The three of them kept getting in each other's way until they were at Death's door, all trying to enter at once à la the Three Stooges.

"He's not here," Hilly cried. She was crouched over Death, still in the apron she'd worn to oversee breakfast, holding fistfuls of his pajama top, her nose an inch from his. "He's not here!"

"Let go of his shirt, Hilly," Skye said calmly.

"He's not here!"

"He's there, Mom. He's right there. In your, um, fists."

"He isn't, you ridiculous child!" Hilly wrenched her attention back to her husband. "You come back to me, Reaper," her mother commanded the unconscious—

*Please only be unconscious or even a coma not that I want my father to be in a coma but please please don't be dead I'm not ready no one is ready.*

—body on the bed. "Come back to me, bone man! Freyja Brunhilde Göndul demands it, you eater of souls, you king of the graveyard. Lord of crossroads, return to me at once!"

"I wish my folks had cute pet names for each other," Gray said faintly, and Amara bit her lip, hard, to lock back the hysterical giggle. The pain helped her get a grip, and she crossed the room, gently moved her mother aside (thank God Hilly went easily), and felt for a carotid pulse.

*Has his skin always been so papery, so fragile?* Death's hair had faded further in the hours since she'd seen him, his closed eyelids so purple they looked like bruises. And he was thinner than the night before, which should have been impossible. Worse, far worse . . .

*How can he look so small? He was the giant of my childhood, one of the biggest men in the Midwest. Even when I was old enough to drink, I had to look up to him.*

"He's not dead," Amara said. "His heart is beating. Possibly in irritation because Mother keeps shouting and shaking him." But she softened the sarcasm by taking her mother's small, cold hand in hers. The screams had terrified her, but her mother's desperation and anguish were as frightening. "Mother? Do you hear me? He's alive."

"There's no point in calling nine-one-one, right? You guys?

Even if we took a car to drive to the nearest cell tower for service?" Gray had his phone out, but made no move to do anything with it. "I mean, who would we even call?"

"No one," Skye said firmly. "This is a family issue. It always has been."

"Has anyone reached out to Paeon?" Amara asked.

Her mother's shocked reaction gave the answer. "Surely it hasn't . . ."

"Mom. It's crazy that the night I got here, I had to remind you that Paeon was an option. Death has been sick for a while. Long enough to call me home, so I'm guessing at least a month. And now he's unresponsive." She understood that her mother was using denial to cope, and she also understood that she couldn't keep indulging that delusion. "Paeon could be our only option." To Gray: "He's an ancient doctor who took care of gods so well, he eventually evolved into the god of godly medicine."

Gray was already nodding. "Well, yeah! Definitely call that guy."

"No one has needed his art for decades," Skye pointed out. "Possibly centuries. It will take time to find him. It will take time for him to come to us. In the meantime, the question before us is . . ."

*Oh, hell.*

"—what does it mean when Death is unresponsive? And what happens next as a consequence?"

And they all looked at Amara. Even Gray.

*Dammit.*

# CHAPTER NINETEEN

"First things first." Amara rubbed her temples and willed the migraine back the way you'd fend off a rabid weasel. *Back! Go on, git!* "Where does Dad keep the scrolls these days?"

They were in the kitchen, because Amara couldn't bear talking about taking on her father's duties with the man in (unconscious) earshot. It would have been like divvying up a person's belongings while you were at their funeral. Skye had volunteered to sit with him, which was the only reason Hilly agreed to leave her husband.

Hank and Penny had been nowhere to be found, no surprise, and no one wanted to go looking for them. Arawn was putting the houndlets through their paces. And La Croix had also vamoosed, which was unlike him. Usually when he was in residence he was on Amara or Hilly's heels. Had he left the property? And if so, when? If he hadn't left, why make himself scarce?

She'd ponder the mystery later. For now . . .

"Mom? The scrolls?"

"We're out of bacon but I can heat up some venison stew. Or a salad? I could make a big harvest salad with arugula and squash and goat cheese and bacon. You like salads, Amara. With sunflower seeds, and I've got bags of them in the pantry. Or something sweet? Belgian waffles—which aren't Belgian, but never mind . . . or perhaps some fudge? I could make homemade ice cream, is maple nut still your favorite?"

"Unfortunately," Gray replied.

"Mom. Please." Amara crossed the room and gently closed the fridge in her mother's face. "Nobody's hungry. If I eat anything larger than a sunflower seed, I'll vomit. Where are the scrolls?"

"Oh. Those." Hilly's head was cocked to one side and her gaze was vague. "We don't—your father doesn't use those anymore." She forced a laugh. "It's the twenty-first century, darling. We have all new equipment."

"You do? That's great! Show me?"

"It's this marvelous device that receives information via—how did your father put it?" Hilly closed her eyes, then opened them and smiled for the first time since she discovered Death at death's door. "Telephonic transmission!" At the look on Amara's face, Hilly elaborated. "I know, it sounds complicated—my understanding is, the machine takes data and forms it into something called a bitemap."

"Bitmap, ma'am," Gray said with a determinedly straight face.

"Yes! And it's all done by transmitting the bitmaps through telephone lines. Think about that! And then a machine reassembles it on our end and spits out a copy. Quick as all that!"

Amara blinked. "You're talking about a fax machine."

"No, it's a telefacsimile machine."

*Not now, migraine.* "Okay. Where is your telefacsimile machine?"

"The library!" Gray piped up. "I saw it when I was poking around there earlier. It's in the cabinet with—"

"Another obsolete device?"

"Don't be such a whatever-our-generation is called," Gray said. "Plenty of people still need printers."

"It's that archaic mindset that has kept us from the paperless offices we've been promised for the last fifty years. All right, I guess I should take a look and see what the telefacsimile has reassembled on our end."

"Stay here with your mom, I'll get it for you." Gray paused. "If—if that's allowed? A regular person intercepting Death's bitmaps?"

"Gray, you don't have to—"

"I want to, Amara. My best friend is in a mess and a half. I want to help."

"You're a good boy," Hilly said. "If Amara has no objection, I don't, either."

After Gray scampered out, Hilly added, "You have fine taste in friends."

"Thanks." She spread her hands and smiled. "What can I say? I love that delightful weirdo to death."

". . . Does he know?"

Amara said nothing.

"Ah, my poor poor dear. Why are you chasing heartbreak?"

"I like to keep busy?"

"Is he, ah, prepared?"

Amara said nothing.

"If you wish, I could talk to your fath—" Hilly choked off the word, then buried her face in her hands.

"Mom! Dad's not dead." Amara wasn't used to the role reversal; it felt odd to pull her mother into a hug and make ineffectual soothing noises. "He's just, um, resting. Which he wholly deserves. When was the last time he went on vacation? Or took a mental health day?"

Her mother pulled back. "What on earth is a mental health day?"

"Never mind. I'm crap at the comfort thing."

"You just need more practice."

*Perish the thought.* "But I meant every word. You wait. He'll be coughing up backhanded compliments and sneaking Cokes when he thinks you aren't paying attention in next to no time."

"I wasn't prepared."

"No, of course not. Who is? Plus, you're not an ordinary woman married to an ordinary man."

"No, I mean . . . this wasn't supposed to—" They could hear Gray galloping back along the passage, so Hilly forbore to finish her sentence. "That boy can move when he gets the urge."

"You should see him on Free Scoop Day."

"It's good to have you both here what with all this—I mean, especially since—we didn't plan for *this*, obviously . . ."

"Mom?"

Hilly shrugged.

*She didn't used to cut off her own sentences like that. If anything, she'd babble until I got tired and gave in. Is there something she's holding back? Or is it just stress?*

*And, again: NOT NOW, MIGRAINE.*

# CHAPTER TWENTY

Three-point-two million people die in the United States every year.

"The good news is, I only have to worry about the Midwest. Fifty-two thousand in Minnesota, thirty thousand in Iowa, one hundred and eighteen thousand in Michigan, a mere five thousand in North Dakota . . . then there's Nebraska, parts of Kentucky . . ."

"But that's still . . . what?" Gray narrowed his eyes. "At least five hundred fifty a day."

"Yes, that's correct," Amara said, pretending she hadn't been reaching for the calculator on her phone. "So I'd best get started."

"Shall you take the crown, dear?"

"*No.*" Amara cleared her throat. "Was that loud? I think it may have been loud. I won't touch that thing, Mother." *Not today. Not any day.* "I'm surprised La Croix touched it. He hates crowns. And things that aren't purple." *Shouldn't have said his name. Now watch him reappear and irritate the shit out of me, like Beetlejuice. Or a Kardashian.*

"Well." Her mother had the look of someone about to argue, then shrugged. "It's not like you *need* it, per se. It's just a symbol. That's all we have, in the end. I thought you might—never mind."

*How can someone who made me—half of me—still not understand me? It has to be willful.*

"Crown stays here, got it. Okay, here we go." To her horror, Gray was flipping through the paperwork with an expression she knew well. It was his *well, this'll suck but let's get it over with* look. "Ha! Amara, look. It's not just a fax machine, it's one of the first fax machines. The kind that used thermal paper." He held up the curly printouts. "I'm barely old enough to remember the rolls that always curled up the second the machine spat 'em out, doncha love it? Remember how fax paper used to be in those big rolls?"

"Put the curly printout down and back away, Gray."

"Yeah, right. Who's first? Do we do it alphabetically or logistically? Do we rock, paper, scissors this thing?"

"What? No. *We* aren't doing anything. *I'm* barely doing anything. This is only temporary until we figure out how to make my father well."

"Amara, at some point you're going to have to—"

"Don't presume to tell me what I will and will not have to do, Graham Gray," she snapped. "You are a guest. *My* guest."

"Ours, technically," Hilly put in.

"Not an apprentice. Not an intern. A guest. And guests do not accompany Death on Reaps. You will stay here. Have some pastries, catch up on whatever graphic novel series you're currently obsessed with, eat lefse until butter and brown sugar are swimming in your veins, and stay put."

He laughed at her. "I'll bet that works better on people who don't know you. And I can eat lefse on the way to . . . to wherever we're going. The first one is at Trinity Homes; sounds like a hospital."

Amara reached past him, opened the breadbox, and withdrew two cinnamon knots, each as wide as her outspread hand. "Here, Mother. Slap these over your ears like you're cosplaying Midwestern Princess Leia."

"Amara, I really don't think—"

"Slap them on!" Amara seized a fistful of Gray's shirt and pulled him close. "Understanding the process of death intellectually is not the same as viewing a Reap." *It'll change you.* "It will *fuck you up*, Gray, are you hearing me?" *You'll never see me the same way.* "For that, and a thousand other reasons—"

*We might remain friends, but you'll be terrified of me.*

*And that's how you'll spend your last few months in this world. Terrified. Of me.*

"—I'm going alone." When he made no response, she repeated herself. "Are you listening to me?"

With mingled despair and admiration, she observed Gray's eyebrows rush together as his jaw tightened. "I'm aware we're not going on a joyride. But this is your literal worst fear. The thing you've been having nightmares about for years."

"I never told you about the—"

"You talk in your sleep. Scream, sometimes."

*Oh. How mortifying.*

"I . . . I think you keep having the same nightmare. There's a woman, and she's terrified. But you're terrified of *her*. It's . . . weird. And it sounds awful."

"It's—"

*"Don't! Please, it can't be. It can't be my time yet! It's a mistake, please. Please, I'll do anything. Take my mother. Take . . . anyone. Just not me. Please."*

"—just a bad dream."

"I know it isn't." He was giving her his straight gaze, the

unflinching examination that always meant No Bullshit. "And you do, too."

"Well. I'm sorry you had to—had to put up with that."

"There's nothing about being with you that amounts to 'putting up.' It's all good on my end. Mostly."

She was still mortified, but she was also starting to see how it was. They were platonic pals, had always been so, but they'd slept over at each other's places plenty of times, and even in the same bed now and again. Hell, they'd shared a bed the night they met.

She hadn't known she screamed in her sleep, though. It's not like she brought men home all the time. Or some of the time. Or ever.

"You've been running from this all your life. I won't let you face it alone, no matter how many cinnamon buns you force your mom to wear."

"*Such* a nice boy."

"Not now, Mother." To Gray: "You don't know what you're in for."

"I'm aware I'm dog-paddling in a sea of ignorance. I'm loyal, not omnipotent. We're wasting time. Places to go, people to psychopomp." At their stares, he added, "What? It's not a verb? I feel like it could be a verb."

And Amara laughed, to keep from screaming if nothing else.

# CHAPTER TWENTY-ONE

She'd driven from her folks' house to Minot hundreds of times. But always as Amara Morrigan. Never as . . . whatever the hell she was now. And never with the delightful Graham Gray beside her. So the ride was simultaneously too long and not long enough.

Amara pulled into the lot with great care, checking blind spots no one in the world knew existed, and finally parked in the Trinity Homes lot.

Then she sat and sat and sat.

"Are you hoping whoever it is will die of old age instead of a heart attack so you don't have to take care of him right this minute?"

Amara said nothing. Amara said nothing. Amara said—

"Hon? You okay? Relatively speaking?"

"I know this one." She could see the sweaty marks from her fingers on the curly printout. "She was my middle school music teacher."

"Oh. Does that make it easier or harder? I guess it depends on who it is. Or how you feel about music. Given that you listen to way too much nineties pop garbage, I'm not optimistic."

"I will not hear one word against Ace of Base or En Vogue," she said absently.

Gray reached over and gently pried open her white-knuckled grip on the steering wheel. "Maybe that'll be a comfort for her. An old student. Someone she knows."

"I was a crap singer. So, no."

Gray let out a snort and then clapped his hand over his mouth. He rolled his eyes to look at her and let out another muffled snort.

She had to smile. She'd never adored anyone more, or been more infuriated by anyone, come to think of it. Well, La Croix was a contender for that last one. And she'd never suffered from inappropriate laughter with that guy the way she did with Gray. "Come on, you ridiculous dope. Let's get it over with."

✦ ✦ ✦

The grounds were lovely, even at this time of year: lots of trees and flower beds, wide paths and even a fountain. In a month, residents would look out at a riot of color.

The inside was nice, too; once they were through the double doors, they could see it was closer to a fancy apartment complex or a high-end hotel than what people thought when they imagined a state-run nursing home.

Gray slowed and stopped at the registration desk, then hurried after Amara when she didn't. "Don't we need visitor badges or something?" he stage-whispered.

"When you do that, everyone can hear you."

"Sorry. My first time."

"Everyone heard that, too. Lesson the first: Death Lite can get in anywhere."

"Okay, let's nip that in the bud right now. That's not a nickname you want. Try to picture it on a T-shirt. See? Terrible."

Amara made no reply as she neared the residence rooms, just swerved, seized a small plastic trash can outside the women's restroom, and dry heaved.

"Oh my God. You never throw up. I've never *seen* you throw up. And you chased vermouth with chocolate milk that one time."

"I'm not throwing up now, either. Hurrrrggggnnn!" Dry heaves: all the unpleasantness and exhaustion of vomiting, none of the release.

"Let's head back to the car." Gray displayed his essential fearlessness by putting an arm around her heaving shoulders, ignoring her long, rattling belch. "Give you a minute. Come back, hit the nurse's station for some ginger ale and crackers—"

"It's not a cafeteria, Gray."

"—and we'll try again."

"No point. To anything, really." Amara tucked the trash can close to her side like a football, shrugged off Gray's comforting arm, then rapped gently on the door to Room 196. In response to, "Jesus, finally," they entered.

The room was about the size of a hotel single, with white walls and mint accents. Amara pushed past the discreet curtain, noting where the en suite bathroom was in case her frazzled system wanted to offer up something more substantial than dry heaves. There was a couch at the foot of the bed, but it looked like it had been assembled from cinderblocks, right down to the squares and gray fabric. Amara gave it a wide berth.

There was a mountain in the bed swathed in crisp white sheets: Agatha Lindstrom, DOB 2/14/1975, DOD today. Class III obesity, type 2 diabetes, hypertension. Cause of death: myocardial infarction.

Amara cleared her throat. "Hi, Ms. Lindstrom. You might not remember me, but—"

"Amara Morrigan. You sang like a cat set on fire."

"Yes, but when I started in your class, you said I sang like a *rabid* cat on fire. So, improvement?"

"I'll take my small victories where I can find 'em." Ms. Lindstrom's clear gaze shifted to Gray. "Who's the stud?"

"You can see him? Never mind, he's *my* stud," Amara snapped, then recovered herself. "I mean, this is my friend, Graham Gray."

"Hi! I have no official role here, ma'am."

"I was . . . expecting your father. The jumped-up redhead with the crazy eyes."

Amara spread her hands in the universal gesture for, *Yeah, but what can you do?* "He's . . . indisposed. I'm, um, filling in."

Ms. Lindstrom let out a wheezy chuckle. "Listen to us and our fuckin' euphemisms. It's time, isn't it? You're getting me out of this shithole."

"It seems like a nice enough—"

"You're here to kill me."

Stung, Amara replied, "I think maybe your diet and accompanying lifestyle killed you."

Lindstrom flapped a chubby hand in Amara's direction. The fingers were so swollen, the rings had long been cut off. "Don't you judge me, you rotten brat. I don't haveta take shit from Death's still wet-behind-the-ears kid."

Amara could almost read Gray's mind: *This woman was a teacher?* Amara was pretty sure Agatha was like this *because* she'd been a teacher.

"I appreciate you making this easier on me," Amara deadpanned, and got another chuckle.

"Remember when you 'accidentally' burned all the sheet music for 'High School Confidential'?"

"Jerry Lee Lewis raped and married his thirteen-year-old cousin. And possibly killed his fifth wife."

"Still a bangin' song, though."

"Oh my God."

"Look here, brat: If you don't wanna listen to problematic—"

"*Problematic*?" Wait. Was this the way it was supposed to go? Did people argue with her father? Did they talk about problematic pop stars with Death?

Seemed unlikely.

"—music, you better go through your playlists with a fine fuckin' comb. Betcha half the assholes in your phone did somethin' terrible. Ozzy Osbourne? Tried to kill his wife. Jim Morrison? Indecent exposure. Axl Rose? Assault. Elvis? Where do I fuckin' start? James Brown? Same problem."

Amara rubbed her temples. "We're getting off course."

"Naw. I was pissed when you set all that stuff on fire, but I always admired your guts. S'why I'm glad to see you now. I did my fuckin' job for thirty-eight years. Now you do yours."

# CHAPTER TWENTY-TWO

"Okay. I'm done not throwing up."

"You sure? I'm in no rush. Take all the time you need to not barf."

Amara rested her head on Gray's shoulder. As they left Trinity, he'd glanced at his phone (ever the enthusiastic intern, Gray had put all the, um, clients' addresses into his GPS), then took the wheel while she clutched the garbage can that was her new best friend and struggled with the nightmare that was this long long *long* weekend.

Gray pulled into the lot for Roosevelt Park, empty save for a few maniac snowshoers, cross-country skiers, and ride-or-die zoo visitors, and she perked up a bit as he parked, came around, opened her door, and helped her out.

"Awwww. All chivalry, all the time."

He took her hand and steered her toward the nearest bench, where they sat in heavy-yet-companionable silence. She could see camels and bears and the tiger, and the flash of red in her periphery was a fox.

After a bit, Amara ventured, "I used to come here all the time as a kid."

"I knew it. You were a closet pickleball fan even then."

"God, no. I'd check out the sloth and the reticulated giraffe, my mother would utilize the trails, and my father would fish off the docks."

"How normal."

"We had our moments."

"More than I had, y'know." Gray gave her an affectionate nudge. "My mom never took me to a park, but if she ever did, it would only be to ditch me. Not that it's a contest. But if it was a contest, which it isn't, I'd win. Handily."

"What's your prize, then?"

"Therapy."

She snorted. "Actually, this place was more like Apology Park, no offense to Teddy R. Whenever they screwed up or felt bad for me when someone else screwed up or I was having a bad day, they'd bring me here. Rain or shine. January or July. Like the time Death brought me here to cheer me up after Take Your Daughter to Work Day."

"Ohhhhh boy."

"Do I really scream in my sleep?"

"Yes."

"Oh." Pause. "Do I say anything?"

"'Let her go.' 'Don't take her aunt.' 'Don't take her daughter.'"

"Oh."

✦ ✦ ✦

Amara giggled, then clapped a hand over her mouth so Daddy wouldn't hear. He'd been so busy lately, no time for her *at all*, but that was okay, she was a big kid now, second grade next year, and big kids had to do that thing Mommy talked about, that opp thing, they had to . . .

*Make your own opportunities, my darling.*

. . . be brave and clever and she *was* brave and clever and someday she'd be the boss of everybody like her daddy but for now she was still small.

So she snuck into the back of Daddy's car, way down under the blankets from the Fourth of July picnic and *urgh* it was hot but she didn't care because Daddy worked sooooo much and she wanted to help and she *would* help. His job was too big for one person. Mommy said. Better yet, Skye said!

And now shhhhh, the car was slowing and stopping, and when she heard the door slam she waited a few seconds and then peeked over the seat and they were in Robinsdale Trailer Park where Jenny lived and it had that awesome playground but no time for that, because Daddy was going into one of the fancy trailers, the wide fat ones that almost looked like real houses and she waited until the door closed and then waited a little more and finally scooted out from beneath the blanket and slipped out of the back seat and didn't slam the door and ran quietly and it was hard to run quietly but she did and the screen door was closed but hopefully unlocked and she heard screaming and froze and froze and unfroze because she had to help so she . . .

She . . .

She went in.

And Daddy was there and a pretty blond lady she didn't know was on her knees in front of him—did she fall? Was it a game?

"Don't!" the lady cried, because it wasn't a game. "Please, you can't," she said, and she was crying hard, so so hard. And Daddy was just standing there looking sad and she said, "It can't be my time yet!" and "It's a mistake, please."

And Daddy saw Amara standing by the door and his red

eyes were wet and he shook his head and the pretty lady was scrabbling on the carpet in front of him and then she grabbed his belt and said-shouted-screamed, "Please, I'll do anything. Take my mother. She's old, she can—or my aunt, my God, that bitch has been smoking for thirty years and it's *my* time? How is that possible?" And now the pretty lady was crying but she was mad-crying, like Mommy did when Amara broke her crystal swans. "How can it be my time? Take . . . anyone. Just not me. It doesn't have to be me, don't you understand?"

"I'm very sorry," Daddy said in his terrible-deep-sad voice.

"My daughter! She's with my ex-husband most of the time, I almost never see her, it's like she really isn't my kid anymore, and I can—I can have another one! Just not me. Just—"

And then she stopped talking. And crying. And everything.

✦ ✦ ✦

"Jesus Christ."

"She offered up everyone she loved in a selfish scrabble for more time. I dreamed about her for years. Still do, apparently. And here's the thing: I couldn't blame her. I don't think you would have, either, for all you endured in your childhood. She was just so . . . despairing. It was the worst side of her, and I like to think that when she wasn't about to die, she was a good person. A caring mother and daughter and niece."

"Sure, that tracks."

"But I didn't see any of that in the trailer. Neither did my father. And after that day, no one else did, either. And that's what my family does. That's what we are. We bring out the worst in humanity. And it's my job, now."

"First, that's not what you do, and second, it's a temp job. And you've had a million of those."

"A sizable false equivalence. And it'll be a full-time gig soon enough. I'll be the one to Reap away everything a person is, and leave nothing behind."

"That's not true! Amara, I love you, but you don't always pay attention."

". . . Thanks?"

"Look how happy your old music teacher—Agatha—was to see you. Y'know, under all the bitchiness. She knew what you won't face: that what you do—that what your dad does—is good and necessary. You helped her!"

"Will you sleep in my room tonight?"

If the abrupt question surprised him, Gray didn't let on. "Of course."

"Okay. I love you. Thanks for listening."

"Love you, too, Death Lite."

"Hey!"

"I was wrong, before. I think you should own it. We're definitely gonna make it a thing. I'm getting T-shirts made."

"Good God, you're not kidding, are you?"

# CHAPTER TWENTY-THREE

"Can you believe it?" Jimbo Muller picked himself up off the cement cellar floor and staggered over to them as he brushed himself down. "Whoo, adrenaline rush! I can't believe I didn't break my damn neck! Embarrassing, right? Breaking my neck changing a lightbulb? It was only a three-foot fall, Crissakes. Goddamned shaky two-step ladder . . . the guys on my work crew woulda laughed themselves stupid." Muller blinked. "Who the hell are you two, and what are you doing in my basement?"

"I've got some crap news for you," Amara said.

"Aw, man." Muller ran his fingers through his short gray hair and sighed. "Look, if it's about my ex-wife, just tell her I'm still waiting on the bonus from my last job. The guy promised it to me by Monday, and if he doesn't bring it by, tell her I'll personally make sure—huh." Muller looked at the sprawled figure on the floor, then at Amara, then at the sprawled figure on the floor. "Aw, shit. That's me."

"Yes."

"Lying still on the floor."

"Yes."

"But also standing here talking to you."

"Uh-huh."

"Well, fuck."

"Yeah."

"Can I ask you something?" Muller asked.

"Of course."

"Why are you carrying a little garbage can?"

"Oh. Hi." Beverly Lundergard struggled to sit up in bed, but was overtaken by a racking cough so deep and drawn out, it sounded like she was vomiting up a lung. Her swollen face, with its unhealthy yellowish cast, got steadily darker as the coughing fit went on and on. As Amara and Gray approached the bed, she waved them back, whooped for breath, and seized the nearly empty bottle of water which was, thank God, uncapped.

After a few gulps she lay back, letting out the occasional wet gasp. "Not too close," she croaked, flapping a hand at them. "You two don't wanna catch this."

We *two*? The first time was odd. The second . . . well. She'd have to think about what that meant.

Gray cleared his throat. "We won't catch your double pneumonia, ma'am."

"Don't take chances." Beverly had to rest for a few seconds before she could finish. "Not even a chance of a chance. This sucks; you've got no idea. Sorry, I didn't hear the doorbell. And I forgot to—" Another series of retching coughs; Beverly groped for the near-empty Kleenex box on the table beside her and hacked up a golf ball-sized lump of green phlegm streaked with blood. "Forgot to lock the door," she finished, dropping the befouled Kleenex into the overflowing wastebasket beside the bed. "Is that for me?"

Amara clutched her garbage can tighter. "No."

"Okay. What can I do—" Another cough, and she gulped the last of the water with a wince. "For you two? My God, someone lined my throat with razor blades while I slept. Was it you guys? Better not have been."

"Ms. Lundergard—"

"Bevvie. And whatever it is, I don't need it and I'm not buying it. My roof is fine, my windows are fine, my car windshield is fine, I don't need Girl Scout cookies, I don't want to buy band candy, I hate my cell phone provider but they all suck anyway. Sorry you wasted a trip."

"We didn't."

"Good for you, I guess." Beverly closed her eyes for a second. "I am. So sick. Of being sick. Before you go, could one of you refill my water bottle? Sorry again about not being able to buy anything."

Gray started to do it, but Amara put a hand on his arm and shook her head. Bevvie pulled in a deep breath and her eyes popped open. "Actually. Um, actually, I think that last bunch of coughs knocked more than phlegm loose. I feel . . ." She started to sit, waited for the bone-deep ache to steal her energy, the waves of dizziness that made even the thought of going to the bathroom beyond exhausting. And the relentless tickle in her throat that would, soon enough, turn to a fishhook.

But it seemed she was getting a respite. She tossed the covers aside and stood, feeling lighter and happier than she had in months. "Wow! I really do think that did the trick. Holy shit, it's like I got a jumbo shot of penicillin or something. Can I get you two anything before you go? I've got a fridge full of iced tea and a freezer full of pudding pops. I know, not great, right?

They're the only things I've been able to keep down in forever but I'll tell you what, kids, I could murder a stack of pancakes right now. You guys want some pancakes? Will DoorDash bring pancakes?"

"Probably, but no thank you."

"God, I don't know what I should do first, shower or eat." She looked down at herself and sniffed. "I don't actually stink, though. Or is it one of those things where you can't smell your own bad smells, but everyone else can? You kids would tell me if I stank, right?" As Amara opened her mouth to reply, Bevvie rushed ahead: "I feel so *good*, you have no idea. Why *are* you here?"

Again, Amara began to answer just as Bevvie's brow furrowed and she turned to look at the bed she never left.

"I look so . . . frail," she said softly, gazing down at her wasted body, the puffy, waxy face, the sunken eyes. "And a little gross, to be frank." She bent and sniffed. "And I *do* stink, apparently." Then, to Amara, "I know who you are now. I can't think why I didn't recognize you earlier."

"It happens that way sometimes," she replied.

"I, ah, didn't know you worked in pairs."

"She doesn't. I'm just shadowing her this weekend," Gray said. "Part of the Death Lite Internship Program."

"Good God, Gray."

"So . . . what now?" Bevvie asked, and reached out as if she wanted to shake hands.

Amara took her hand and held it. "Now is when you find out what comes next, Bevvie."

She smiled. "I feel great. I forgot what being healthy was like. Though I guess I'm *not* healthy." She spared the corpse one more glance. "It's weird I'm not scared, isn't it?"

When neither replied to the rhetorical question, Bevvie

squared her narrow shoulders. "Whatever's next, it's not a lonely, smelly sickbed with neighbors who slowly forget about you. So I guess we'd better get going."

"It's your journey, Bevvie. I'm just here to see you off."

"I'm gonna meet the Almighty in my nightgown?" Bevvie looked down at herself with a shrug. "Well, He's probably seen worse. Thank Christ I didn't die in the bath."

And then Bevvie Lundergard was giggling beside her sick-bed, and her smiling eyes were the brightest things in the room.

# CHAPTER TWENTY-FOUR

The sun was sliding away and the dark was rushing in after they finished their last Reap du jour. Gray broke the silence with, "I'm confused."

"Warned you."

"No, you freaked out about it fucking me up. You didn't say anything about upending the laws of space/time. And possibly physics. And how confusing that would be. To me. Or anyone, I bet."

They were back at the compound. Gray had coaxed the small garbage can out of Amara's grasp and they had an early supper of lefse and brown sugar, which they gobbled while standing over the sink.

"Hurry, if my mother catches us, her wrath will be terrible, she'll have questions I don't want to answer, and the lefse supply might get cut off."

"I get that you want to avoid your mom while you process living your literal worst nightmare, but there are about a hundred better spots to eat than over the sink. Especially in this place! And it's not that I don't like a dessert for supper, but there are three pies in the fridge: chicken, apple, *and* chocolate cream. We could be gobbling down pies over the sink like kings of old."

"Faster, dammit!"

Death was still comatose, and Amara had her suspicions. So she washed the butter and brown sugar off her hands, grabbed Gray, and led him down the kitchen stairs into the main basement.

"This wasn't on the tour."

"There are a lot of things that aren't on the tour."

"Awww. Thanks for making me feel special."

Amara hit the lights, then led him to the wooden doors beneath the stairs, unlocked them, and slid them wide like a barn door.

Gray peeked over her shoulder. "It's a small fake cave! For some reason."

"It's not fake. It's an actual cave. The house was built around it."

"A death god thing?"

"A death god thing. Crawl in." Amara turned, closed and latched the double doors, and turned back to find Gray hadn't moved. "Well?"

"The last time you told me to crawl somewhere, my shorts got soaked and I wound up kneeling in dog shit."

"That was three years ago! What, *I* should have crawled into the culvert? It was your errant basketball."

"You had jeans on! I was in shorts."

"You're always in shorts!"

"My point!" In response to her glare, Gray sighed and got down on all fours. "They've set it up so you have to crawl in, but your folks couldn't put down some carpet?"

"Jesus, you sound like an old woman."

"Always have, always—ow! Even Berber carpet would be—hey, there's a tiny waterfall in here!"

"We supplement the underground spring with well water."

The waterfall was bracketed with flowstones that resembled icicles, making it look like winter had been trapped inside the cave with them.

She crawled past the cave popcorn, the clusters of calcite crystals that looked like bouquets of diamonds in the low light, and the dogtooth spar, which always looked like a pile of sea sponges to her. Above them, boxwork had covered the low ceiling with honeycombed weathering, and cave bacon draped the opposite wall. Amara assumed the scientists who had named such things were perpetually hungry.

"Cool, you have your own indoor grotto."

"I loved coming in here, especially when I hit my teens. It's very peaceful."

She settled in next to Gray who (shocker!) had questions. "Not that your chilly, misty secret indoor lair isn't lovely, but is there a reason we aren't having this meeting in a room with heat? And/or blankets? Or in your Mustang? We could drive to Dairy Queen and then watch our ice cream melt before the power of your car's heater."

"Do you remember when I suggested my mother reach out to Paeon?"

Gray blinked and focused. "The thing that happened a couple of hours ago? Vaguely. He's the god of godly medicine, right?"

"Yes."

"Am I gonna get to meet him? Because I have this thing with my elbow he could maybe take a look at . . ."

"Apparently you won't meet him, since I assume Mother still hasn't contacted him. Which makes *no* sense. She doesn't need me to remind her to take action, and she'd be the first to tell you that. So is she doing this—or not doing this—on my dad's orders? That's the best-case scenario, and it sucks."

Gray frowned. "So what are you thinking?"

"I'm thinking this is a woman who was fully prepared to gut my sixth-grade teacher for not letting me check out books from the adult library. And she's as protective a spouse as she is a parent. My middle school got pissy when my dad took me out for two weeks, and when Mom saw the letter they sent him, she went right down there and tore a few strips off their hides. So believe me when I say Freyja Brunhilde Göndul ignoring a viable option is *unbelievably* out of character. Why wouldn't she pull out all the stops?"

"Is that why we're meeting in your chilly grotto? You think there's mischief afoot?"

"Nothing works in here. Not cell phones, not walkie-talkies, not radios or fax machines or electric can openers."

"Wait, why did you bring an electric—"

"It's a black hole of No Service. Best of all, no one can sneak up on us; there's only one way in or out."

Gray studied her in the low light. "Wow. You *do* think there's something afoot. Or you're about to murder me in the perfect place to stash a body."

"If I didn't murder you when you gobbled up my secret stash of Little Debbie Swiss Rolls—"

"You should have put them out. I had to go hunting for them."

"*Secret stash*, Gray."

"It's not my fault you're a shitty hostess! And for the record, my stance on this is the same as it was two years ago: I regret nothing. So are you thinking conspiracy or attempted murder or what?"

"It's got to be the first, because the second doesn't make sense. No one in their right mind would want to kill Death, because no one in their right mind would want the job, or to live in a world of eight billion people who can't die."

"Well, no."

"What?"

Gray spread his hands and shrugged. "*You* don't want to get rid of Death. *You* don't want the job. But there are 7,999,999,999 other people on the planet who might not share your opinion. And who might want a world where their loved ones can't die."

"Most of whom have absolutely no power over Death. Wanting a world where loved ones can't die is just a motive. It's not power. I know I'm biased, but, again: no one in their right mind. Which narrows the suspects down to people who *aren't* in their right mind. And in Minot, that's about six thousand suspects. Nine thousand if it's a long winter."

"Can we circle back? Are you saying that's how it works? If there's no Death, there's no . . . death?"

Amara waved away the concept. "It's moot. Death has been with humanity since before the caves. His avatar might change, but Death is always, always a force."

"So with your dad off his feet, are you the avatar in question?"

*Well?*

*Are you?*

Amara heard a roaring in her head and doubted it was the underground spring.

"Okay, I'm assuming by that long silence that you are, in fact, Death's avatar-in-waiting, since your dad's the current avatar . . . is it because you're an only child? Which is weird, by the way. Your folks have been together for centuries but only had one kid?"

"I had siblings," she replied shortly. "They all died before I was born."

When he was quiet for too long, she took his hand. "Now who's responsible for a long silence?"

"You had sibs and never told me?"

Amara shrugged, and ignored the pang Gray's wounded expression brought.

"Are you telling me that all of Death's avatars-in-waiting have died except for you?"

"Yes."

"And that didn't seem suspicious to you?" Gray asked in full-on skeptic mode. "Any of you?"

"Not really. Being an avatar-in-waiting isn't the same as enjoying the protections of being Death. One of my brothers died of an infection three hundred years before penicillin was invented. My sister got caught in a blizzard and froze to death. Like that."

"Jeez. I'm sorry, that sucks. But it also makes sense, I think. Death's avatar has to be tough. I guess the thinking is, if you can die of exposure, maybe you wouldn't have made a good Death? This isn't my area."

"No, it is not."

"Give me a break, I was a computer science major." Gray drummed his fingers on his knee in a rapid tattoo because she'd long since destroyed his fidget spinners. "I'll bet they had coming-of-age stuff, too, back then. Your folks and their . . . tribe, I guess?"

"Tribe?"

"And not cool ones, like bat mitzvahs. Terrible ones, like having to kill a huge wolf like Gerard Butler did in *300*. That's probably why your folks liked keeping you around. They must have been worried when you moved out."

"Yes, my other siblings stayed close. I never knew how they could stand it. One of my brothers died when he was only sixty. He *never* moved out." Amara paused as the implications of Gray's observation penetrated. "This will sound awful—"

"Noooooo."

"—but I never thought about it like that. I saw my folks as anchors and they saw themselves as life jackets. Ugh. Not my best analogy."

Gray reached out, took her hand. "So we both had older siblings who died. Why didn't you tell me?"

Amara couldn't meet his gaze. Anyone else would be irked, and maybe Gray was, a little, but he seemed more concerned than angry. "It's like you always say. It's not a contest, but if it was . . ."

"I'd win," he finished.

"I both love and loathe being the person who one-ups everybody. 'You think that's bad, one of my brothers was mauled to death by a pregnant mountain lion six hundred years ago.'"

Gray brightened. "But that means your parents could have another baby. You'd be off the hook. Do we dare speculate about procreational activities among the very, very elderly?"

"No. Let's stay focused instead. We have to solve this *now*; we can't hope my mom suddenly gets morning sickness and refuses to make lefse while simultaneously serving pickled pigs' feet with every meal."

"Jesus Christ!"

"Well put. Dreadful in so many ways."

Gray rubbed his forehead. "Your mom's superhuman ovaries and your dad's ancient-yet-perky sperm aside—"

"Good God."

"—here's one of the other things I can't figure out. If you do the math, a *lot* of people died in your territory or demesne or whatever, way more than we could get to on our own in just one day, *plus* we only Reaped half a dozen or so. How does that work?"

"You didn't think Santa really visited three hundred million houses in one night, did you?"

"Annnnnnd you're already losing me. Also, are you implying Santa is real? I . . . don't know how I feel about that. He gave me a *lot* of bad presents when I was a kid. Dental floss? A gift-wrapped bottle of Windex? Paper towels? Fuck's sake. Though our windows *were* incredibly clean . . ."

"Of course Santa's real, but we're getting off-topic. It's a bubble."

"Sorry, I thought you just said it's a bubble."

"Listen: I was there for Agatha and Jimbo and Beverly. But I was also there for Tanya, Scott, Renee, Dean, Shelly, and the others. It's like . . . it's a ritual. And by performing that ritual for Agatha, Jimbo, and Beverly, the others were able to pass on, too. I was with them, even though my physical body wasn't. And it's not just me and thee in the bubble. Each person we saw today ended up in the bubble, too." Amara sighed. "I'm sorry. I know it doesn't make sense."

"Death-god shenanigans?"

She nodded. Better to call it shenanigans. A lighthearted word for the darkest agenda. She didn't give a shit that her old music teacher was ready to die. The young woman offering her daughter's life as a bribe to Death was much louder than Agatha's grouchy bitching.

*And this is it. This is my life now. Every day. If Dad . . .*

*If Dad . . .*

Gray shifted his weight, leaned against the cave wall, wriggled for a few seconds, then leaned forward. "Argh, my kingdom for a back support pillow. I'm guessing a furnished, carpeted ancient cave over an even more ancient spring is dumb because of the damp alone."

"Quite dumb."

"And it's not that I don't love your cave, but why are we meeting here again?"

"Privacy. And while we're speaking of death-god shenanigans, let's consider our suspects."

"I like how you used 'our' as if I knew what the hell was going on and was capable of being helpful."

"You're helpful. Look at the chain of events. My father got sick and not only stayed sick, but worsened. He was stable this morning, but sometime after breakfast, he lost consciousness."

"We were all together in the dining hall, but I'm pretty sure everyone split up right after."

"Correct. So: Penny and Hank."

"Probably banging the whole time. It was obvious to everyone that they were in a rush to finish breakfast, but probably not so they could kill Death. Also, whaaaaat are those two even doing?"

"Persephone and Hades's relationship is deeply problematic and has lasted for centuries and I cannot advise you strongly enough to stay out of it. Focus, please."

"I'm trying! There's a lot going on. Okay, La Choy was there, too. He showed up late—sometime after Penny and Hank—and he bugged out right after. Which is why when your mom screamed the scream that could be heard for miles, he didn't come. He was long gone by then. We know why Penny and Hank stayed put, but why didn't La Choy stick around?"

"Good question. Remind me to hunt him down and ask him."

"Is it because of you?"

"What? No. What?"

"You guys have some history. Don't glare; anyone who's been in a room with you two for longer than ninety seconds would pick up on that."

"Pffftt." Amara shrugged off all the La Croix nonsense. "He's just a jackass. He's always gotten on my nerves but, like all assholes, sees it as a challenge."

"So you two never . . ."

"*No*. He's an annoying, overprotective chauvinist, which is the nicest thing I can say about him. More important, he doesn't like the winters here, so I can't see him engineering a scheme to kill Death, get rid of my mother—which would be almost as difficult as doing away with Death—and then live in NoDak for the next several centuries. He's from down South and bitches when the temp dips below sixty."

"Wait, what? Why would La Croix have to kill your mom?"

"Do you really think Freyja Brunhilde would meekly accept the murder of her husband? Trust me, anyone who takes on Death would have to kill my mom, and I don't see La Croix doing that. He adores her."

"That's a good point, though. If someone's plan is to get Death out of the way, and they're strong enough to do it, do they have similar plans for your mom?"

"Horrible thought," Amara replied, more than a little taken aback. "One I should have had before. And all the more reason to figure out what the hell is going on. This is why we're friends; you always think of stuff I should have but didn't."

"That and you keep me in Little Debbie Swiss Rolls. Scratch La Choy. What about Skye? She showed up late for breakfast. She even joked about it."

Amara shook her head. "She was sparring with me. We were in each other's company after breakfast, and she was right behind me when I ran to my father."

"And Chernobog only comes at night."

"Chernobog only comes at night."

"Maybe you're—*nngh!*—wrong." Gray wriggled a bit, still trying to get comfortable. "Stupid stalactites or whatever the hell they are . . . why would death gods want to hurt or kill a death god? And if they did, how would they know it would work? And for what?"

"What do you mean?"

"Revenge? Expansion? A fucked-up version of 'The Most Dangerous Game'? They've all got their own kingdoms, right? Sounds to me like taking on another chunk of territory would be nothing but a pain in the rectum. And, like we speculated, what happens to your mother?"

"Which brings us back to the beginning: No one in their right mind wants this job." She chewed her lip and pondered. *Maybe we're making this more complicated than it has to be. Maybe there really is a simple explanation: It's Death's time and I'm just being paranoid.*

*Oh* please *let it just be that I'm clinically paranoid . . .*

"I can't be the only person who feels like that," she finished.

"No, but you sure stepped up."

She rolled her eyes. "Stop it."

"Nope. You were incredible today. It was completely awesome."

"It wasn't and I didn't. Not really. I wasn't being me. But it would have been much harder if you hadn't insisted on inviting yourself along."

"That's what I do."

It was. Most people wouldn't have gone on *one* Reap, never mind half a dozen. For that matter, most people wouldn't go out of their way to be besties with the Grim Reaper's kid. But her situation was untenable. Gray wasn't going to set his life aside to help her Reap indefinitely. And even if he wanted to, she wouldn't allow it. And even if she allowed it, his time was running out.

Amara shivered a little and scooted closer. "We should have brought cardigans."

"Naw, don't need 'em." Gray slung an arm around her shoulder and she leaned into his warmth. "Listen, I don't know what's going on, but I'm with you until we figure it out, whether it takes days or months. You know I can work from anywhere. Having a programmer on-site wasn't necessary even before the pandemic. I can find a work-around for your family's lack of internet and hilarious reliance on fax machines."

"I love you."

"Back atcha."

And then she ruined everything.

# CHAPTER TWENTY-FIVE

*Stupid stupid stupid stupidstupidstupidstupid!*

Amara shot out of the cave, through the double doors, and galloped up the stairs like there was a horde of zombies behind her. Which would have been preferable to the horde of Gray behind her.

La Croix jumped when she burst into the kitchen, then closed the fridge and beamed. "Just the avatar I was looking for. If you don't mind terribly, I should like to watch you eat something delicious."

"Private chat *now.*"

"I am, as ever, at your serv—ouch."

"A long-overdue private chat. C'mon, you."

"I am delighted, despite the fact that your nails are sunk into my tricep like claws."

"Crybaby."

*She leaned in and . . .*

*She leaned in and . . .*

*Stupid! She leaned in and did something really, really stupid!*

She pulled La Croix into the wine cellar off the kitchen,

all but slamming the door as he sighed, his gaze sweeping over dozens and dozens of bottles, everything from a Markus Huber Reisling Eiswein, made by harvesting and pressing frozen grapes at night, to (urgh) frosé.

"I will not deny I find your urgency intriguing and worrisome."

"Why were you late to breakfast? And why'd you leave after breakfast?" she demanded. "And where did you go? And why are you back now?"

La Croix paused before answering. "Such behavior is not unusual for me. I am often late—everyone will wait, after all—and I rarely linger. You have loudly commented on those habits."

"Really? Because when you intrude into my life, you often linger. It's one of your more aggravating traits."

"What can I say? I live for the company of your family. The compassion, the generosity of spirit, the vast—"

"Stop it."

La Croix snickered. "In this case, I wished to visit some of my people. Brave souls who left the love and light of their homeland to live on the tundra."

"Sometimes people move, La Croix. Live with it."

For that she got an ostentatious shudder. "Their choice, of course. But I refuse to live anywhere 'wind chill' is a factor in my day-to-day life. That was not my only task, however; I was also needed to assuage some concerns. Apparently some of my people have gone missing."

"So you left to chat with your worshippers?"

"I prefer 'followers.'"

"Not better, La Croix."

"Why the interrogation? And where is friend Gray?"

*She leaned in and pressed a kiss to his mouth . . .*

*A stupid stupid stupid stupid kiss!*

*And then he . . .*

*And then he . . .*

"He's busy," she replied shortly. "I needed to talk to you in private."

"Wonderful to hear. Dare I inquire if you finally have tender feelings for me? Or anyone?"

"What? No." She'd ruined what she had with the only person she had tender feelings for, and there was only so much tenderness to go around. "Why do people keep assuming that? So you hung out with your followers and just now came back?"

"Yes, to check on your father and see if your dear mother needs anything. Again: Why the interrogation?"

"Never mind, I've got everything I—"

"Amara Morrigan." The wiseass grin disappeared as his tone dropped at least ten degrees, and though he hadn't moved, he loomed over her, a good trick since he was three feet away. "Answer my question."

Amara took a few seconds to respond. *I'm so used to dismissing him as a jackass, I forget he can be a* formidable *jackass.*

"Something's not right," she admitted. "And not just with my father. I think a person or persons might be doing this to him."

La Croix frowned. "That is . . . an extraordinary accusation. For what purpose?"

"That's where I keep getting stuck."

"And who could do such a thing?"

"Same problem. I'd think only Death can kill Death, but I might have that wrong."

La Croix studied her for a few seconds, opened his mouth, paused to consider, then said, "I was late because I did not get the invitation in a timely manner."

"Understandable, since you're the worst." Bitchery aside, Amara didn't like the sound of that at all. Why wouldn't her mother want all the support she could get? "My mother's under immense pressure. I'm going to give her the benefit of the doubt—"

"As did I."

"—and put it down to stress. I mean, you drive *me* nuts, but my folks always liked you. No reason to cut you out."

For that, she got another one of his mocking bows.

# CHAPTER TWENTY-SIX

*Years earlier . . .*

When Sophie Perry died, Amara knew her plan had failed. So she ran to her cave and sat and sat and awaited the inevitable summons.

"Amara? Come out, dear. Your father needs to speak to you."

*Hmmm. Mom doesn't sound* too *mad.*

"Now? I'm . . ." She groped for an excuse. "I'm doing homework."

"You're eight, darling, you have no homework."

"That's not true!" She had *two* Seek-and-Find worksheets to fill out. Those apples weren't going to seek and find themselves.

"Even so, I doubt you're doing homework in a lightless cave near a waterfall. Though if you are, stop at once because that's terrible for your eyes and the waterfall will ruin your work. Out, please."

She sighed and crept out of the cave, then looked up at her mother from her hands and knees. Mom had the stern-yet-loving expression that meant Amara was in trouble and she was disappointed, but not *too* much trouble and not *too* disappointed.

Or she just had a bellyache.

She followed her mother upstairs, through the kitchen, and into the dining hall, stopping short when she saw the evidence of her crime on the table.

Her father's crown.

"Did you think if you hid this from me, I wouldn't be able to Reap?" he asked kindly.

Amara shrugged. Her father's deep red hair was getting long again; he always grew it out, along with a beard, for winter. His red eyes were warm, like banked coals.

"I guess I should be glad you didn't try to destroy it. It was a bitch tracking down all those owls for all those feathers. Especially the secondary wing feathers. Never been pecked so hard in my life."

"Good!" Amara snapped, then burst into tears. She heard a sigh and squinched her eyes shut as Death rose to his feet. She shouldn't care he was disappointed. She should care about stopping him.

Then he was gently dabbing at her tears with one of Mom's scratchy linen napkins. "It's Sophie, right? She missed a lot of school, and when she came back, you knew she was going to die."

"And she shouldn't have!"

"Oh, sweetie, you'll get no argument from me. But we've been over this, and we'll keep going over it until you understand: I did not kill your friend. Remember when we talked about psychopomps? I helped Sophie with her inevitable death, which is not the same thing as killing her. And my obligation to her doesn't come from a pile of feathers. My crown is like every crown. It's not a tool, it's a symbol. Do you understand?"

"But it isn't fair! She was sick for so long and she was happy to be back at school. Remember when I accidentally dumped my pudding cup all over my sweater? She was the only one who didn't laugh. And she helped me clean up. She's nice!" Amara took the scratchy napkin from her father, who was on one knee in front of her. "Was nice."

"You're absolutely right, it's not fair. Not even a little bit. But it was always going to happen."

"She'll never come over to make cookies again. She'll never go sledding with me again or pick me first for dodgeball—*why*?"

"Because it was her time, hon. And now that you can see people's deaths, that means someday, when you're ready, you—"

"I won't! Not ever! It's *your* dumb, dusty crown. *You* keep it. I'll never take it. I'll—I'll chuck it into the pond. I'll burn it up!"

"Hon, you're not listening."

"'Cuz you're still saying the same stuff you always do! Someday I'll be you and have to kill everybody!"

"Well, yes. But not everybody. And not until you're ready."

Amara rubbed her face with the stupid scratchy napkin. "So who decides when that is?"

"You, hon."

She looked into his kind, creased face. "Well, I won't ever. So there."

"Fair enough." He straightened with a sigh. "Your mother's making lefse again. How about we go help ourselves?"

"I hate lefse," she lied, and swiped at the stupid tears rolling down her stupid face.

"Now, now," he said mildly. "Say what you like to me, but never traduce your mother's cooking."

"I hate everything!"

"I don't blame you, hon. Today of all days."

# CHAPTER TWENTY-SEVEN

Amara paused, looked up at the million billion stars gleaming at her from the dark, then trudged through snow toward her tower. She'd known the weekend would be awful, but it was now a full-on calamity galloping toward a debacle.

*She leaned in and pressed her mouth to his, pulse hammering so hard she could feel it in her temples. Quick as thought, his arm came around her as he leaned in and—*

"Amara?"

"Gah!" Her pulse was hammering again, but for the wrong reason. "Jesus, Cherny, don't do that!"

Chernobog, the Black God, took half a step back. "Sorry," he rumbled, because he had a voice like a gravel truck. "Thought you saw me."

"No one ever sees you until—never mind. Sorry. Didn't mean to snap." She extended a hand. "It was nice of you to come. It's been a while."

Short, blunt fingers engulfed hers and squeezed. Like all of them, he was physically unchanged, still rocking the bulky physique, sweatshirt, and jeans that were his unofficial uniform.

He had the build of an NFL athlete who'd retired a decade ago, thus the beer belly (gin belly, technically) sheathed in muscle.

His black eyes were so bright the corneas looked blueish, and his hair was a pale helmet. Like La Croix, he could loom without half trying.

"Saw your father. No change," he added before she could ask.

"I know. It's a problem."

"Heard you Reaped."

"Of course you did. Death gods gossip more than BuzzFeed."

"Who?"

"Never mind."

A short silence fell, because the god of darkness was the opposite of chatty. As she had many times before, Amara felt obliged to shatter the silence. "So you probably also heard about my friend."

. . .

"Well, I kissed him today. Yes! That's right! I orally mauled my best friend."

. . .

"Not a peck. A full-on, all-lips-on-deck sort of kiss."

. . .

"And he started to kiss *back*! That's the part that's screwing me up."

"Problems."

"You're damned right."

"Change things?" At her blank stare, Chernobog pointed to his yellow head. "You can be something else."

"Oh. No, we've been best friends forever. I know that's an overused phrase, but it's an overused phrase that happens to be true. What we had was perfect and I was stupid to risk it. Change is bad, especially now. Oh, and your attempt to dye your naturally black hair platinum looks entirely natural, so don't worry."

. . .

"Well, thanks for listening. Goodbye?"

A nod, and then he was gone, doubtless back among the shadows from whence he came. Or he was going to hit the kitchen for some cold venison. Either way: not her problem.

Scratch Chernobog, she thought. He wasn't around for any of the death-god shenanigans. *I can't wait to tell Gray I was able to elim—*

She cut herself off. She wouldn't be able to look at him right now, much less have a conversation.

*I've ruined it. I ruined everything.*

Her first instinct—to annihilate the memory of her blunder with copious amounts of booze—was (maybe?) a bad plan. She would, however, indulge in a long, mostly booze-free soak while she figured what the hell she would say to Gray when she saw him. Thank God the compound was . . . well, a compound. She should have no trouble avoiding him. She'd managed to avoid her aunt for most of the summer back in ninth grade, and dodged a subpoena her senior year.

*Oh, you piece of shit coward.*

She opened the tower door, took care to creep past Gray's (closed! yes!) door, then trudged up the stairs to her room. She flung the door open with a sigh which was immediately cut off by her yowl of surprise.

"Jeez, finally," Gray said. He was wearing what she instantly recognized . . .

*Oh no.*

. . . as one of his sleeping outfits.

*No no no no.*

Flannel shorts, a T-shirt (Jim Gaffigan's *Barely Alive* tour), and his *Shrek* slippers.

"What are you doing up here?" she cried.

He had the complete gall to look surprised. "You wanted me to sleep with you tonight."

"And you came?"

Even more surprised: "I said, didn't I?"

"Well . . . yes . . . but then . . ."

"'But then' nothing. Don't worry, I grabbed some extra blankets since I sleep clammy, and I saved some midnight lefse for you."

"My mother sent that up here for me!"

"There's still plenty here."

"Not your call!"

"Don't you dare shame my stress eating!" Gray sighed and ran his hand through his brutally short-but-coming-in-nicely hair. "This is a lot of shrieking, even for you. Is something wrong?"

*"What?"*

"It's about the kiss, isn't it?"

She was so humiliated/furious/confused, all she could do for a few seconds was gulp like a walleye flopping on a dock. "Of—of course it's about the kiss, you beautiful imbecile!"

Gray shrugged. "Well, you've got a lot on your plate this weekend. I'm not so egocentric to think I'm your biggest problem right now."

"You idiot, you've never been any sort of problem, never mind my biggest, now get out."

"Nope."

"Gray!"

"How many times have we crashed in the same bed together? Five? Ten?"

"Twenty-six." The blood rushed to her face as she realized that, quite unconsciously, she'd been keeping track.

". . . Twenty-six, okay. So if I leave now, it'll get weird."

"It'll *get* weird?"

"Weirder," he amended. He crossed the room to her, and she had to fight the ridiculous, simultaneous urge to back away and step closer. He took her hands and looked at her, really looked. And she couldn't pull her gaze from his. Couldn't even yank her hands out of his grasp. *When did Gray get magical hypnotic cobra powers?* "Look, Amara, I get it."

"That makes none of us."

"You had a crap day, one significantly more awful than I thought, and were forced to live through your worst nightmare, and turned to me in a moment of extreme—"

*Yearning? Horniness? Unrequited nonsense?* "Stupidity?"

"—stress. So we kissed. Who gives a fuck? I'm not reading anything into it. You prob'ly shouldn't, either. It's like that time I got hopped up on gummy bears and went to a noncostume party dressed as Baby New Year and you saw my dick. No big deal." She snickered; she couldn't help it. Gray, stone sober, nude but for a too-short sheet, had been a sight indeed. "Grow up, idiot."

"So, no big deal?" she asked.

"No big deal."

"It's just that easy, huh?"

"Sure."

✦ ✦ ✦

It wasn't.

"Dammit! I need more blankets."

"Pretty sure every blanket within a five-mile radius is on you right now, Amara. I can barely hear you; pretty sure the quilts are pressing the air from your lungs."

Amara thrashed beneath her quilted cocoon. Before this

evening, the fact that Gray slept clammy had been hilarious. He could draw body warmth from a cucumber.

But there was nothing hilarious about current events. She was aware that he was only a few inches away, that it would be the easiest/scariest thing in the world to roll toward him and kiss him again, to reach below his waist and yank down his . . . *argh.*

She was afraid to look at the clock, to see just how many hours of awkward they'd been enduring.

She sat up and glared when Gray giggled. "Sorry," he continued. "It's just I'm amazed you can move at all with that weight on top of you. Oh, shit, did I just do a metaphor?"

"You did not. Isn't this bothering you?"

"I'd endure any amount of awkward with you."

She sighed, and not just from frustration. "All right, that's sweet and stupid."

"And it's not like this is the first time things got weird between us."

"Yes, but those other times were related to death-god shenanigans. Or ordinary shenanigans, like when you bet merch you didn't have and lost."

"I *swear* I had *New Mutants* #98. Double-sleeved!"

"Yes, yes, the first appearance of Deadpool, I remember."

"Pretty sure my mom took it, but it's not like I was going to reach out and ask her. Easier to just pay up and clean your damned oven. Who uses an oven like a microwave, then forgets she uses the oven like a microwave? A week later, I could still smell the burned plastic."

"Don't remind me. I still feel bad about ruining that fried chicken."

"My point is, things have been awkward before. And my other point stands—you were stressed beyond belief. I knew it, and you did, too. So obviously I would never—"

"I'm aware." Was she ever. Gray didn't have to spell out his revulsion.

"You didn't let me finish. I would never—"

"Let's move on, shall we? I was dumb, you were dumb, all were dumb, forever and ever, amen."

"Let's put that on some T-shirts," Gray suggested. "No, I've got enough T-shirts; let's make hoodies instead."

"I can't wait until Chernobog scares the nonsense out of you."

"Oh my God! I forgot about him. He comes at night and it's night!"

"He does and it is and he's here."

"Why didn't you lead with that? I've been wondering about him since yesterday. Have you seen him? Did he admit to a plot to kill your father?"

"Yes, and no. And he's a platinum blond now. So calm down."

"Calm down? The creepy death god who runs around at night dyed his hair and you think that makes him less terrifying? Is he here right now? He is, isn't he?" Gray shot upright, and the move seemed instantaneous as he wasn't encumbered by a dozen quilts. "Oh my God, is Chernobog in the bathroom? Is he standing right over us? I can't see shit, he could be here right now! Why the *hell* don't you have a night-light?"

"Because I outgrew them decades ago?"

"Well, the fact that you're calm is helping me get back to calm. And lefse would make me more calm. I know you hid some from me, you perfidious bitch."

She smacked him in the face with a pillow and he obligingly laughed so they could pretend nothing had changed.

# CHAPTER TWENTY-EIGHT

*Years earlier . . .*

When Amara realized her favorite teacher was going to be dead by dinner, she kicked over the recycling can in the front of the room and set the papers on fire. This provoked several reactions from the audience: the bully she'd stolen the lighter from, the track nitwit who'd never liked her, and the teacher who did.

"Damn. That's hard-core."

"Oh Em Gee, *why* are you so weird and crazy *all* the *time*?"

"Amara Morrigan!" Mrs. Mickel had tossed her cardigan on the small blaze and was now stamping wool into the embers. "Hallway, *now*. And Karen, use the latte I know you smuggled to class to put out this mess."

"It's not a latte. It's a flat white."

"Empty it all and I won't ding you for detention. As for you, young lady . . ."

"I know. Detention." Even better, detention on Mickel's watch.

"My own fault," Mickel grumbled, scribbling the dreaded blue slip while Karen dumped out her overpriced coffee du jour. "Saw there weren't any students in detention today and foolishly made plans."

"That *was* foolish," Amara observed.

"Just for that, *two* hours."

"Yes, ma'am."

"That was as unlike you as anything I could imagine," Mrs. Mickel said hours later. There was a run in her pantyhose, her updo was well on the way to being an updon't, and her glasses magnified her pretty brown eyes so they looked comically huge. She was, as always, an adorable wreck with a fine brain. "What got into you? Is there tension at home?"

"I'm a teenager. Of course there's tension at home."

Mickel chuckled. She was young, about a decade older than Amara; she'd gotten her degree just two years ago. "Right. Silly question. And I understand if you don't want to discuss it, but I'd hate to see 'firebug' go into your permanent record."

"My permanent record is the least of my problems." *And yours.* "I just needed to make a fiery statement denouncing tyranny in all forms that would result in Karen having to dump out her drink and then whine about it for an hour afterward."

"Is this about the cafeteria running out of tater tots again?"

"It only happens to *me*. Three weeks in a row I had to make do with a lack of tots!"

"Oh, Amara. You've got to let Totgate go."

"Never!" Amara realized she'd jumped to her feet and sat down. "Everybody else is drowning in tots but they run out when it's my turn? Three times in a row? How does Principal Hecker not see what's happening?"

"I have some chips, would you like some?"

"I'm not a child to be placated with—oh, cheddar sour cream? Yes, please."

So they argued for two hours and detention was jolly, which Amara hadn't expected but should have, since Mrs. Mickel had a rep for relaxing the rules.

Amara loved Mrs. Mickel for her kindness, knowledge of Greek mythology—Mickel could give Hilly some competition in that area!—and sense of humor. But mostly because on the second day of school, Amara had her first period, and Mrs. Mickel helped with the humiliating and painful cleanup, lent her clean shorts from Lost and Found, slipped her some Advil, and never told a soul. And made it all seem like NBD.

And it *was* NBD; biological functions were nothing to be ashamed of, certainly not in the twenty-first century. But still. People could be stupid and cruel; thanks to Mrs. Mickel, no one found out, so no harm done, except to her shark underpants. But Amara hadn't been able to see any of that until Mickel calmed her down and pointed it out.

Mrs. Mickel didn't deserve *any* kind of death, but especially not being broiled alive due to an ancient oven's gas leak. Amara wouldn't have it; simple as that. So when she heard the sirens, her entire body relaxed; she nearly oozed out of her desk chair into a puddle on the floor.

"I live just a couple of blocks from here," Mickel murmured, opening the shades and peering out the window to see where the fire trucks were headed. "Amara, we only have ten minutes left for detention, why don't you head home?"

"Sure, Mrs. Mickel. See you tomorrow."

But she didn't, since Mickel was killed in a car crash on her way to the fire Amara had saved her from.

# CHAPTER TWENTY-NINE

After a sleepless night spent lying a foot apart like ill-tempered, exhausted dolls, they were both awake before Amara's phone went off.

Gray had time for a couple of irreverent questions before Amara kicked him out.

"Does Death need to set an alarm? Or does he just wake up on his own? Or is he like a rooster, who gets everyone else up? Wait, people die at night. Does Death even get to sleep?"

*It's the bubble,* she thought groggily. *It's time-walking. It's hard enough to explain when I'm wide awake. Which I'm not just now.*

She stumbled into the bathroom and began the day by splashing ludicrously cold water on her face. It wasn't enough, so she filled the sink with more cold water and essentially went snorkeling. She could almost feel her pores slamming shut in self-defense.

She got dressed and groaned in horror when she saw her reflection. Her dyed hair leached color from her face, and the dark circles made her look like the Crypt-Keeper, if the Keeper favored leggings and red wool sweaters.

*Fuck it. Gray doesn't give a shit and neither do I.* Not that a man's opinion—or anyone's, really—dictated her outfits. But Gray put up with her frosted tips ("You're like a sexy hedgehog!") and athletic-socks-with-penny-loafers phase.

She rapped on Gray's door on her way down to the kitchen. "My mother will have another breakfast feast waiting," she shouted from the ~~wrong~~ right side of the door. "See you in a few."

She heard the expected yelp of alarm; in sharp contrast to Amara's ten-minute prep, Gray needed a minimum of half an hour to get ready. Two hours, if he showered.

As expected, her mother was putting the finishing touches on several pounds of food and beamed as Amara came in.

"Good morning!" The trill was jarring given how white and strained her mother looked; Amara could have sworn the woman's laugh lines had deepened overnight.

"Looks wonderful, Mom. I can only assume by the ham *and* the turkey *and* the bass that you're expecting seventy-five guests." Amara got a patented Morrigan shrug for her trouble, then continued with, "I'm going to check on Dad and come right back." When her mother simply nodded, Amara asked what she knew was a dumb question. "No change, I assume?"

"The bacon will be ready by the time you get back," was the nonresponse.

"Okay, Mom. And I know I wasn't here much yesterday, but when I was, I noticed you didn't eat anything. And I'm betting you haven't had your own breakfast yet, since you're focused on ours."

"Oh, well. Busy-busy, you know."

"What I know is you're no good to us if your low blood sugar forces a swoon."

*That* got Hilly's attention; she didn't stop rolling out dough but her head came up at once. "I wouldn't swoon on a bet, Amara Morrigan, and you know it."

"Just checking."

Normally the walk to Death seemed to take forever; today it felt like five seconds. And there were worse horrors to contend with than a comatose death god.

"You!"

La Croix was on his feet the second he saw her. "And a very good morning to you, Amara." He paused and considered. "As good as can be expected under the circumstances. Would you like my seat?"

"You don't want to know what I'd like."

"Au contraire."

"What are you doing here?"

"Spelling your dear mother."

"Oh." Amara could have smacked herself. La Croix set her teeth on edge, but she couldn't deny he'd been . . . not helpful, exactly. There? Was that it? He'd been there? "Well. I know she's not eating much, so. It's nice of you to give her a break from the grieving not-quite-widow at the sickbed thing. Thank you."

"I live for your praise."

"A mistake."

"And friend Gray? Where is he?"

"I don't know, how would I know? Why would you even ask me that? I'm not the attendance taker, dammit!"

"Er." La Croix seemed taken aback, which was odd. Nothing ruffled that fucker's feathers. "All right."

"Sorry. Long night. As you could probably tell."

"Not at all; you look radiant."

She snorted. "I have access to mirrors, so I know you're even more full of shit than usual." She came closer to the bed, reached down, and took her father's hand; normally tan and strong, this morning it was like a small bundle of sticks. "Hey, Dad. Thought I'd check on you before I went out on more Reaps. Oh, and I've been Reaping. Which, by the way, I'm certain I'm screwing up. It's not like I've had any training." But her conscience wouldn't allow the disingenuous comment, so she clarified: "Wouldn't allow any training. So that's on me. But there's still time to make a complete recovery and save the Midwest from my piss-ignorance."

She watched his face. Nothing.

"Now you're just being stubborn. Did I mention I've temporarily taken your *job*? The one you've been executing—heh—flawlessly for centuries? And never wanted to give up? I've got no business in the field and even the swans know it. Now wake up and micromanage me, dammit!"

Nothing.

She let go of his hand and began to pace. "Remember when I lied to you about opening night so you wouldn't come see my middle school play? Wasn't that obnoxious and unkind?"

. . .

"And the time your ten-gauge shotgun ended up on the bottom of the swan pond? And I said the swans did it? Well, it was me. I didn't just lie to my father, I traduced innocent swans. Don't you want to give me what for?"

. . .

"How about May of my junior year, when I accidentally backed the truck into a ditch and left it there? And then convinced you it was an early Halloween prank? Or a late Halloween prank? It wasn't a Halloween prank."

. . .

"And the time I—"

"By all the gods, stop." La Croix wore a peculiar expression, like he didn't know if he should sob or giggle. "If the shotgun thing didn't rouse him, nothing will."

"Jesus." Amara stopped pacing and stared down at the wasted figure on the bed. She knew it was impossible, but he seemed to be shrinking before her eyes. "Maybe he *is* dying."

"We must, of course, consider the possibility."

"Because it *is* a possibility," Amara finally admitted. "Did you know the old Death? The Death before my dad?"

"No, my predecessor did. All I know of your grandfather is that he was born in Bornholm sometime during the ninth century. And that he never died."

"Sorry, what?"

"According to your dear mother, he simply faded and allowed his son to assume the mantle."

"Oh." *Why didn't I know that?* But she knew why: She never gave enough of a shit to ask. She sighed and spared the bedridden figure a last look. "Last chance, Dad. Open your eyes or La Croix and I are going to keep talking about you behind your back right in front of your face and you'll have to *deal with it*."

. . .

Amara turned back to La Croix, splendidly arrayed in purple and black and managing to slouch even when standing tall. She came closer when she spotted the brown crumbs on his lapel. "Who'd you get to have lefse while you watched, you weirdo?"

"I reminded your dear mother that her duties as hostess prompted her to accede to a guest's desires."

"Sorry, I didn't get a lot of sleep last night." *Argh. Why do I keep bringing that up?* "What are you saying?"

"I told her I wanted her to eat something."

"And she did. And she let you watch, like any good hostess."

La Croix gave her the one-shoulder-modesty-shrug. He had always been a bundle of oddities; she was just a teenager when she found out he could only enjoy vices like food and smoking if someone indulged right in front of him. She remembered thinking that was sad and weird and a little bit hilarious, like La Croix himself.

*No wonder he stays skinny.* "Thank you," Amara said. "God knows she was ignoring my gentle demands that she eat a fiftieth of what she's cooked so far."

La Croix inclined his head. "At your service, always. But I trust you will excuse me now. Skye offered to spell me, and then I must away."

"Big day of watching people smoke and shoot up?" La Croix raised an eyebrow, and before Amara knew what she was going to say, it was out there: "Sorry. I'm thankful for all you're doing for my folks."

He smirked. "I can only assume we're in Hell, and it has indeed frozen over."

"I know you're just being a wiseass, but this really *is* Hell and it *has* frozen over," she said, pointing out the window.

La Croix shuddered at the chill March landscape. "Indeed. I should like nothing better than to flee south; New Orleans is lovely this time of year."

"According to you, Nawlins is lovely every time of the year."

"Never pronounce it like that!" he nearly shouted, and she had to laugh.

# CHAPTER THIRTY

"For the love of everything, Mom, *stop cooking*."

"I know, I know. You see the repast and are fretting because you think there's no rice pudding."

"That is not what I'm fretting about, Mom."

"Not to worry," Hilly continued, tapping the slow cooker with a wooden spoon not much older than she was. The runes carved into the bowl preceded Christ. "Ready in five."

"Ready in five. Sure, sure. Totally on the same page. Such a relief." Amara rested her face in her hands and began counting to ten. "Gaaaaaah."

"Is Gray coming soon? He mentioned he liked smoked turkey so I made him another one."

Amara sighed. "No. He needs a couple of hours at least. Possibly three if he shaves. It's an adorable inversion of the guys-don't-need-hours-to-get-ready trope."

Her mother laughed. "I always liked your own inversion. Ten minutes to get ready, even at the height of your cat's-eye makeup phase."

"You know they have a stamp for that now? It looks like a

Sharpie and is almost as cheap. You pop the cap off and lean in—a mirror is still crucial—and stamp yourself. The whole thing takes about half a second and you get a perfect cat's eye. Gray's the one who told me about it."

"Ah. How handy."

Amara had to smile, remembering the bathroom chaos.

*"Hold still, you silly tart! Now you've got a perfect cat's eye in your eyebrow!"*

"Poor boy. Poor, poor, boy."

"Mom. Don't."

"What will you do?" Hilly asked softly. "When the time comes?"

Amara was already shaking her head. "I can't talk about that, this weekend of all weekends. I can't even think about it."

"Oh, darling . . ."

Amara burst into tears and hid her face in her hands again, this time for shame.

Her mother clucked and pulled her into a hug. Resistance was futile; Hilly could hoist a twenty-five-pound sack of flour on each shoulder and jog up a flight of stairs. "You kissed him, didn't you? You gave in and kissed that doomed boy."

Amara gritted her teeth in mid-snivel. "Graham Gray is a lot of things, but 'boy' doesn't apply." Then she *really* showed her mother a thing or two by ugly-crying harder.

"Oh-oh-oh, my poor darling." Her mother patted her back, and Amara was petty enough to want to burp in response. "I'm sorry. I'm so sorry."

"It's not fair. I know that's childish."

"But true. It's *not* fair." Her mother pulled back and held Amara at arm's length. "I'm proud of you."

"What?" Amara dropped her hands. "Why? All I've done

since we arrived is give you sh— Uh, be more hurtfully sarcastic than usual."

"You Reaped. And you did a splendid job. Not a splendid job for your first time; splendid, period."

The praise made her glow, but she was compelled to honesty. "It's not like there was any choice. What with your other children being long dead."

"Yes, that's so."

"We've never really talked about it."

"No, we haven't."

"I'm very sorry you had to outlive most of your kids."

"Thank you, darling."

"And had to return to the drawing board to get me."

Hilly frowned. "Is that what you think we did? I once was the goddess of fertility, did you forget? I wanted another baby because it's my nature, not to bring forth a spare to fill a job opening."

"Oh. I guess I owe you another apology."

"Mm-hmm."

"Stop feeling my forehead, I'm not sick."

"Just checking. It would be an utter catastrophe if you, too, fell ill."

"Whatever Death has, I don't think it's contagious. But until he recovers, I'm on the spot."

"You are, indeed. And I say this with all love and admiration—"

"Oh, boy."

"—but I fully expected you to spend at least three or four days resisting your duty."

"I was tempted. So, so, so, so tempted. But I had Gray. He made it almost bearable."

"Ah. Yes. It's very brave to allow yourself to get close to someone knowing he's . . ." She tilted her head to one side. ". . . ready for breakfast!"

Amara turned just as Gray loped into the kitchen. "Oh my God. That's another smoked turkey, isn't it? Hilly, I love you more than I love Milky Ways."

"Wow. Half an hour," Amara said with a smirk. "I'm impressed, Gray."

"I can be speedy when it suits me." He opened the fridge, pulled out a pitcher of fresh-squeezed orange juice. "I love that sweater on you. It's like a blanket with sleeves."

She looked down at the vast green field she was wearing. "It's not 'like' a blanket, it *is* a blanket. With sleeves. Oh, no. I'd know that curly paper anywhere."

Gray held up the printout. "Yeah, I took the liberty of swinging by the libe and grabbing today's list."

She stared and stared and, for good measure, stared. "I don't deserve you," she muttered, then was mortified she'd spoken aloud.

"Well, yeah. What've I been telling you all these years?"

*And I ruined it. Couldn't resist making a bad situation exponentially worse with a bungled lip lock.*

"Good morning, Hilly." Skye came into the kitchen with a wave, sporting her trademark braid. She was wearing cargo pants (she adored all the pockets) and a black sweater with plain shoulder epaulets. In deference to the house, she'd left her hiking boots at the entryway. "Hi, Amara. Gray."

"Hi, Skye! I was reading about you yesterday."

"Thoughtful, Gray." Skye's smile faded as she looked Amara up and down. "How are you doing? I took a look at the scroll—the faxes—in the library earlier. I'm sure yesterday was rough."

"Rough, torture, never-ending torment . . ."

"But we stopped at Dairy Queen on the way back," Gray put in. "Which made it all worthwhile. Who knew they'd be open in March?"

"Still. I imagine it was unbearable."

"You're not wrong. Thank you, Skye." As always, Amara was grateful for Skye's kind interest; more than once growing up, Amara was convinced the only ally in the compound wasn't *of* the compound, but lived on the Isle of Skye. "I'd come up with a self-deprecating platitude like 'it wasn't all bad,' but it was."

"Well, I might have a little good news. Check this." Gray handed over a stack of printouts. "Only a couple dozen people die today. Well, more like six hundred, but apparently when we Reap one, we're really Reaping a whole bunch. Or something. So it's practically a vacation."

"Not for them."

"I think it can be argued that it's a vacation for them, too."

"Yes, but we won't have that argument, will we?" Amara replied. "Let's eat and get back to it."

Skye gaped, which was amusing for no other reason than she was not the gaping type. "You're going back in, too, Gray?"

"We're a team," Gray replied. "Ever since I swan-dived into a giant mud pile back in college."

Amara snickered. She'd never told the full story of their meeting to anyone, and never would, without Gray's leave.

"Wow. Okay. I—good for you guys." Skye shook her head. "Sorry, I just didn't expect you to be so . . ."

"Competent?"

"Don't answer that," Gray advised. "It's a trick."

Skye nodded. "Excellent advice." To Hilly: "La Croix asked me if I'd sit with your husband a bit. He had to flit off and deal with . . . whatever he deals with."

"Probably looking for someone to devour a lobster omelet while he watches," Amara muttered.

"Speaking of devour, breakfast is ready," Hilly announced.

"Woo-hoo! I call the smoked turkey!"

# CHAPTER THIRTY-ONE

"Something's wrong."

Gray raised his eyebrows. "You're gonna have to narrow that waaaaaay down."

"She should be here." They were in Fargo's Manchester Office Building, a hive of activity. Amara's hands were on her hips as she turned in a circle, surveying the large room. "Tanya Bergen should be in this office at this moment, pissed about her vacation being cut short and about to die of a stroke."

"In this oddly stinky mailroom, no less," Gray observed.

"But she's not."

"So . . . do we go look for her?"

"That's not how this works. C'mon."

"Sure, sure. Where are we go—oh. You're grabbing me and hauling me to the elevators. Gotcha. And speaking of 'how this works,' here's something else I don't get. You can go anywhere to Reap, I get that. But how can I? I'm not Death. I'm not even Death's intern."

Amara stabbed the button for the lobby and they rode down in silence.

"Amara? Did you hear all that stuff I just babbled? Or are you too busy plotting your next Reap? Which is also fine."

"Mmmm?" She was doing her best to project "so focused on the task that nothing else is getting through" because she was pretty sure she knew the answer to Gray's question, and it was equal parts ludicrous and frightening. "Next?"

"What?"

"Who's next?" She was through the elevator doors before they opened on the way, and Gray jumped out and trotted to keep pace.

"Oh. Um." Gray dug for the paperwork. "God, this curly paper is the—okay, if we're going alphabetically—"

"Closest. Who's closest?"

"That'll be Sergeant Wayne Perryman, Minot Air Force Base."

✦ ✦ ✦

"Holy shit," Gray muttered. "We are walking past so many people with guns right now! And they don't care! Or at least haven't noticed."

The Minot base was a few miles outside the city proper. Amara had driven past the comforting warning sign (Only the Best Come North), and the airman on duty raised the gate without asking for ID, speaking to them, or looking at them. She had the impression that the airmen were so used to accommodating Death, it was just another chore they barely had to think about.

The size of a small city, the AFB sprawled across the prairie, boasting its own golf course, movie theater, and Minuteman III missiles. There were plenty of service personnel outside soaking up the sunny day, and not a single one noticed Amara or Gray. Possibly because they were all focused on the fox picking its way through the slush, doubtless looking for a tasty rabbit. Or a garbage can.

"He's supposed to be here." They were in the headquarters for the 91st Missile Wing, and Amara was pacing again. "He's supposed to be excited because they're inducing his new wife's labor tomorrow—"

"Oh, man."

"—and he's getting a head start by handing out cigars and beef jerky. Then he's supposed to go have a heart attack in the break room, since his arteries are clogged with cigars and beef jerky. But he's not here. What. The. Hell?"

"Should we ask? Maybe he's been assigned somewhere else."

She was already shaking her head. "Not how this works. I might not know much about the job, but that part I internalized pretty quickly. In all the time my father has done this, he *never* had to find someone to Reap. If you have to look to Reap, you're not Death, you're just a serial killer."

Gray reached out and plucked the elbow of a passing airwoman. "Excuse me, we're looking for Sergeant Wayne Perryman. Do you know where he is?"

The airwoman, dressed in crisp blues, her long brown hair pulled back into a sleek bun, stared at Gray like she was trying to focus, and when she finally answered, it was with the slurred speech of a drunken sleepwalker. "Hmmmm . . . nnnnnoooo. Should be heeeeere."

"That's right," Gray said with a vigorous nod. "He *should* be here."

"Mmmmmmm . . . not here."

"Do you know wh—"

"Nnnnnnnot here."

"Stop it," Amara said. "You'll break her brain. Come with me."

He did, and they sat in the Mustang while Amara tried to

figure out what to do and Gray tried to take a picture of the fox with his phone.

"I know weird is relative, but a fox running around an Air Force base is weird."

"They're not uncommon. We're only fifty miles from the Canadian border. Now. Going forward—"

Gray was ahead of her. "Number three is Melanie Chamber. Seven miles from here. Minot City Hospital. The, um, pediatric oncology ward."

"Oh, fucking swell."

✦ ✦ ✦

Melanie Chamber stirred in her small hospital bed and turned her head to look at her visitors. Her eyes were sunken pits, her skull bald and yellow, her elbows like windshield wipers. Eaten alive, day and night. Poison the only cure, and not much of one. The ward was hushed, which Amara found equal parts appropriate and sad. "Hi. Are you looking for my mom?"

"Oh, thank God." *Whoa. Did I just give thanks because I can Reap a fifth grader?*

"She means no," Gray said. "We're here for you, hon."

Melanie somehow produced a smile. "My grandpa told me about you. How I shouldn't be scared when you come. But you're not what I thought you were gonna be."

"Tell us about it," Gray replied.

"I thought you'd be older. And a guy."

"My father's sick," Amara said, taking Melanie's hand in hers, careful not to jostle the IV or dislodge the tape. "I'm filling in."

"Will he get better?"

"I don't know. But you don't have to worry about that."

Melanie's small hand was essentially one giant, red-black bruise. She looked as if a breeze would blow her away. She looked as if a breeze would *hurt*. "I'll take care of you."

"Okay. That's . . ." Her tentative smile became fixed. Her chest fell and did not rise again. Alarms began to shrill, and Amara stepped back so the code team could begin their fruitless tasks.

# CHAPTER THIRTY-TWO

"This will shock you," Gray announced, "but I have thoughts. And questions. Some thoughts. And many questions."

"Hit me."

"Okay, but first, how fucking brave and awesome was that kid? I can't imagine going through a tenth of that."

Amara said nothing but, like Gray, had thoughts. *Your childhood wasn't exactly all awesome all the time, my love. Your mother almost accidentally killed you more than once. And your father was worse.* Time had shown Gray didn't welcome comparisons, or discussion of any kind, about his childhood.

She would never understand how such hateful wretches produced someone so loving and kind. *I'm constantly whining about my parents, but they never threw a hot pot of elbow macaroni at me. They never made me drink glass after glass of raw eggs until I threw up. Never locked me out in the snow, or made me sleep in the car during a heatwave. Though Mom's lutefisk* is *pretty awful, and her feelings get hurt if you don't ask for seconds . . .*

"So of the people who died," Gray was saying, his expression adorably intent, "some of them know exactly who you are. Or who your father is. Sometimes they know you right away, and sometimes they recognize you after you start talking to them. But a few have no idea who you are. What's up with that?"

"The older families know Death, and pass that knowledge to the younger generation."

"Older families like Native Americans? The Mandan and the Sioux?"

"No, Natives have their own death gods. Europeans—immigrants from France, Norway, Germany, Sweden, to name a few—have been here for centuries. And they bred fast, since 90 percent of their children died before they could walk, and also a splinter could lead to your lingering demise. So they wanted their line to continue, no matter how quickly it aged their wives. Which is why there are still Le Sueurs and Radissons running around. Pike and Carver have descendants, too; offshoots from the original settlers. And some of them passed down what they knew about Death."

"Huh. Okay. Thanks for explaining. What's the plan for the Reap-ees who were MIA today?"

"Reap-ees?"

"Well, we have to call them something, and the Reapettes sounds like a 1950s girl group."

"We really don't. And I need to think about it."

"D'you want to think about it while gobbling a fistful of Buster Bars?"

"I do not." Some things, even Dairy Queen was no good for.

# CHAPTER THIRTY-THREE

". . . and then we came back here. Primarily because I don't have one fucking clue about how to proceed. Dad? I dropped an F-bomb. It's out there. The F-bomb is out there. Better wake up and lecture me on how profanity is a sign of limited intellect, for fuck's sake."

"Well, it is," Hilly said, entering Death's sickroom with a tray. Amara was more than a little amazed the tray was laden with washcloths, not food. "But you're an exception to the rule. Remember when you took every vocab-building exercise you could find, and memorized the seven words you can't say on TV? In ten languages?"

"No, that doesn't sound like me at all, you *puttana marcia*."

Hilly flapped a hand at her in a 'get out of here with that' motion. "How are you holding up, my darling?"

"About as well as a tower made of toothpicks. You?"

"That covers my situation as well." She set the tray on the nearby end table, grabbed a cloth, disappeared into the bathroom, returned with the washcloth dripping. "But we prevail."

"You should cross-stitch that onto a pillow."

"I have."

Amara snorted as Hilly folded back Death's bedcovers and began washing his face.

"No change, obvs."

"'Obvs'? Is it that much more difficult to pronounce the entire word?"

"Fair," Amara admitted. "That's what happens when I'm around Gray for too long."

"Where is he? Does he want a snack?"

"If he does, he's covered. You can't take two steps into the kitchen without being caught in a blizzard of snacks. And if you smoke another turkey, Mother, I swear to all the gods . . ."

"There can always be more snacks," her mother said, because she was sweet and clinically insane.

"He went to the library to do more reading and fell asleep in there. We—he didn't get much sleep last night, so I left him snoozing and came to talk to Dad. Well. Talk *at* Dad."

"All right. To answer your question, there are no changes, but only in his case. It would seem everyone *but* Death is changing."

"Tell me about it. Mom, this might sound like another odd question—"

"I'll be the judge of that, dear."

"—but did you ever go with Dad on Reaps?"

Hilly paused in midscrub and straightened. "You were right. That was an odd question." She tilted her head, studying Amara, and they both let several seconds go by. "And the answer is, as you must know, *of course not.*"

"I figured."

"Death has his territories and responsibilities, as I have mine. What's the saying? 'Ne'er the twain shall meet'? Something like that."

"Close enough." Amara watched her mother work, and did

not offer to help roll Death so she could scrub his back. Partly because, hey! She was helping *plenty.* And also because Hilly could have hoisted Death out of his bed, carried him downstairs, and then jogged with him for the better part of a mile. "You have separate fiefdoms. You always have."

"Dare I ask why you dare ask?"

Amara scooched the chair closer to the bed and thought how best to answer. "You know Gray's been Reaping with me."

"Yes, to our surprise and pleasure. Not only did you show up when summoned—"

"Oh, c'mon. I'm not that bad. Obviously I would have come home. Um. Eventually. Within a week at most, depending on how my new job at the RV park was going. Those garbage bins won't empty themselves, Mother. I have to call to get someone to do it."

"—you immediately dove in and seem bent on smashing any norms in your path. The only surprise is that we're surprised."

"Yes, yes, I'm a grumpy rebel and always have been. They can see Gray, Mom."

"Beg pardon?"

"The ones about to die answer Gray when he talks to them because they can see and hear him. Except he can get in anywhere, like me, so in that respect, they *can't* see or hear him. He even pointed out how we walked past any number of armed airmen and neither of us were hassled, or even stopped."

Hilly straightened and rubbed the small of her back. "What are you saying?"

"Why is my best friend Death's appendage? Why is he enjoying the same shield I am?"

"Oh, Amara." Hilly's expression was typical of mothers everywhere: equal parts exasperation and adoration. "When will you outgrow the need to ask questions you've answered yourself?"

She sighed. "I was afraid of that. Your truth *and* your

nonanswer. Here's the other oddity: I couldn't find everyone on the scrolls."

Hilly, who had bent to resume Death's bed bath, paused in midscrub. "I don't—what?"

"There were people on the list I couldn't find. They weren't where they were supposed to be. Where the scroll said they would be. The infallible scroll that has never, ever been wrong even once throughout history."

"But that's—"

"Exactly."

Hilly sat down, hard. *Yikes. Thank goodness the chair was there.* "It's forbidden. It's near impossible. And it's unthinkable."

"And yet."

"Amara, Gray will die."

"I'm aware." She was, but she still nearly reared back at her mother's bald statement. "And I get why you felt the need to reinforce that. Ouch, by the way."

"Amara . . ."

"Because if people on the scroll are missing, that might be a loophole. It's possible Gray could be one of them. Named but not Reaped. So there might be a way to save him."

"Except it's forbidden!" Hilly shrilled. She caught herself and got to her feet. "Forgive me, both for the outburst and the necessary reminder that the man you love will not live to see the summer solstice."

"Ah, yes. The 'sorry but it was necessary' nonpology."

"Tell me how he leaves this world."

*"This world." Like there's something out there, as opposed to the abyss.*

"Aneurysm," Amara replied shortly. "The brain damage sustained from years of child abuse combined with high blood pressure means that a chunk of his brain will pop like a balloon.

They killed him. Those abusive psychopaths killed him when he was too little to fight back. It just took two decades to take effect."

Hilly held out her arms, but Amara shook her head. "I've done enough crying all over you for one day."

"Tomorrow, then," her mother replied, and though it wasn't especially funny, Amara laughed.

# CHAPTER THIRTY-FOUR

Later, as the sun began to slip away and her stomach began grumbling to itself, Amara looked up from *Celtic Legends* to see Hades and Persephone standing over Death's bedside, holding hands like frightened children and looking woeful.

"So it's true. He's comatose," Hank breathed. "He isn't waking up."

"He hasn't woken up *yet*," Amara said.

"It's not supposed to be like this," Penny said in a small voice.

"Tell me about it." Amara closed the book. "Thanks for coming. It's nice of you to visit again."

"We haven't actually gotten around to leaving yet," Penny said, then stretched up on her toes to nuzzle Hank's nose.

"I'll tell Hilly to lay in more Gatorade."

"Pardon?"

"Never mind."

"How goes the Reaping?" Hank asked.

"Well. It's Reaping. So there's really only one way it can go."

Amara held her breath, but neither of them had notes. Excellent. Hilly had kept her confidence.

*The Reaping is going fine. Why wouldn't it be going fine? When has a Reap ever not been fine? As far as Reaping goes, nothing strange or worrisome is happening at all!*

"It's good of you to be such a help to your family," Penny said. She was still using her wardrobe to channel college cheerleaders, right down to the oversized letter jacket slung over one cashmere-clad shoulder. Which raised questions: Did she pack it? Or just happen to have it with her? Also, when did Hades go to the U of ND? "I know it's been a comfort to your mother."

"Thanks. Did you two come up for air long enough to ring the figurative dinner bell?"

"Yes, and your mother asked—"

A shriek cut him off, and Amara was out of her chair and the book thumped to the carpet before she realized she was already moving. It wasn't the first time her reflexes kicked in before her brain.

"By all the gods, who is *that*? And are they on fire?"

"It's just Gray." Amara was intimately acquainted with all Gray's noises. "It's dark out, so."

"I'm sorry, what?"

"He'll be fine, Penny. But we should head to the dining room anyway. If our tardiness results in congealed gravy, my mother will see to it that we'll all be shrieking like Gray."

✦ ✦ ✦

"It's night! It's night!" Gary shot out of the library so fast, if he'd collided with anyone he would have knocked them on their ass.

As it was, he had the attention of everyone in the hall. "Chernobog comes at night!"

"Dusk, actually," Amara pointed out.

"Sorry." Chernobog had been right behind him, and now Gray was right behind *her*. "Didn't mean to."

"It's fine," Amara replied. "Your reputation precedes."

"Chernobog," said Chernobog, holding out a slab of a palm. His fingers were an interesting dichotomy of stubby and strong; she'd seen him twist off bottle caps that weren't twist-off. "Paying respects."

"This is my friend, Graham Gray." When Gray didn't move, she added, "He's very pleased to meet you."

"Just because I'm cowering in terror doesn't mean I can't speak for myself," he snapped. "I'm not *very* pleased to meet him, I'm just . . . pleased."

Chernobog waited. Amara could picture centuries sliding by as Chernobog quietly went about his business while ignoring the flow of time.

"I, um, like your hair," Gray ventured. "It's a . . . a striking contrast to the, uh . . ." The flannel, the black jeans, the swarthy complexion, the dark stubble, the large, long limbs. "Everything else."

Chernobog's lips twitched, the closest he ever got to a smile. "Light hair, not scary."

"Oh. *Oh.* Say, that's nice of you. Going blond so as not to scare people. Amara colors her hair for the exact opposite reason."

"I'll thank you to leave my hair out of the conversation, Graham Gray. And supper's ready."

"Sauerbraten?"

"You know it, Chernobog. *Rode Grütt*, too, I bet. C'mon, Gray, stop cowering and let's eat."

"I wasn't cowering." Gray was already smiling; she adored the man's resilience above nearly all else. "I was guarding your flank. I'll guard it all the way to the dining hall, too."

"Good job. My flank never felt safer."

# CHAPTER THIRTY-FIVE

"Look, I don't want to play games. The emotional kind, at least. If you wanted to bust out the *Anti-Monopoly* board, I'm all in."

"Gray . . ."

"Hey, I get it. You hate being a free-market competitor, but you're really good at being a monopolist."

"Gray, this isn't about—"

"So I'll just say straight out, I want to sleep in your bed again tonight. Mostly to keep you company, because I know today was even worse than yesterday, and I know you're probably too stubborn to ask for comfort again. But also because, maybe we could take turns?"

"Um." Why did that spark so many filthy thoughts? With an effort, she shoved the sudden surge of erotic images to the back of her brain. "What?"

"I'm just saying I wouldn't mind being the sooth-ee in addition to the soother."

She stared at him.

"If you don't want me, I get it."

"That's—that's not—"

"And I'll take your answer seriously. So be very, very sure you don't want me in your bed, because this can't be one of those 'I'm saying no for form's sake but maybe I could be persuaded' situations. Like when you pretend you don't want a Big Mac."

"They're so bad for you, Gray!"

"I know! I saw the same documentary you did. We threw McNuggets at the TV to show our disdain. But you still want one every now and then, even while insisting you don't. Hell, I've seen you insist you don't want one while you chomp into a Big Mac. Like me and McNuggets."

"Like you and McNuggets," she parroted. Gray was often an open book to her, but sometimes she had to puzzle over him a bit. Reason #26 why she'd been fool enough to fall for the delightful yutz.

"Exactly. So. Assuming I'm not giving off inadvertent creeper vibes by implying no might not mean no, do you want me to sleep in here again tonight?"

She pretended to think about it. "Well. You do deserve being the sooth-ee for a change."

"Right?" His face lit up, and she wasn't sure why, but in that moment, he was dazzling. "Right."

"Besides, staring at the ceiling for hours while your eyes get grittier and grittier and you worry dawn will never come is more fun with someone next to you."

"That's the spirit."

✦ ✦ ✦

"You mom told me you were looking for La Croix."

"Hmm?" It was after midnight and Amara was almost asleep. *Perhaps somewhere in my heart, I've always known Gray and I should be together, so instead of freaking out, I'm finally relaxing.*

*Or I'm just really fucking tired because it's been a nonstop stress train and I only got two hours of sleep last night.*

*Yes. The latter. Definitely.*

"Your mom," Gray was saying beside her in bed, because he wanted her to endure *two* sleepless nights. "She let me watch her make lefse. You know how experts make a task look easy? Your mom is an expert who makes it look hard. I was seriously worried she was going to burn herself."

"She does. All the time."

"I figured." Gray propped himself up on an elbow. "There's so much to keep track of! There's that long stick, first of all, and she's got to thread the hot lefse on the stick."

"Gray. I've observed the procedure. I've even helped."

"But first she's got to roll it all out with a fancy roller that makes stripes, which takes forever, and meanwhile, the lefse grill—it has its own grill!—is getting hotter than Hades. That's not me exaggerating. Hank told me! Hotter than Hades!"

"All right, I'm going to ask you to calm down."

"It's like a slo-mo nightmare that eventually ends up slathered in brown sugar and butter! How can I enjoy lefse knowing your poor mom is nursing second-degree burns?"

"You'll just have to reconcile yourself, I guess."

"Yeah, well, I got off track."

"Noooooo."

"Kindly shut the hell up, Amara. While I was slathering salve on your mother's palm, she mentioned you'd come looking for La Croix."

"Hmmm. She's ever the helpful font of info these days, isn't she?"

"Which is weird, because he's not exactly your favorite person in the world. Or even your favorite death god. Do you mind telling me why you wanted him? I promise not to get jealous. Or, if I do get jealous, I won't show it . . . yeah. Let's go with that last one. I'm only human, for fuck's sake."

"Why would you be jealous of Baron La Croix?"

"Exactly! No reason, no reason at all!"

"Are you all right?"

"Fine! I'm fine!" In the darkened tower bedroom, his shouting seemed louder than usual. "Nobody's jealous! Seriously, why did you want him?"

"He said something yesterday. And again today. I'm still trying to figure . . . never mind."

"Oh, come on!"

"My point is, the one time I actually wanted to see him, he was nowhere around. Probably holed up in a furnace somewhere. He doesn't do well with cold."

"Amara."

"Nighty-night."

"Amara." Gray sat up in bed. "You *gotta* tell me what's happening. I've seen you furious and hurt and drunk and flirty and dreadful and sexy and giddy and vengeful and pissed, but I don't think I've ever seen you so apprehensive and scared."

"And . . . and you're not now. Seeing that."

"And not just apprehensive, but mysterious, too. You've answered every one of my dumb questions over the years, even the weirdly personal, but suddenly you're a clam. A great-looking clam, but still."

"You think I'm an attractive bivalve?"

Gray would not be swayed. "You didn't seem this freaked even when you were staring down the barrel of the dreaded fax machine. I mean, *I* knew you were freaking out, but you kept a lid on it, especially when we were in the field. Please, please tell me what's wrong. I won't make you laugh with the 'maybe I can help' routine, but I need to know why someone I love is terrified."

*Love?*

*Yes. I knew that. Of course he loves me.* As a friend. As a friend. As a friend.

*Jealous. He said he'd try not to be jealous of La Croix. Which is ridiculous.*

*Jealous?*

*Huh.*

"Amara?" He peered down at her. "Are you in there? Blink twice if you understand."

"I haven't quite figured it out yet. The scope of the problems. Or solutions." Truth. "But when I do, you'll be the first to know." Lie. "Also, please stop looming." *Pretty please? Because the urge to grab you by the ears and kiss you is goddamned overwhelming.*

"That's not really an answer."

"Because I'm not really sure what's going on. I'm not being mysterious, I just need to let the other side of my brain work on it for a bit. All I've got right now are vague suspicions. Babbling my half-formed bullshit theories is dangerous. I need more data."

He studied her in the dark and she held her breath. After a few seconds that felt like hours, he lay back down. "Fair enough."

*Hmmm. Not like him to give up so easily.*

The ludicrous part? She was disappointed he had.

# CHAPTER THIRTY-SIX

*Mmmmm . . . warm . . .*

Oh. One of *these* dreams. That was fine. That was just fine. She couldn't remember the last time she'd had sex. Well, she could, but counting up the years was too depressing. Normally she dealt with her biological urges with assistance from her trusty Hitachi. But alas, there hadn't been room for Señor Shaky *and* all the boxes of hair dye.

She wriggled closer to the warmth and mumbled appreciatively when strong fingers threaded through her hair, felt warm breath, heard deep, contented humming. Then there was a warm mouth on hers and she had no interest in waking up. Instead, she luxuriated in the kiss, burrowing still closer for warmth, and her fingers skated across cotton and delved lower as . . .

. . . as . . .

She cracked an eye open and found herself staring at Gray's eyelids, and yelped into his mouth.

"Shit!"

"What? Ow, fuck!" Gray was as horrified as she was, going

by his appalled expression and how he'd pulled away so hard he'd tumbled to the floor.

She peeked over the edge. "Are you okay?"

"I—I—" He gaped up at her and did the goldfish thing a few more times. "Fuck."

"Well put."

"I'm sorry."

"Me, too." She blinked down at him and cast about for something—anything—to explain herself. "If it helps, I wasn't molesting *you*. It was the dream man."

"I was just about to make the same excuse."

The mortified hilarity hit them both at the same time. "It's my fault," she tried to explain between giggles. "I haven't had sex in ages—"

"Same. It's been almost a year for me."

"—and I was having this lovely dream . . ."

"I know! I guess we can be grateful our terrible morning breath woke us up before we got, um, dreamier? Our timing is terrible."

"So is everyone else's," she replied dryly. She glanced over at her phone and nearly groaned when she saw the time; more Reaps beckoned. Every day of her life. Forever.

And so no time to waste.

"What a fucking bizarre weekend."

She shrugged as she rolled out of bed. "Ready for more? After we've brushed our teeth?"

"And after coffee, sure." Gray yawned and sat up. "Our ritual humiliation aside, I slept great, so that's something."

She smiled. "I did, too. And I imagine Hilly will have several gallons of coffee for your slurping pleasure."

"I'm really glad you let me come along."

The subject change—if that's what it was—gave her pause, and she shrugged. "Like I could have stopped you."

"Yeah, Amara," he replied seriously. "You could have. I think you could stop pretty much anyone you wanted. But you didn't. You indulge me all the time, not just this weekend. I need to remember not to take that for granted."

"Do you always get maudlin after you make out with your best friend?"

"Apparently," he admitted, and that set her off again.

Two children. A new mother. A happily married man in his forties who wept, not for his own demise, but the family he was forced to leave behind. ("My twins graduate tomorrow.") A teenage girl who'd gotten her driver's license two hours earlier.

"Jesus Christ!" Gray collapsed in the passenger seat beside Amara, rubbed his eyes with his fists, glared at the roof of the Mustang. "How did your dad do this for a million centuries?"

"No idea."

"Oh, man, the kid who went through the windshield. Can't get her out of my head. She wasn't even begging to live, just to talk to her mom for a second because they'd had a huge argument . . . fucking *brutal*."

"It is." Almost . . . too brutal?

Gray straightened in his seat and in the almost-telepathic flash shared by best friends, plucked the thought out of her brain and put it out there where it couldn't be ignored: "It's almost like someone is manipulating events to make a shitty job everyone knows you don't want even harder so you'll quit."

*That . . . sounds right.*

Which wasn't just insane, but impossible. The idea was so large, so bizarre, it seemed to bury her brain in dread. She had to work to keep her reply calm and even. "It *does* seem like that."

"Which is impossible, right?"

"I . . . would have thought so." And here, the hideous irony: The one person she could have discussed this with? Was in a fucking coma.

"And also paranoid?" Gray continued. "Because Death's whole thing is that you can't change if someone's gonna die, right? If they're on the scroll or Death's fax or app, that's it? So shall it be forever and ever, amen. Right?"

"As good as. It's actually more forbidden than impossible. There aren't many who could even try it." Amara was staring out the windshield, hands clenched at ten and two, thinking about the same girl Gray couldn't get out of his head. How the argument with her mother made her late, how she got lost, drove too fast to make up time, panicked, skidded, over-corrected, and then got even more lost. Permanently lost.

She felt Gray's hand cover her two o'clock hand and gently squeeze. "Shitty as this is, it's good you feel bad."

"Not the 'numb is worse' cliché."

"Yes, the 'numb is worse' cliché. Don't you think being dead on the inside is worse?"

"I'm thinking a lot of things, actually."

"Oh ho. At least all the Reap-ees were where they were supposed to be today. Unfortunately," he added in a mutter.

Amara mentally conceded the point, then started the car and answered Gray's unspoken question. "I had a word with my mother before we left this morning; she's calling a conclave on my behalf tonight."

"You and the death gods are gonna elect a new Pope?"

"Death gods were holding conclaves long before the Catholic church muscled in on it. This one belongs to our family and Death's colleagues."

"Okay. Good plan."

"Yes, I thought so." Necessary plan, more like. She was reminded of being stuck with a long crochet project, like an afghan. Fun to start, but the middle was a drag and took forever, though it was only a few days. Then you blinked and realized you'd made a huge blanket from a pile of wool.

Not her best analogy. But things had seemed impossibly mysterious when she and Gray got off the train a few days ago. Subsequent events only added to the conundrum. And then she came to realize the problem wasn't the puzzle she was trying to solve, nor even the design. It was that someone put the puzzle pieces in the wrong spot.

Or maybe she was just clinically paranoid. Either way, the conclave had to happen.

"And I know you're going to explain why I think it's a good plan. You're great at that."

"I could," she replied, summoning a grim smile. "Or you could just wait and be surprised."

# CHAPTER THIRTY-SEVEN

*Holy shit, holy shit, holeeeeee shit!*

Graham Gray tried to calm the hell down for the dozenth time in three days. And for the dozenth time in three days, he failed.

He should have been terrified. Or at least worried. Apprehensive? But nope; seeing Amara in action robbed him of all fear. Hell, he couldn't even be nervous. Okay, he could, but it was nothing to do with death-god shenanigans, and everything to do with how he finally knew how Amara Morrigan tasted: warm and sweet, with a sharp, almost metallic undertone. Vanilla beans wrapped in tinfoil, except the tinfoil wasn't as prickly as it looked.

*Maaaaaybe don't be hanging out in Death's bedroom thinking about how his daughter tastes?*

Good advice. He tried to give them all a quick once-over without giving away the fact that he was giving them a quick once-over. Luckily, once they got over the shock of Amara showing up with a guest, they'd politely ignored him most of the time. Given that the enduring goal of his childhood was to be politely ignored, he was fine with it.

So! All the suspects in one room, probably. *Let's start with Hades and Persephone, draped all over each other.* Not a chance in hell (argh, unintended pun!) those two were plotting anything beyond who gets the next orgasm.

La Croix? He looked cool as a cuke, which was apparently his thing, and that tracked right now: If he was up to shady shit, why come to Minnesota to fetch Amara? He wasn't sent; he as much as told them over dinner that night in Minneappolis that he felt it was his duty, not an order. He could have steered clear of the drama, but didn't. Plus, he *really* liked Amara's mom. Hard to see him going all in on destroying her husband. Gray still remembered her wild despair when she found Death comatose. Hard to picture La Croix being fine with it.

Arawn? Anyone with adorable hellhoundlets probably wasn't plotting to do away with Death. All right, he knew that didn't necessarily follow. *It's possible the houndlets are clouding my objectivity.* Still, hard to see Arawn caring enough to try and murder Death. He looked intimidating as shit, but seemed super-detached pretty much all the time. Gray wasn't sure Arawn cared about anything, never mind glomming new territory.

Skye? Amara's beloved teacher looked mildly interested in the goings-on, like it was a tennis match you'd bet money on, but not real money. Plus, she was probably the closest thing Amara had to a friend besides himself. Why would she hurt her?

Chernobog? Who the fuck knew?

"Is this the best place to do this?" Penny asked, slipping an arm around Hank's waist. So weird to know you could blame winter on them. Okay, that wasn't entirely fair; it wasn't Persephone's fault her mom overreacted. Punishing two-thirds of the planet with months of blizzards? *Not cool, Demeter!*

He turned his attention to the bed. Blizzards aside, Death looked worse each day—you could chart the deterioration—and no one knew the fuck why, except Gray was pretty sure Amara *did* know, and all the suspects were gathered because she had a bit of a Sherlock streak, for which he blamed Benedict Cumberbatch.

"Penny has a point. Wouldn't the dining hall be more appropriate?" Hank asked, and Gray couldn't get over the man's resemblance to Steve Martin. It wasn't just the short white hair. It was the man's resting tense face, and how his rare smiles were always strained, like he was amused but also constipated. "Roomier, at the least."

"Too many temptations for Gray to feed my hounds," Arawn said with a snigger. And he was right, dammit. The hellhoundlets were locked up somewhere, which sucked because if ever a sickroom needed hellhoundlets, it was this one. Boo! They were born to be free, dammit! Free and cute!

"We're doing it here," Amara replied. "The scene of the crime, so to speak. The corpus delicti. Plus, my mother doesn't need the distraction of tending to our culinary demands."

"Why?" Hilly asked at once, already rising from her chair. "Are you hungry?"

"Only for the truth," Gray said. He tried for sincere, but it came off like a TV prosecutor mugging for a jury. Not that he would have minded if Hilly had produced another smoked turkey. The woman was a friggin' kitchen sorceress. Possibly literally. But Amara was right. Everyone had to stay put.

Almost everyone. He was perfectly aware he was a glorified bystander. "If you're hungry, Hilly, I'd be glad to bring you something."

Amara's mom waved his offer away. "Absolutely not, you're a guest here."

So weird that Hilly had set the standard for pale Midwestern homemakers everywhere, centuries earlier and almost by accident. Martha Stewart would give every one of her teeth to apprentice here for a week. Well. Supervise Hilly for a week, maybe. That could be fun to watch, in a death-match kind of way.

Gray made a concerted effort to focus on what was happening right now as opposed to imagining cage matches. If the worst part of the weekend was seeing Death get sicker while helping Amara kill people, the best was solving Amara mysteries, which were his favorite mysteries.

He'd wondered for years about her suburban studio apartment and crap car, just like he'd wondered about her taste in food. Amara favored bitching about McDonald's while sucking down a Filet-O-Fish with a McNugget chaser. If she cooked, it was ramen noodles and Campbell's tomato soup. Credit where it was due, she could make a mean grilled cheese and a perfect omelet . . . and that was about it. No interest in cooking, or even grocery shopping. Takeout, but never from anywhere good.

In other words, Amara's entire living situation was a collection of knee-jerk reactions to her growing up as Death's heir, in a luxurious compound where she slept in a tower bedroom, drove a Ford Mustang, and ate homemade *everything*, and plenty of it.

Oh, and the jobs. It had taken him way too long to figure out why someone with a trust fund was always hustling for temp work, never stayed more than a few weeks, and often jumped into industries she didn't like or actively loathed.

All that to say, the weekend was worth it just for a deeper glimpse into the life and times of the woman he loved.

As a friend.

*As a friend.*

The kiss was irrelevant. She'd been under a huge amount of stress and strain and, going by her extreme mortification afterward, deeply regretted it the second she laid one on him. The *last* thing he wanted to do was make things worse by suggesting they not only cross the line between friends and lovers, but pole-vault over the fucking thing.

God, he'd adored her from the moment she shoved him off the roof and into a haystack-sized pile of mud. But Amara was like a porcupine: Sharp quills hid the soul of a sweetheart. Dangerous . . . but only when provoked. Sexy, but . . . no, that's where his metaphor broke down.

"When did you decide?"

That brought him back to the present. If he could have gotten away with it without looking like a total ass, he would have rubbed his hands together. Gray had heard the same pleasant tone when Amara was zeroing in on a #MeToo fuckface. Her targets got the same bland questions and pleasant demeanor right before she torpedoed their lives.

"Beg pardon?" Hank asked.

"When did you decide to go along with my parents' scheme to make Death sick and trick me into my birthright?"

Dead (heh) silence. Penny and Hank looked at each other. Skye looked at the floor. Hilly looked at Death. Chernobog looked at Hilly. And La Croix . . .

*"What?"*

Holy shit, La Croix was *surprised.*

Amara was eyeballing La Croix with her "hmmmm" face. "Did you decide as a group? Perhaps in this very room? Or did you all come to the decision separately? Not that it matters. I'm just curious about how we got here."

Cue the awkwardest of awkward silences.

"Will no one answer me?" La Croix yelped. "I say again: What?"

"Why would you make such an accusation?" Hilly said, still looking down at Death.

Hilly was too calm. And she'd asked the wrong question. Amara took a breath.

"Well, let's see. I had no warning, despite the fact that Death has allegedly been ill for months. You were willing to take your time before reaching out because you assumed you had total control of the situation. You were far too calm and civilized about the whole thing. Very much out of character."

"I resent that," Hades said indignantly.

"I don't," Skye said with a chuckle.

"If this was real, my folks would have been in touch the second Death sneezed. And well before he became bedridden. But they didn't say a word before this week. Because it's not real. And their choice of messenger was telling, too. Giving him Death's crown was a nice touch."

"It's been a lie?" La Croix sputtered. He turned to Hilly. "You used me to perpetuate an illusion?"

*Wow. He sounds genuinely hurt. Huh.*

"I don't think—" Penny began.

"Two: You told me you never called Paeon, despite the fact that nothing like this has happened in the history of human events. Despite the fact that he's the only person still living who might have been able to help. I understand why you wouldn't lie to Paeon—too many ways that could have blown up in your face—but at the least, when *I* brought him up, you should have agreed to bring him in. Even if you didn't mean it. But you didn't. *I* reached out. That was a red flag the size of a quilt right there. You ignored my suggestion because you knew exactly what was wrong. And Paeon probably would have, too."

"Told you," Skye said to the room. "Didn't even take her the weekend to smell a rat."

"All fine to say this *now*," Hades muttered. "You were on board, as I recall."

"Shush, peanut gallery. Hold all questions and comments until the end. Three, you all vary from incredibly freaked to weirdly calm. And when you voice a concern, it's never 'This shouldn't be happening.' It's always 'It not supposed to be *like this.*' Because while you expected him to be sick, you didn't plan on him being *this* sick. And it's obvious that the coma took every one of you by surprise."

"Oh, I said 'like this' one time," Penny huffed. "Hardly damning."

Amara nodded. "I concede that. It's not damning on its own. But if I pull all the oddities together and consider what I know about you, all of you, and what you think you know about me, it's plenty damning. But that's not the worst of it. Is it?"

"Nope." From Chernobog, who'd been leaning against the far wall, arms crossed over his chest, quiet as a grave marker. Just being around the big lug was intimidating; small wonder he did what he could to seem less terrifying. The dye job was downright adorable. *What is that?* Gray wondered. *Nice'n Easy Boy Band Blond?*

"It's gotten away from you, hasn't it?" Amara asked. "Whatever spell or poison or trick you colluded to pull. Whatever nonsense scheme you came up with. Death's not getting better. *That's* what you're all freaking out about. Not that Death is sick . . . but that he's visibly decaying before our eyes."

"Oh, but—"

Amara ignored Penny's timid interruption. "There was supposed to be a reveal, right? As if this was reality TV and not, you know . . . reality? Once I stepped up, Death was supposed to make a suspiciously miraculous recovery, I would have faced my fears and then I could leave with a calm acceptance of my future, blah-blah. Which carries its own problems—clearly none of you thought past Death's recovery. And his miraculous recovery would have raised red flags, too."

"You're right," Skye said, holding up her hands in what Gray had to assume was an uncharacteristic placating motion. "It was juvenile and insulting, and we—"

"You fucking idiots."

"Amara," Skye continued, more than a little taken aback, "we never—"

"Don't you understand?" Gray asked. "Hilly always backs Death, so that's not such a surprise. But your betrayal is the worst, Skye. Because Amara loves you. Because she thought you were friends."

"No one hit your buzzer, new guy," Penny said. "You shouldn't be here, much less with our Amara. You're not suited."

"I'll have you know, her eccentricities blend perfectly with my clinical insanity," Gray snapped back. "And I'm not *with* her. Not like that. Amara will back me up."

"Goodbye," Amara said, which wasn't the backup Gray had been looking for.

Hilly's head snapped up. "You're—"

"This is your scheme and your headache," Amara replied. "Best of luck fixing what you put in motion. See you in another six years."

Gray cleared his throat. "I guess that's my cue to go pack. Thanks again for all the lefse."

# CHAPTER THIRTY-EIGHT

"Don't go anywhere," Amara ordered La Croix as they were leaving the room, and half an hour later, she snagged him by the sleeve and dragged him to the indoor cave.

"What in all the worlds—"

"In."

"Amara, what is—"

"In, in."

"Very well, don't *shove.*" La Croix stumbled, caught himself, and nearly fell into Gray's lap.

"What's up, La Choy?" Gray held up a small tray. "Don't worry, I brought snacks."

"That is not what I was worrying about; thank you all the same." La Croix glanced around the cave and shivered. "Shouldn't you be packing?"

Gray's response was muffled by a mouthful of *szarlotka.* "'Course not. It was a bluff . . . my *God*, these are good. Amara wouldn't abandon this mess, no matter how much they deserve it."

"Oh." La Croix loomed over Gray, perhaps by accident, as he pondered. "I hadn't considered that."

"Have a seat," Amara said, settling beside Gray. She couldn't remember wanting a drink so badly in her life, which is why she didn't dare fix herself one or five.

"No, Amara, thank you."

"You can't want to stand like that, all hunched over," Gray pointed out. "What if we're in here for an hour?"

"I shall cope. Everything in here is chilly and damp and I only just got this jacket back from the cleaners."

"I'm not sitting here craning my neck up to talk to you while you lurk over us like a beautifully dressed gargoyle," Amara snapped. "Have a seat already."

With a put-upon sigh, La Croix fussed about and carefully, gingerly, *finally* sat across from them, as far from the tiny waterfall as possible.

"Thank you."

"I'm already damp and sad."

"Sure, but only one of those is our fault," Gray said cheerfully.

"Not just for meeting us here," Amara continued after digging her elbow into Gray's side. "Thank you for declining to join Team Scheme."

"I cannot." La Croix rested his forehead on his knees, then straightened. "I cannot believe Hilly would so deceive me."

"And all the others," Amara prompted. "Who also deceived you."

"Cahooting like crazy and leaving you out," Gray added.

"Yes, yes, death gods can be treacherous, it's in our nature, all our natures, but Hilly? Unfathomable." La Croix sighed and studied his palms. "I must now reexamine all I thought I knew about your lady mother."

"Sure, sure. Perfect timing. You've got all the time in the world to brood and ponder my mother's motivations. Only maybe do something else first?"

"Such as?"

"Tell me about the people who disappeared," she replied. "You told me you had urgent business with your followers. You said you had to address their concerns about recent events."

"You *do* pay attention. How nice to discover new facts about old friends."

Amara gritted her teeth but kept a pleasant expression on her face. "You told me you thought some had gone missing."

"And you think this has to do with what's been done to your father?"

"With what *else* has been done to my father. Remember, he was all in for the first part of the plan. Things didn't go to hell until he couldn't fight an 'attack' that wasn't sanctioned by the group."

"I still cannot believe—"

"La Croix, we don't have time for you to come around on this. Please, *please* stay focused. When Death succumbed to a coma," she continued, "you were nowhere around. Everyone else—except Chernobog, for obvious reasons—stayed. But you did a fade right after breakfast."

"I remember. You already interrogated me about this. Ah! And that's why you did such a thing," he tsked, and actually shook a finger at her. "You thought I was in on it."

"Yes. But since you probably aren't—"

"How dare you!"

"—what *have* you been doing?"

"Soothing my followers. Some of the ones who relocated to this frozen wasteland had lost loved ones, but their death rituals weren't working. It was as if—"

"They disappeared," Gray put in.

Amara nodded. "The same thing happened to me. People who are supposed to die can't be found. Which is impossible. Right?"

La Croix's elegant brow furrowed. "You believe it's connected."

"You don't?" she replied.

"I had not thought—" La Croix cut himself off and fumed in the gloom. Finally, he looked up. "What is happening?"

"Something worse than Death not being able to wake up."

"How vague and horrifying."

"One way to put it."

"So what's next?" Gray asked.

"I have to interrogate my mother."

"Okay. Bring back more snacks."

# CHAPTER THIRTY-NINE

"There isn't enough *frikadelle* in the world for me to forgive you," Amara announced. "But I'll take an apology anyway."

Her mother. Freyja Brunhilde Göndul. Goddess of sex, love, gold, and fertility. Currently scrubbing the shit out of one of her ovens.

She looked up, stood, and tossed the blackened washcloth over her shoulder into the sink. "You shall have one, darling."

"Yes, well. That's not an apology."

"I'm very sorry." Hilly's undereye shadows were beginning to match her husband's. "Truly."

*She never apologizes this quickly. Go for the kill! She is entirely at your mercy, FINISH HER.*

"I deserve all your vitriol and more," Hilly continued. "Worse: How can I face your father after this? I failed him. That's if I'm even allowed to face him." A lone tear trickled, fell off Hilly's cheek, and hit the counter. She snatched a clean washcloth out of her apron and scrubbed it away like it had personally wronged her. "What if he never returns to us?"

*FINISH H— Aww, nuts. No fun at all.*

"You have to assume things will work out, Mom. The way you always have."

"So ironic that this is all happening now. Your sweetheart is the perfect mate for someone whose duty is to meet people at the point of their death, several times, each and every day."

Appalled, Amara replied, "I'd never ask Gray to shackle himself to the family business. Bad enough I have to do it." Though she had to admit her mother had a point. "It's moot, anyway. For a couple of reasons. This isn't like you, Mom. Where's that 'the flagon isn't half empty, it's half full' attitude that drives me absolutely bugfuck?"

"Gone. Possibly forever. Like your father."

"Oh, come on! You can't give up, he's only been in a coma for a couple of days."

"My darling, do you hear yourself? Death has 'only' been comatose for two days. That's a bit like the cancer 'only' spread to your lungs and lymph nodes."

"There's an off-putting analogy. And it's too soon to be so pessimistic. Like when my siblings died; you were determined to be a mother and hung in there and voilà! Here I am! You know . . . eventually."

Several more tears joined the first. "Odd that you should mention your poor doomed brothers and sisters." Hilly dashed away more tears and glared at the washcloth. "The last time I did something this shameful, your sister died."

"Oh." Idun. The girl Amara would never, could never, know. She'd looked like Amara, apparently, except she had white-blond hair, almost silver, and topped out at four feet eleven. Small enough to escape notice and seek all sorts of mischief. "Mom, I can't imagine it was your fault she died. You would have done everything you could and then some. On your laziest day, you make mama bears look indifferent."

Hilly was already shaking her head. "I failed her, as I failed your father."

"Idun's the one who got caught in a blizzard, right? Froze to d— Uh, succumbed to hypothermia?" *A painless death*, Amara thought but didn't say. And maybe it was, but Amara bet it was lonely and scary, too. Especially for a kid.

"Yes, during her coming-of-age ritual. She was so confident—from the moment of her birth!—but I should have followed her."

"But wouldn't that have been against the rules?"

"She died alone. And I don't doubt she called for me, in the end." Hilly sniffled, then blew her nose into the washcloth. "I'd rather have a live disgraced daughter than the alternative. Thank all the gods Skye was there to help me through my grief. What a pity she never had children of her own."

"Definitely a pity and also, that's going straight into the wash, right? You won't use it to wipe down counters on the way to the laundry room?"

"I think you should snatch Gray to your bosom and leave. Now. Tonight."

Amara blinked. "Okay, first, I'm not snatching Gray anywhere near my bosom. Second, leaving was a bluff. I just wanted to see what everyone would do once they thought I was bugging out. Obviously I'm here for the duration."

"*No.*" Hilly threw the repellant washcloth into the sink. "You have to flee, Amara. You must. I will not go down this road again, not for every ounce of gold in the world. Whoever's trying to steal your father's job will lose interest in you once you're gone."

"How does that follow? Disappearing is no guarantee of safety. No. I'm not fleeing, and no need to point it out; the irony isn't lost on me. Besides, you have no way of knowing that."

She took her mother's hands in hers. "I promise not to freeze to death, Mom. The Mustang is loaded with blankets and hand warmers, and in the winter I live in Gore-Tex. But to figure the rest of this mess out, not to mention the agenda of the member of the conclave who went rogue, I need more details of your terrible, terrible plot. I'm guessing it was one of those 'it seemed like a good idea at the time' situations."

Hilly reclaimed her hands and resumed scrubbing with (whew!) a new cloth. "Actually, one of those 'keeping to my oath to obey my husband in all things' situations."

"So it was Dad's idea."

"Yes."

Amara drummed her fingers on the counter and thought. "But you didn't try to talk him out of it."

"I did try." Scrub-scrub-scrub. Rinse. "For days and nights." Scrub-scrub. "Which is why he was eventually compelled to remind me of my oath."

"Oh. Huh. I . . . hadn't considered that."

"The only time he had to do such a thing in three hundred years."

"Wow. Okay. Lots to ponder here. Still not your fault." *I'm pretty sure. Not* entirely *her fault, at the least.* "It's a textbook example of a cockamamie scheme, and you should all feel silly, but something bigger is simultaneously happening."

"Can it be so, darling? Perhaps Death is simply failing because all things end."

"Maaaaaybe. And it's not like he doesn't deserve a break after all these centuries."

Her mother summoned a faint smile. "Why, Amara. How empathetic."

"Yes, yes, it's been a weekend of growth and change. Dad's trapped, too, in a job with pretty good health bennies but no retirement plan. And it's tempting to think maybe it's just his time. But I don't like all the accompanying shenanigans. You don't have anything else to share with the class? No inconvenient details left out?"

"No. On my oath, no."

"Let's keep your oath out of it. Look, just . . ." Amara gave her mother a brisk pat on the shoulder, because she was, at times, exceptionally lame. "Keep your chin up. Or whatever. It ain't over until it's et cetera. Fear not, your youngest and most screwed-up child is on the case."

Hilly smacked her with the washcloth, which was fine. Anything was better than tearful breast-beating and a wooden spoon across the knuckles.

# CHAPTER FORTY

"Sorry."

Amara's heart stopped, thought it over, then rebooted. Hard. "Jesus Christ, Chernobog!"

"Not my full name."

Amara had been tower-bound; now she leaned against the fence to wait for her heart to fully commit to getting back to work.

"If you won't wear a bell, at least consider tap shoes. While I'm recovering from the heart attack, let's chat. Why'd you go along with Team Scheme?"

"They asked."

She groaned and got ready to yell, or at least whine. Then she took another look at him and reconsidered. "They didn't freak out around you or make jokes about how scary you seem. They just politely asked you to help them. And you said yes, because you're the living embodiment of the 'dark is not evil' trope."

"They were nice."

Amara nodded. "I get it, I think. Dumb plan, dumb reason, but . . . okay."

"I try not to be," he said earnestly. "But. I'm frightening anyway."

"You're like Jessica Rabbit. You're not scary, you were just drawn that way."

"What?"

"Pop culture reference. One of Gray's favorite movies."

"He's nice."

"He's wonderful. And still *here*, can you believe it? I'm not sure I do. I haven't ruled him out as a hallucination. Like that movie *The Tale of Two Sisters* where—spoiler!—the youngest sister was dead the whole time. You would tell me if Graham Gray was a hallucination, right?"

"Yes."

"Excellent. One less thing to worry about. Now switch to pastels and give real thought to tap shoes."

"No."

"Have it your way. Listen, it was terrifying running into you, and I'm glad we caught up, but I've got miles to go before I sleep or have a nervous breakdown or however the cliché goes."

"Bye."

✦ ✦ ✦

Gray heard the staccato rapping at the bedroom door and put aside *The Invincible Red Sonja* #1 to answer. He opened the door and beheld a sight that would buckle the knees of ordinary men: Amara in her sleep outfit of mauve velour pants, black thermal top so old and well-washed it was nearly transparent, and fuzzy green socks.

She smiled. "My turn to demand an impromptu sleepover, don't you think?"

He laughed and swung the door wide.

# CHAPTER FORTY-ONE

"In my professional opinion, Death is fucked."

So pronounced Paeon, god of godly medicine and skeet-shooting enthusiast.

He'd bustled in, fended off Hilly's culinary offerings, and made the proverbial beeline for his patient.

"Not helpful," Amara said. "And your bedside manner remains awful."

"Beggars and choosers, Amara. It's nice to see you. I appreciate the call." Paeon was short, about five foot six, with blond curly hair and an immaculate gray suit. His monochromic wardrobe coupled with the wild frizz of his curls made him look like a dapper dandelion. "But it's also quite frightening. If you're here, it must be bad indeed."

"No offense, Paeon—"

"You often say that as a precursor to something really very offensive."

"Ha!" from Gray. "He knows you, Amara."

"—but I could have made that diagnosis."

"And yet, here am I."

"Mmmm. Did Team Scheme fill you in on what's happening?"

"Just now." Paeon gave Hilly some side-eye, but forbore to comment further. "Death wanted to trick his last living child into embracing her birthright."

"Nutshell," Gray said.

"And how are *you* feeling, young man?"

"A little hungry," Gray admitted.

"Cripes, half an hour ago you devoured a stack of waffles so high I couldn't see your face," Amara cried. "Forehead-high waffles, Gray!"

"More an amuse-bouche than a meal, though."

"That's not how you pronounce that. I mean, you're not even close."

Gary shrugged off her devastating correction. "I think you're just pissy because my idea didn't work."

"A little," Amara admitted. Gray's plan. A stupid plan. A "there's no way this can work but let's try anyway" plan: No one can resist the smell of freshly cooked, crisp bacon. Not even comatose Death. So he'd piled a plate with it and brought it to her father. Who was still in a coma. A bacon-resistant coma.

"Never mind me," Gray replied to Paeon. "Though it's nice of you to ask."

"Yes, never mind him." Christ, did *everyone* know Gray would be in the dirt a few months from now? Stupid question. Just death gods and the god of godly medicine, apparently. "What's the prognosis for my father?"

"How did you do it?" Paeon asked Hilly.

"That's the question," Amara replied. "Because I've got no idea."

"Ah." Paeon plopped his pink wheeled suitcase, which looked like a giant shiny Canada mint, on Death's bed. It was a king, so there was plenty of room for him to pop it open and rummage, but it was still jarring. To Amara he said, "The fact that you don't know gives credence to Death's foolish, idiotic plan."

"Thanks for the lecture, don't trash my comatose dad, your medical bag is ridiculous, please answer my question."

"Ichor, I would guess." Paeon looked up. "Yes?"

Hilly, cupping her elbows as she observed the proceedings, nodded.

"Fast-acting, not necessarily controllable," Paeon commented. "You—and I include Death in that 'you'—likely assumed someone of such powerful longevity would be able to fight it off before he succumbed. That he could ingest enough to look ill, and be ill, but not *so* ill that he would lose his faculties. Or be in any real danger. But it's the simplest thing to take too far. As we see here."

"Ichor?" Gray asked.

Amara sighed. "They poisoned my father with their blood."

Gray's expression almost made her laugh: nausea warring with fascination. "Ichor is blood?"

"God blood. Yes."

"And they *fed* it to him? He went along with this?"

"Behold, my family," Amara said dryly. "Not that it's a contest."

"Ichor is toxic to humans," Paeon explained. "And not especially good for gods, either. It would kill you instantly, Mr. Graham."

"Gray, please. So no god-blood cocktails for *moi*. Warning noted. But here's where I keep ending up in the weeds: Death isn't human."

"His avatar is. It's complicated," Paeon said, kindly enough. "I'm guessing he deliberately made himself vulnerable. Allowed the ichor to begin to work."

"Because he's walking around in a human body," Gray guessed. "So because physics—or would that be biology?—Amara's dad can let himself be vulnerable?"

"Very well, Gray, perhaps *not* complicated."

"Not to brag, Dr. Paeon, but I read a ton of graphic novels and I've got over a decade of D&D under my belt."

"Splendid," replied the underwhelmed god of godly medicine.

Amara let out a sudden yelp: "Fuck!" Everyone flinched, including Hilly, who was too surprised to snap out a reprimand. "God, I'm so blind. I was *supposed* to figure this out, wasn't I? This isn't just a scheme of Scooby Doo–esque stupidity. It's my rite of passage." She let out a groan of pure irritation. "If I came on the run, remained to help, figured out the scheme and 'saved' Dad, I would be worthy of taking Death's musty, feathery crown."

"Oh," Gray said. "Another reason for your mom to put off calling Dr. Paeon. Seeing as how he figured out what they did and how and why in about thirty seconds."

"Yes, well." Paeon didn't quite shrug. "I am outstanding."

"But someone here—well, not just the people in this room, all the death gods in town—they saw their chance, and kept feeding him. Kept him under. Watched him sink lower. They needed Death off the board. Maybe . . . to clear the way for me?" Or not. Which was the more intriguing and sinister possibility.

"Who, though?" Gray asked. "Also, it's not me. In case you were wondering."

"Thanks for setting my mind at ease. And if we knew who, we'd know why. Stupid, stupid, stupid." She punctuated each stupid with a hard forehead tap. *If I don't let up on my skull, I'm asking for a migraine.* "Why not just let me go hiking in the snow for three days? Rhetorical, Mother. I know why."

Hilly nodded. "Your father's idea. A rite of passage that, if failed, wouldn't be fatal."

Amara wasn't sure how to feel about that. One hand: What

happened to her long-dead sister had been an appalling waste. Other hand: Amara resented being coddled. *Maybe just admit that no matter what the situation, you'll find a way to complain about it?*

*No. Asking too much.*

"Not fatal to me, anyway . . ."

"How are the migraines?" Paeon asked, apropos of nothing.

"What? Oh. Painful yet nonexistent," Amara sniffed. "According to some."

Hilly sighed. "Will you never let that go?"

"I needed help, Mother."

"And you got help, Daughter."

"Telling me my crippling head pain was all in my head was the opposite of help, Mother."

"Wait, what?" From Gray, who stepped forward so he and Amara were almost hip-to-hip. "Of course they're real. And they suck. Amara usually has to hit the sheets for at least half a day. Plus Dr. Paeon just explained that Death's avatar is human. Migraines are a thing that humans get. And Amara's human. So."

"A ridiculous thing," Hilly muttered. "A nonsense thing."

"Let's stay focused," Amara said. "Mom, there will be plenty of time for us to rehash old arguments and drive everyone mad with our tiresome squabbling."

"I'll, er, make a note of that."

"Paeon, is there anything you can do?" Amara gazed down at Death, who now looked as much like a corpse as he could without actually being dead. Over the years she had loved him, loathed him, resented him, adored him, protected him, attacked him. But now, right now, all she could feel for the husk on the bed was profound pity. "Maybe set up an IV for the gods? Flush out the toxins?"

"It's not a hangover, Amara. And counteracting ichor is beyond even my skills. Your father will recover, or he won't."

"Great. Thanks for making the trip."

"You're so welcome. And don't take that to mean I'm leaving. I remain at your lady mother's disposal. And Death's, of course. Does anyone mind if I eat that plate of bacon?"

# CHAPTER FORTY-TWO

Despite the treacherous shenanigans, the day's business couldn't be put off. She and Gray used the time waiting for La Croix to notch half a dozen Reaps—a fatal myocardial infarction, a GSW, two car accidents, an accidental asphyxiation, and a deliberate asphyxiation—and when they got back to the house, La Croix was there.

"I regret to confirm your suspicions," he told her. He'd stopped long enough to kick off his boots in the entryway before he tracked her to the kitchen. He'd turned on all the kitchen lights, which was painful and irritating . . .

*Not now. Do not get a migraine now!*

. . . but she let it go, not least because he returned with a crapload of valuable intel.

Grateful for his speed and the news, she rolled a fat lefse bundle loaded with brown sugar and ate it in front of him. "*Thhnnggss aagghh ack*!" she managed as a few brown sugar crystals went down the wrong pipe.

"Ah, that's lovely," he said with the satisfied sigh of an addict getting a fix. "Truly hits the spot. Another? No? Ah, well. I don't suppose I could talk you into a post-lefse cigarette?"

"Mom would kill me. Odd enough that I'm doing this much for you."

"It is," he agreed cheerfully, but sobered almost immediately. "I'll stand with you, Amara Morrigan."

"Of course you will."

He smirked. "But?"

"But it's more about you being pissed about being tricked, and more pissed about being left out, than it is about backing my play. You're irked and have scores to settle."

". . . True."

She clapped him on the shoulder. "That wasn't a criticism. Well, not that big a criticism. I'm in no position to turn down a god's help. Thank you, truly."

"And now?"

"Now I have to go fuck my best friend because there's an excellent chance I'm going to be killed tonight. And I think I'm getting a migraine."

". . . Carry on."

✦ ✦ ✦

"Okay, now *I* want a cigarette."

Amara snorted, groped for a pillow, thwacked Gray across the face with it.

"Yow! Also, it's hilarious that La Croix can't actually indulge his vices unless someone does it for him. No wonder he's so skinny. Other people chow down the calories for him. What a racket."

They'd thoroughly trashed the tower guest room and Amara could not recall caring less about a mess. "How about we don't talk about Baron La Croix right now?"

"Okay. Can we talk about how awesomely hot our first-time

sex was?" Gray leaned over her, propped up on an elbow. If it had been anyone else, she'd have felt crowded. Since it was Gray, she wished he would wiggle closer. "You've got to admit, that never happens. It's usually awkward and you're both self-conscious and there are lots of accidental elbow pokes and maybe even a fart and/or queef. Or both. A feef! No, wait. Quart."

"Dodged a bullet," Amara said dryly. "And farts."

She'd been on him the second he opened the door, and the kiss was more like a grapple. She came up for air long enough to beg for consent, and his response—yanking his clothes off, then hers—was gratifying.

"Crazy-crazy-crazy," he muttered, touching and kissing her everywhere.

"We're ruining this friendship," she gasped, reaching down for him and gently squeezing his lovely long length.

"Definitely should stop," he agreed, nuzzling her nipples, then coming up for another deep kiss. He slid back down her body and rained kisses along her inner thighs, then nuzzled her pubic hair, carefully parted her, and spent a good five minutes licking and kissing while she clutched at his hair and groaned at the ceiling.

"Nuts," she gasped as she shuddered through another orgasm. "This is deeply nuts. I never come this fast."

"Yeah, well." She tasted herself as he came up for another kiss, as she spread her knees and arched to meet him. "Been a while for both of us." Before he could elaborate, or she could answer, he stiffened and his eyes rolled back, Amara's second favorite part of sex. *What can I say? Watching that particular involuntary reflex is scorching.* "Aw, hell. I swear I usually last longer than two strokes." Then he'd collapsed over her and it was many minutes before either of them felt like talking. Or moving. When they did finally move, it was for the obligatory bathroom break and grumbling about the wet spot, which Gray gallantly covered with a towel.

Now they were cuddled together in his bed, lovers who wouldn't share the summer.

"Thanks for acceding to my demand for sex."

"Thanks for demanding sex." He leaned down, grabbed the blankets in his fist, pulled them up and over them. "Why'd we wait so long?"

"The friendship," she yawned. "You've long made it clear you had no interest in taking it further."

Gray sat up. "What?"

"I'm not complaining," she assured him. "Truly. I wanted you, but I was fine with respecting your boundaries. Sexual and otherwise." *Gah, I sound like a dirty after-school special.* "It was worth it to me. Worth it to you, too, I think."

"*I* wanted *you.*"

"Gray. Stop. Our default is friends. The status quo has always been friends, and not the kind with benefits. Which you made clear again after our disastrous cave kiss."

"First, not disastrous. Second, my ass!"

"You said!" Now they were both sitting up and tenderly glaring into each other's eyes. "You said you would never want to have sex with me."

"No. You didn't let me finish. I said 'I would never' and you cut me off. So I tried again. I even pointed out that you didn't let me finish. But—"

"I don't—"

"See? You're doing it again. And when I tried again, I only got as far as 'I would never' before you insisted we move on. *You* made it clear you wanted nothing past friendship."

"Oh, fuck me."

"What I meant, what I kept trying to say, is that I figured

you'd kissed me in the cave as a reaction to being stressed beyond belief. So I wanted to assure you that I wouldn't take advantage of you in that state. No matter how much I wanted to feel you from the inside."

"Is that a Nine Inch Nails reference?"

"I wanted you. From. Day. One." Each word was accentuated with a poke in the ribs. "I. Have. Loved. You. From. D—ow!"

"Let's just say, going forward, that we were both utter idiots."

"Agreed. You more than me, though."

"Shut up, I hate you."

"No. You don't. Not even a little."

"I have no comeback for that."

"Thank *God*."

They snuggled back together and Amara was beginning to wonder if Round Two was feasible given the time constraints, when there was a sudden thud at the door, which then opened so fast it rebounded and nearly slammed shut in Hilly's face.

"Alas," Amara sighed. "Round Two is *not* feasible given time constraints."

"La Croix told me you expect to be murdered tonight!" Hilly was a flour-dusted vision of maternal wrath as she stomped into the room. "I insist you get up immediately so we can deal with this mortal threat."

"Jesus Christ, Hilly. What's the rolling pin for? You know what? Maybe don't answer that."

Amara squashed the urge to clap her hands. "Hooray, La Croix came through." To Gray: "He really is a shameless gossip."

"Amara Morrigan!"

"I'm up, I'm up. Also, you could be a bit more scandalized."

Hilly blinked. "You're an adult who finally had sex with someone you love."

"Awww." Gray looked up from trying to cover his unmentionables and grinned. "You lurrrrrv me!"

"Shut up, you knew that."

"And I'm happy for you," Hilly continued, exasperated as only Amara could make her, "but we have much more pressing business."

"Fair. I assume everyone's here, or you wouldn't be."

"In your father's room, as La Croix requested. On your behalf, I now realize."

"Good. Thank you. Uh, Gray, after you find your sock, could you find my sunglasses?"

"On it."

"I apologize for the intrusion, darlings," Hilly continued as Gray rolled out of bed, then crawled halfway beneath it to rescue one of his socks. Which he waved at her, then fled to the bathroom. "Necessary though it was. Time is not on our side."

"Which is ironically hilarious. Time is always on Death's side. One way or the other, everyone goes down."

"Yes, well." Hilly stepped to the bed and began making it, then stopped herself. "Perhaps you and Gray will have the chance to couple again later."

"Perhaps," Amara agreed. By midnight, she would either be dead, or straddling Gray, so. Textbook win-win.

# CHAPTER FORTY-THREE

"Wait," Skye said. "I thought you were leaving." To the group: "Did she not tell us she was leaving several hours ago?"

"Changed my mind. You know how capricious I can be. Flighty, yet dour. Easily distracted, yet glum."

They were back in the sick room and her dad was front and center, so to speak, in a huge bed that would have made anyone look small, and made Death look still more frail. His deterioration over the long weekend was as sorrowful as it was shocking.

*I never thought he'd die. And even if I did, I never thought he'd die small.*

"Yes, yes, you're *good* little hellhoundlets. Who's the best little hellhoundlet? You are! And also you. And you, too!"

"I do appreciate your lover, Amara," Arawn said. He'd pulled up a chair beside the fireplace and stretched his long legs out in front of him. La Croix was also beside the fireplace, as close as he could get without actually climbing into the flames. "No one in recent memory has ever been so charmed by my beasts."

"Lover?" Gray asked.

Arawn flapped a hand at him. "Oh, please."

"Oh." Gray nodded. "Death god thing."

"You're both still sex-flushed and sweaty," Penny pointed out with a giggle. "Not a death god thing. It's a 'having eyes and not being entirely stupid' thing."

Gray ignored the needle. "Sensing when people have banged is another death god superpower, I guess," he said, gazing into a hellhoundlet's large liquid eyes. "Yes it *is*. Yes it *is*! Awww, your ears are so silky."

"*Anyway*." Amara fought the urge to kiss and kick Gray, not in that order. "I've got good news for all of you. Death is just fine."

"What?" From Hank and Penny, in amazed unison.

"Good." Chernobog.

"This is news to me." Dr. Paeon.

"Graham Gray, do *not* give my dogs whatever you've hidden in your pocket."

"This is your fault." La Croix to Hilly. "You let her read too much of that Arthur Conan Doyle pop culture dreck."

"Have you gone completely crazy?" Skye cried. She'd been the last to arrive, and either was wearing what she'd worn the day before, or she had lugged several identical pairs of cargo pants and black sweaters with epaulets to the compound. "Aren't any of you listening to her?"

"That's true, Skye," Amara said. "They're not great listeners. But then, they don't have to be."

"Hush, Amara . . . Death is not 'just fine.' Oh, gods, I knew this was going to be too much for you," Skye moaned. "Oh, you poor kid . . ."

"And the reason Death is fine is because *that*," Amara continued, pointing to the body on the bed, "is no longer Death. *I* am, for all my remaining days, however long they be, and retroactive to my first Reap. My parents were right; it's time I embraced my responsibilities regardless of my father's state of health. Or his state of death."

Chernobog: "Good."

Penny: "Wow!"

La Croix: "Well done. Could someone throw fifteen or twenty more logs on the fire?"

Hank: "Congratulations?"

Arawn: "It strikes me that this could have been a conference call."

Amara turned to Hilly with a smile. "Did I pass, Mother?"

"Do you even need to ask me such a thing?" Hilly hugged her. "With flying colors. With every color in the spectrum and a number invisible to the naked eye. I'm so proud of you. And so sad for you. For all that makes no sense."

Skye: "*What*?"

"That's not to say we're giving up on Dad," Amara said, ignoring Skye's pained yelp and wiggling out of the hug to hold her mother at arm's length. "See my face, Mother. My word on it, we will never give up on Dad. But the goal now is simply to cure him—"

Paeon snorted. "Simply."

"—as opposed to the time-urgent emphasis on curing him so he can instantly return to his sworn duties. Which makes your job a bit easier, doesn't it, Paeon?"

"Well." The god of godly medicine considered. "Yes."

"Has everyone in the room lost their minds?" Skye cried. "Amara can't do it. She herself said so over and over and over. For years!"

"You're sweet to worry about me. And obviously I can," Amara replied. "Have been, in fact. It's not as awful as I imagined. To be fair, a big reason I got through it was because Gray was with me."

"Awwww! Thanks, babe. Still can't get that poor teenager out of my head, though."

"I know. Don't call me babe. But . . . it's my job now. Unless." Amara gazed around the room. "There are objections? Not that those mean anything. I'm the heir and I'm stepping up; it's nothing you can vote on. I just want your objections on the record. If there are any."

"None." Chernobog.

"Oh, that's not for *me* to say," Arawn said with a not-quite-nice smile. "As you said, this is yours. It was always yours."

"I mean, congratulations?" Penny said. She lifted her arms as though she would hug Amara, as she had done many times when Amara was a child. But didn't step closer. And let her arms drop back to her sides. And Hank reacted to her discomfort, and put an arm around his wife, queen of the dead, author of winter.

*So it begins*, Amara thought, sad and proud and wary at the same time. *I'm no longer Hilly's annoying little girl who could be amused with tickles and candy. You don't just rush up to Death and give them a hug. You keep your distance. Even when you don't want to.*

"Well done, Amara," La Croix said. "I would rise and take your hand but I cannot feel my extremities."

"Jeez, La Choy. Hilly, d'you mind if I . . . ?" Gray left the hellhoundlets alone long enough to cross the room, fish a quilt out of the open closet, and drape it around La Croix's shivering shoulders. "Just FYI, it's at least seventy-five degrees in here and climbing."

"I cannot believe what I'm hearing!" Skye just about shrieked. "Why are you all standing around simpering at her? This is a disaster!"

"No, Brexit was a disaster." Gray smirked. "This is just inconvenient."

"Shut *up*, you twittering imbecile!"

Amara wasn't sure who Skye was referring to. "Are you all right? You look like you're going to stroke out."

"Am *I* all right? Do any of you hear her? Or yourselves?" Skye clutched her head, then grabbed her braid in both fists and yanked, hard. Once, twice, and again. It was a startling, almost disturbing thing to watch. "She can't do it! She has long said so!"

"Well, as I also said, dreading the Reaps was worse than doing them. I'll never get over how odd that is. And I'm new, obviously." She spread her hands and shrugged. "But I'll learn. My father was new, once. And I have help. I'm not so proud I'll go it alone."

"You are not your father!" Skye practically screamed.

"Skye," Hilly began tartly, but subsided when Amara shook her head.

"You only got through one Reap before you *and* your luckless paramour fled to the zoo, for gods' sake! Like children ducking class!"

"Right. The zoo. That *was* relaxing. And you knew that how, Skye?"

"I—what?"

"How did you know Gray and I went to the zoo?" Amara's tone was pure honest curiosity. *Just asking a simple question. We're all still friends. Nothing amiss anywhere.* "You weren't with us. And we didn't tell anyone what we did or where we went."

"It's not like your activities have been a secret," Skye snapped. "And La Croix gossips like a fishwife."

"I knew nothing of a zoo." La Croix was rubbing his hands together before the roaring fire that was making everyone sweat. "And I demand you leave me out of whatever this is."

"Amara, we've been friends for years."

"Have we, Skye?"

That checked her. "Yes! Obviously! It's why you must listen to me now. I'm the only one in this room who has your best interests at heart."

"Oh, I do beg your fucking pardon," Hilly snapped.

Skye unwisely ignored the growing wrath of Hilly. "Haven't I always looked out for you?"

"No, Skye."

"Yes! See? I—what?"

"You've always looked out for yourself. Sometimes our needs aligned, and when I was younger I mistook that for empathy and friendship."

Scáthach, the guide to death for the Isle of Skye, pulled herself up to her full height, which was intimidating, but only if you had never met Death. Or Chernobog. "What are you daring to say to me?"

"It took me a long time to see what you were doing. Partly because you fooled yourself into thinking you had my best interests at heart, which made it easier to fool *me*."

"Of course I have! I always have! Fool you? You would come to me when you couldn't go to your own mother."

"True. But it doesn't change the fact that you used our faux friendship as a means to secure your fondest wish: more territory. It's always been your goal. I'm just wondering when you decided."

"That is an absurd and hateful lie!"

"You *have* always been there for me," Amara admitted. "Constantly following me and pushing me. It's why you encouraged me to hide in Death's car when I was a little girl."

"I didn't—I just said—"

"You knew it was too much for any child, and you made sure to linger long enough to comfort me when it was over. You also promised to do all in your power to see to it I would never have to take Death's mantle. And I think that's how it started, for you. I think that's when you decided."

"Jesus." Gray's expression was pure revulsion. "You talked a little kid into crashing a Reap so you could profit from her emotional scarring?"

"That was years ago! Why are you fishing for an apology now?"

"That's not what I'm after. I'd like to talk about the foxes," Amara continued.

Skye threw up her hands. "What are you babbling about now?"

"I saw one at the zoo, which was odd enough, and another one at the Air Force base during my second Reap."

"Odd?" Hank asked.

Amara nodded. "I double-checked when Gray and I got back. The Roosevelt Zoo doesn't have a fox exhibit. They never have. And foxes belong to you, Skye, the way the night belongs to Chernobog and the hellhounds belong to Arawn. It's how you could keep an eye on me while poisoning my father."

"Y'know what?" Gray asked, rumpling one hellhoundlet's ears while scratching another's belly as the third butted her hard little head into his leg for attention. "I'll bet if we went back the last couple of days and dug up CCTV footage, we'd see a fox in the vicinity of everyone who disappeared."

"No doubt. Once I found out about the foxes, I started to notice other things. Like when you claimed La Croix asked you to sit with Death. Except La Croix told me a different story: *You* were the one who offered to relieve *him*. Which gave you the chance to slip Death more poison. It wasn't even that hard, was it? Manipulating us into repeatedly leaving you alone with Death? We trusted you. Why not? All this time, we've been such good *friends*."

Skye had gone so pale, her freckles stood out in blotchy relief. "And you've convinced yourself I would indulge in such treacherous behavior because . . ."

"I already told you; you just can't be bothered to listen. But I listened to you. I heard your complaints about the loss of territory. Not just when we spar, but every time you see me. I've seen your envy of the compound, heard you repeatedly, in the guise of friendly sarcasm, tell my parents they didn't deserve such a wide swathe of territory. Heard your resentment that your influence over the centuries had been reduced to the six hundred miles of the Isle of Skye.

"So when I pulled all that together, it was obvious. And I can't even take much credit for figuring it out, because you didn't work too hard to cover your tracks. Even now, you're not really trying. You should be projecting calm reason and logical-but-hurt outrage, but you're shrieking like someone set your hair on fire while not actually denying anything I've said."

"Demeanor doesn't equal evidence," Gray added, "but still."

"I—you—I—"

"You know, in all the years we've been 'friends,' I've never heard you raise your voice. But look at you. You're a seething shitpile right now."

And Amara saw it. Saw the second Skye decide to stop dancing and go all in. "Yes, well. I didn't think it would take much effort, since you have a documented history of being a spoiled, oblivious idiot."

"Only two of those are true," Amara sniffed. "And I'll take 'spoiled idiot' over cowardly poisoner."

"Watch your mouth, girl."

She ignored the warning. "Not just my father, either. You've been poisoning me for years. Every chance you got, you dripped vitriol in my ear. Like with my migraines. Outwardly sympathetic, while telling me they were just another reason I wasn't suited to Death's mantle.

"And for what?" Amara spread her hands. "None of this

was necessary. There's plenty of room here. None of us have to reside in our physical territories to do our work. I can be Death in Minot or Missouri or Moscow. And you know my parents would have let you stay as long as you—"

"I am not a guest and I do *not* accept charity! This territory and all souls in it should be mine by right."

"Should? No," Amara said quietly. "That's only what you told yourself. The blunt fact is, it's *mine* by right, and you know it well. It's why you can't stand it. You never could. So when you saw me at my lowest—the painful fogs of migraine, my despair at family obligations, my refusal to return home—you stopped fucking around and set your cowardly coup in motion.

"And you probably told yourself it wasn't wrong, that you weren't betraying me. 'Saving me.' I'm betting that's how you rationalized it. Well, I have woeful news for you, Skye: I don't need saving."

"Utter bullshit! You need saving almost as much as your father does."

"My father. Mmmm." Amara studied Scáthach like she was a bug under a microscope the likes of which had never been seen. "It was your idea, wasn't it? Presented out of concern for my mother and me. 'Let yourself be poisoned; when Amara fails at least she won't die and poor Brunhilde won't suffer the loss of another daughter.' And Death listened. Of course he did. And for love of my mother and me, agreed. And so here we are. A stupid, reckless plan, like something out of a nineties sitcom. And now this mess."

"It's mine," Skye said defiantly. "The territory and everything in it. Your mother. You. The grounds, the buildings, the hundreds of thousands of souls."

"You're off: seventy million. You want to rule over a territory of people you don't understand? You couldn't even be bothered to Google the population. I'm beginning to see why you're down to six hundred miles and a population of ten thousand. You just . . . half-ass everything. I can't believe I didn't see it sooner."

"It all belongs to me. You could never have held it."

"You're a broken record. And how very Darwinian of you. The polite thing to do would be to wait until I failed before launching Project Treacherous Bitch."

"No, I—"

"But you couldn't wait, and once you started, you couldn't go back. You'd made your decision, you talked Death into making himself vulnerable to ichor. Once you crossed that line, it was either go back or go on. And it's not in you to go back, so: more poison. More faux understanding. What you didn't count on was my competence."

Skye pressed her lips together but said nothing. Amara was more than a little surprised no one in the room took the easy shot, either. The only sounds were the snuffling of houndlets, the crackling fire, and La Croix's chattering teeth.

"I not only came when called, I brought a loved one along for the ride and we took up the scrolls. So now you had two problems: You had to make Death sicker and you had to make the Reaps harder. Drive me away so you could heroically step in. So you manipulated the list, giving me the worst first."

"But I thought that was impossible," Gray said.

"Forbidden," Hilly said, glaring at Skye. "Only a handful of people on the globe would even be able to make the attempt. And it would be difficult—not impossible—even for them."

"Manipulating the list contradicts the point of death gods: No one can avoid their fate and it's not okay to try. But what's a little blasphemy when you're going for a land grab, right, Skye?"

"You're talking to me about blasphemy?" Skye muttered.

"That's rich. And I didn't manipulate the list. I switched out the faxes."

Amara held herself still so she wouldn't slap her own forehead. *So simple it never occurred to me. I assumed she was utilizing death-god shenanigans to fuck with the list, but all she had to do was get to the fax machine first. Bad enough that anyone could have done it. Worse that we made it easy.*

*She might have half-assed everything, but my family hasn't exactly been behaving like rocket scientists, either.*

"You also hid the 'easy' Reaps," Amara continued. "That's when La Croix noticed; his followers knew some of the missing, and came to him for help."

Before she could elaborate, La Croix jumped in. Fair: Skye had fucked with his people. "It did not take overlong to see what you'd done, lending credence to Amara's point about your . . . inefficiency." He seemed to get taller and darker with every word, and if Skye had any sense, she'd be mildly terrified right about now. "And however events shake out now, you have made an enemy, Scáthach, warrior maid of shadows. And there will be a reckoning."

Amara cleared her throat. "Anyway. You didn't anticipate La Croix noticing your little practice runs. To be fair, what were the odds? I was supposed to have fled back to Minnesota by now. Your improvisations shouldn't have been necessary. But you decided to make lemon meringue from lemons; La Croix's running around town just added to my stress, and the missing people gave me yet another thing to worry about.

"They're fine, by the way. If you care. The ones you hid. Well, not fine; they're dead because it was their time. La Croix tracked the last one down a couple of hours ago. You hid them on the base, where it would be almost impossible for civilians to look for them. But in a common area, where their discovery, while delayed, was always inevitable. Because you half-assed it.

"And that's it." Amara looked around the silent room. "Uh, that's the mend of my story. End. *End* of the gory. Story!" *Argh! Stupid aphasia.*

"See?" Skye jabbed a finger at the others, who were staring at her with expressions ranging from surprise to horror. "She's getting a migraine right now! Just *talking* about all this—this bullshit nonsense is making her sick. It's why she's wearing those stupid sunglasses."

"They're not stupid," Gray said. "They're Celine's. Never diss Death Lite *or* Celine's sunglasses line."

Skye wouldn't be moved. "This sickly child? Taking Death's mantle?"

"I'm pushing thirty, Skye."

Skye ignored reality (again). "It's an absurd joke. And you all know it. You're just too fond of Hilly—or too frightened—to do anything."

"You know quite well why we aren't able to 'do anything,'" Arawn said, studying his red, red hands. When he looked up, his visage was as grim as Amara had ever seen. "I'm beginning to see Death's point."

*"Don't you call her that!"*

"You really aren't paying attention, and you have perverted your role in life's eternal cycle."

"They aren't migraines," Amara said. "The symptoms were real, as was the pain, but it was a misdiagnosis. Not that it's relevant. And I'll tell you what, Skye. You did help me in your way. I had bad days you made a bit better. In service to yourself, mostly, but I don't forget it."

"So, what?" Skye said scornfully. "Bygones will be bygones?"

"Yes. I'll let it all go—I've already let *you* go—if you leave now. Get lost, stay lost. Know that you're never to return to my lands. Understand that you are banished forever. And this can be over."

"Everything here is mine," Skye said, because she was a delusional, deceitful twat.

"The only thing that's yours is your life. I'd prefer not to take it, but that's up to you. Everything you've done has been up to you. All your wounds are self-inflicted."

"Such nonsense."

"It isn't nonsense," her father said from the bed. "It's just tedious. And why's it so goddamned hot in here?"

# CHAPTER FORTY-FOUR

The uproar was beyond satisfying.

# CHAPTER FORTY-FIVE

Death was a mess. Withered and gaunt, his hair more white than red, barely able to lift his head from the pillow. Scáthach cringed away regardless.

"Husband," Hilly breathed, taking his hand. Then: "You old fool. How long have you been back with us?"

"I'm not." He grinned up at his wife, baring sharp yellow teeth. "Not really. Amara can explain. You look like hells, woman. Dammit!"

"Keep that up, you'll get another pinch."

"Wow. *Wow*," Gray said, goggling. "I thought you got us all in here for dramatic effect, not because your dad was going to be the surprise speaker."

"Both of those can be true."

"It isn't fair." Skye had gone from too-pale to too-red in about a second and a half. "Your time is done, old man."

"Not your call, Scáthach." To Amara: "It's a trade, yes? A good one. That's all right, hon. I'm tired."

"I'm *standing* right *here*," Skye snapped.

"It doesn't matter. You don't matter. Don't you understand?"

Amara asked, contempt warring with pity. "You tried and you lost. Nothing will change that." To Death: "This is what I've been putting up with."

"What, Death, you think you can just open your eyes—"

"How is he opening his eyes in the first place?" Gray slapped his forehead. "Oh. Because half-assed."

"—and all goes back to what it was?"

"No, Scáthach. I don't think that. I think I'm tired and I think you're tedious." Amara's father sighed. "Good thing I don't have to put up with either of those anymore."

"I did what I had to do," Skye insisted, because she was incapable of reading the room. "To survive."

"Is that what you told my sister when you intercepted her all those years ago in the snow?" Amara took a step closer to Scáthach. And another. "I wonder, did you kill her on the spot the moment you caught up?" She had never been this close to Skye unless they were hugging. Or sparring. Their noses were inches apart. "Or did you weasel your way in close, knock her out, and wait for her to freeze to death? I guess it doesn't matter." Amara's voice was almost unrecognizable to her. The only time she'd sounded this coldly forbidding was when she confronted Gray's mother. Only now she wouldn't have to fight the urge to beat someone to death. "What does matter is something you didn't count on. It. Didn't. Work.

"And the fact that you thought it would just shows you never really knew any of us. My folks didn't give up. They dug in. They risked their hearts to have another child. And another. Until they got me. So you waited and plotted a few hundred years before you tried again. And you *still* couldn't get the job done."

"Dammit, woman!"

"S-sorry, husband." Hilly dropped Death's probably throbbing hand. "Amara, what are you saying?"

"I'm sorry, Mom. I suspected it a couple of days ago, but I couldn't burden you with it until—"

"It was easy, Hilly." Skye bared her teeth. "That yodeling twit could never have taken over."

"—Skye confessed," Amara finished. Then she leaned in and whispered in her mother's ear, and got a shallow nod in return.

To Skye: "Mom mentioned what a comfort you were back in the day. How you helped her get through the tragedy. It stood to reason that your cowardly coup campaign didn't start with me."

"Oh, Skye," Penny moaned. "How could you do such a thing? To attack one of us? Our children?"

"And for nothing," Arawn added. "You killed that lively child for nothing."

"I did what I had to do."

Amara couldn't keep the scorn from her tone. "Self-defense? Is that what you're going with? And when I kill you, what is that, exactly?"

"A pipe dream," Skye snarled, and launched herself.

Amara could see how to block the first blow, dodge the second, and blow Skye's kneecap between the first and second. But overconfidence would be a mistake. Doubtless there were plenty of moves Skye never bothered to teach Amara Morrigan.

And yet, she wasn't Amara Morrigan anymore.

She blocked, but Skye was able to get a swipe in regardless, tearing Amara's sunglasses off. Then, blinking in surprise: "What's wrong with your—"

"They aren't migraines," Amara replied, and then seized Skye with something stronger than the strength in her hands: her birthright. "I Reap thee, Scáthach of the Isle of Skye." The words were familiar, though she'd never heard them before, and certainly never said them before. "I don't take all from you, only your life. And so farewell."

It wasn't especially dramatic, or even drawn out. One moment Skye was a khaki bundle of envious rage, and then she was a husk and when Amara dropped her, no one flinched at the unmistakable *bonk* of a dead skull hitting the floor.

"Your, um, all of a sudden your hair color's new. Red. Really brilliant red. We've been friends forever and I've never seen your hair like this. The color of—" And he cut himself off.

"No, Gray." Amara pulled her gaze from the corpse at her feet. "My hair's not new. It's gone back to the way it always was."

And her headache was gone.

# CHAPTER FORTY-SIX

"He's gone," Hilly said, closing the bedroom door. She looked startled to find them all clustered in the hallway, waiting for her rather than heading for the dining hall or library. "For good and for real this time."

Amara pushed away from the wall she'd been slumped against. "I'm sorry, Mom."

"As am I, darling. But he explained. And I can't get angry with you for acceding to his wishes. Or him for leaving. I just." She stopped and flapped her hands, then let them drop and let out a small, bewildered laugh. "I don't quite know what to do with myself now. Or tomorrow. Or next year."

"You won't be alone, Mom. I'm staying. I'll take the train home tomorrow morning to pack up my things and come straight back."

"No," Gray said. His grip tightened; he'd been holding Amara's hand while they waited for Hilly. "I'll go back. I'll pack up your craphole and bring your stuff back here. Except for those bacteria traps you think are slippers. Those I'll be setting on fire."

"Don't you touch my Homer slippers! Or any of it. You're free, Gray."

He frowned. "I was always free."

"No, I mean free of—you're not going to die this year. You're going to have a lovely long life in southern Minnesota." Amara smiled, which was the easy part. Keeping the smile, that was where it got tricky. Not letting it look like a death's-head grin? Also tricky. "And I'll stay here. And it'll all be fine."

He dropped her hand like it was made of mud. "First, what the hell? Second, there's nothing lovely about life without you."

"Awwww."

"Stop it, Penny!" Amara yelped.

"Third, I'm moving in here with you guys if Hilly lets me. Which reminds me, Hilly, is it okay if I move in?"

"Of course, darling, but it's Amara's property now. And so her decision."

"Well, you can't," Amara declared. *I forgot about that. I'm officially a zillionaire. No more trust fund; I control it all. Might as well take the perks with the responsibilities.* "I forbid it. I banish you to Minneapolis and sentence you to live happily ever after."

Gray had no immediate reply, which was alarming beyond belief. Worse, he wore his I'm-thinking-super-hard-and-just-figured-out-something-huge expression. "Your dad said it was a trade. Did you bargain away my death?"

"Really?" Amara said, but not to Gray. "You guys are just going to stand there and listen to this obviously private conversation?"

"It's interesting," Penny said.

"A better question is, why are you having this private conversation in a cramped hallway outside your father's death room?" Arawn pointed out, even as he snapped his fingers and walked away, the hellhoundlets trotting behind him.

"Point," Amara admitted, even as Gray took her hand and led her away, away, all the way to the tower.

He slammed the door and leaned against it. "Tell. Me. Everything."

"Wow. You didn't say a word the whole time you were hauling me up here. That raises concerns."

"Start with, 'I figured out Skye was the bad guy' and finish with 'and then I lost my damned mind and tried to make Graham Gray go back to Minnesota because I'm a jerk with the heart of a jerk.'"

"Oh, the details." She flapped a hand.

"Amara. I'm supposed to die soon. Or I was."

"How could you even know that?" she cried. *Whoever told, they might get what Skye got.*

*No. Don't joke about that. Not even to yourself.*

"Because death gods all have at least one thing in common," Gray said wryly. "Not a single one of you is as subtle as you think you are. *Everyone* who met me was sad and just had to comment."

Amara glared at the floor.

*He's right. We're idiots.*

When Gray reached out and gently tipped up her chin, she glared at him. "Your parents," she finally muttered. "Your parents killed you."

"Right. Heart attack?" Gray's lack of surprise was heartbreaking. "Because my doctor told me I've got the BP of a Russian CEO in debt to Putin. And a raging vitamin A deficiency."

"Ooooh, political. Aneurysm. A few months from now."

There was a pause while Gray let that sink in and Amara wished she was anywhere but here, having any conversation but this one.

"I'm so sorry. Your folks—they should pay. And they will."

"That's a whole different conversation, Amara. So a tiny chunk of my brain was going to blow like a cheap bike tire, but not anymore. Because it's like your dad said: a trade. Your dad's dead because I'm going to live."

"Yes."

"But isn't that impossible?"

"I always thought so. Apparently when Death is dying and a new avatar is on deck, they receive a 'get out of death free' card." She held up her hands. "I know. It's an absurd deus ex machina."

Worse: She was pretty sure her father could have survived Skye's sinister machinations. But he chose to die. And not just because he was tired.

"And your dad told you this when he woke up . . . when?"

"This morning. I was doing what I did all the time as a kid—whining about my problems for twenty minutes. Startled the hell out of me when he talked back. I told him my suspicions, he wouldn't let me tell anyone he was awake, and you know the rest."

Gray's eyes filled, and he looked away as the tears spilled. "I can't believe you did that for me."

"Yes, well." She reached out, turned his head until he was facing her again. "Sometimes you're an idiot."

"And that your dad did that for you."

"He was an idiot, too. In all the best ways."

"And you thought I'd . . . what? Scuttle back to Minneapolis and live an Amara-less life?"

"You didn't choose this." Her gesture encompassed the room, the tower, the compound, the state of North Dakota. "Any of it. I shouldn't have let you come in the first place, never mind sucking you into Reaps and all that that entailed. But that doesn't matter, because it's like I said. You're free now."

"I think you forgot something."

*Hope not.* "Doubtful."

"The people being Reaped could see me. Remember? It freaked you out a little. I talked to your mom about it. I think the reason they treated me like Death was because I was *supposed* to be there. With you. Death's consort or whatever."

"That's one explanation." One she hadn't dared contemplate.

"Bullshit. It's the only explanation. Otherwise you would have mentioned the other possibilities ad nauseum. Amara. I love you and I'm *in* love with you. Sending me away? That's just another death sentence. Don't roll your eyes. Something can be hokey *and* true."

She squashed the wild joy that bloomed in her chest and was spreading to her extremities. Like a shot of the best rum in the world, times a thousand. "I can't expect you to stay with me."

"I know. But *I* can expect me to stay. Jesus, Amara, after everything I've seen? You really think I could just shrug and say 'smell you later' and hop on your dad's private train—well, your private train now—"

"One car. It's just the one car."

"—and get out of town? Even if I didn't want to be Death's consort, this—all this—the tower, the cave, the people—it's incredible! And fascinating! And there's so much more to know."

"And terrible. And depressing. And shocking. And so much more to know."

"And that's *life*, Amara." He took her by the shoulders and shook her a little even as he smiled. "You're talking to someone who never went out for sports because I was almost always in a cast. And someone who got to eat unlimited smoked turkey and take a bridge to your gorgeous library. No one's guaranteed a good time all the time."

She stared at him. "You really want to stay? With me?"

"Forever," he promised. "Or as good as."

"You're crazy," she marveled.

"I'm gonna avoid the obvious 'crazy for *you*, baby!' and just agree."

She threw her arms around him so suddenly, they both nearly toppled to the floor. "Crazy-crazy-crazy. My God. I love you. I love you. I love you."

"Everything you just said? Same."

"Ugh. Stop that."

He kissed her, hard, and then pulled back. "I guess you'd better tell my mom about the new parameters. She's gotta stay two states away, right?"

Amara stared.

"Oh, c'mon. You had to know I'd figure it out."

Amara kept staring.

"All right, now I'm trying to decide if I'm charmed by your astonishment or pissed at your low opinion of my IQ. Which is *huge*, by the way. The internet told me so after a rigorous quiz."

"Are . . . are you mad?"

"No. It was another reason to love you. And you know I'm not talking about the money. But you should stop pissing away two grand a month. You've got your own fiefdom and I'm your co-fiefer. You don't have to worry about Mom hurting me again. I wouldn't allow it even if I wasn't gonna be Death's sweetie. Also, thanks for not beating her to death."

"It was a struggle," Amara admitted. "I broke all her eggs and called her names and threw money at her and she barfed right after I left."

Gray snorted. "There's a scene to picture. Look, it's up to you, but I think you should stop. There's just no need for it.

And now to clumsily change the subject by asking if me moving in with you means I'm the new Hilly."

She paused and considered. "I guess it does. Maybe not immediately."

"Damn, that's a lot of responsibility. I'd better learn how to make lefse pretty quick."

"No rush." She kissed him back. "You've got years and years to learn."

# CHAPTER FORTY-SEVEN

"And finally, how does one smoke a turkey?"

"Darling, you remember that I'm not the one who died, right? That I'm the widow, not the corpse? I'll still be here. Amara has assured me I can remain for the rest of my life, however long or short. I'll still keep you in smoked turkeys and oatmeal spiked with kale."

*However long or short.* Amara helped herself to more meatballs and wondered if Hilly's longevity would be cut short, as she was no longer Death's consort. Elderly widows and widowers often died within months—sometimes days—of their spouse's death. Would her mother follow the pattern? Or begin an entirely new existence?

Regardless, the lady was right. This was her home, too. However long or short her life.

"Hilly, you know I'm sorry about your husband."

"I do, thank you."

"But I didn't know he and Amara were going to work a trade to save—I mean, to extend my life. I didn't even know that was a thing." Gray looked anxious and had stopped scribbling notes. "But if I had, I wouldn't have agreed to it."

"I know, darling." Hilly gave him a comforting squeeze. "Amara takes after her father in many ways, including her insistence on making life-and-death decisions for other people."

"Still in the room," Amara announced.

"Good to know," Gray replied. "And do I even want to know what you guys did with Skye's corpse?"

"Where do you think La Croix and Chernobog went off to?"

"Cool, cool. If those two decided to buy a van and drive around solving mysteries, I'd like and subscribe."

"I'm the mystery solver," Amara said. "It just takes me a really long time to realize there *is* a mystery."

"And what about your dad? A funeral, right?"

"Oh, yes, Gray," Hilly replied. "And when it's done, we'll burn him and give him back to the earth."

"Oh." Gray, who had just piled second helpings on his plate and scored a big fat strawberry for Amara, took his seat at the table. "While we're talking about this stuff, does Skye being dead mean no one on the Isle of Skye can die?"

"No. There was a new avatar the moment Skye went belly-up."

"Let me guess: It's complicated."

"Well." Amara shrugged.

"And it's amazing that Skye's death was dramatic and an anticlimax at the same time. I mean, you barely touched her. One second she was spitting and the next . . ." Gray mimed slitting his throat with his finger. "Canceled."

"That's not what canceled means, and it was only anticlimactic because I'd finally opened myself to all I could do."

"Like Captain Marvel. You realized all this time you'd been fighting with one hand tied behind your back."

She sighed. "If that helps you."

"You bet it helps me. It's no coincidence that when we got

here a few days ago, the first thing you did was say howdy to your folks, then *instantly* dyed your hair. Even though you just did it two weeks ago."

"It's too early in the day to be psychoanalyzed."

"Ha! Not hardly. Watch me take it further: The migraines weren't migraines."

"Correct."

"I mean, you said it a couple of times, but I didn't get it right away. They were a . . . I dunno, a symptom? A side effect? Of squashing your Death Lite powers?"

"Correct."

"Which I told you!" Hilly cried. "Years ago! But now you hear it from Gray, you accept it?"

"It's not just hearing it from Gray," she grumped. "Can't we just agree it's ancient history?"

"Uh . . . which part?"

"No," Hilly said with a frown. "You're forgetting your Faulkner, dear."

"You bet I am."

"The past isn't over, it's not even past?" Gray guessed.

"Close enough, dear." To Amara: "You'll need to meet with our accountants this week. All that was Death's is yours."

"So, downside, you're the Grim Reaper. Upside, you're a millionaire. It's none of my business, but how are you guys rich? Did Death get in on the ground floor for inventions? Did he know the telephone would catch on? And TVs? And, I dunno, fabric softener?"

"Freyja Brunhilde Göndul weeps gold," Amara replied with her mouth full. Crazy how Death's death was revving up every engine: She was starving, horny, and itching to sign tax paperwork. Itching to file something, even. And Reap, God help her!

"Uh. What?"

"My tears would turn into gold. And over the centuries, I found much to weep over." Freyja waved away Gray's astonishment. "I can't do it anymore, which is just as well. We have all the funds we'll ever need. At some point it becomes outright greed."

"I was thinking your husband invested in the printing press, but that works, too."

"Yes." To Amara: "Everyone is coming over again tonight to fête you."

"Joy. Let's meet in the cave, just to make La Croix miserable." She grinned, picturing it. "I imagine we should all get used to things being a little different."

"It goes without saying your father had his way of doing things," Hilly said, "and you'll have yours. And, as you said, you'll have help. Now forgive me if I'm seen to pry, but will I have the joy of planning a wedding anytime soon?"

"I dunno if it's a joy," Gray said doubtfully. "It looks really stressful. Unless TV and movies have been lying to me."

"We *just* admitted we've been in love, Mom."

"Well, it's not like you two have to get to know each other. Or want to be with anyone else. You've had years to find alternatives but remained with each other."

"True. No surprises. Same old, same old. Yawn," Gray said.

"Snore," Amara agreed.

"The *only* way I'd be interested is if you guarantee we can look forward to 'same old, same old' for at least a century."

"I guarantee nothing. In this you'll be like everyone else. Roll the dice. Take your chances."

"Done," he replied, and kissed her.